The
Treadmillers

The Treadmillers

P. R. BROWN

By the same author:

The Gods of Our Time
Dreams and Illusions Revisited
The Mountain Dwellers
The Mirror Men

First Published in Great Britain in 2018 by DB Publishing,
an imprint of JMD Media Ltd

ISBN 9781780915920

Printed and bound in the UK

1

The Spiral of Consciousness

It had been the warmest December on record, and everyone remarked on it. Now, in the second half of January, things were beginning to take a turn for the worse. But this particular Monday morning you would not have thought so. It was a beautiful morning, the crisp air made congenial by a bright sun, as might happen in the calm before a storm. Not that Jack Barker, who taught history, took much notice of it. For he, like the majority of the teaching staff at Morley Comprehensive, was assailed by the Monday Morning Syndrome and was no more capable of appreciating the beauty of Nature than he was the prospect of the day ahead. He knew, after years of Monday Mornings, that by the time he had cycled to school through the toxic haze of polluted streets, he would be ready to head for home again, his briefcase blissfully unopened. He was in no mood, therefore, to take much account of the cleaner air of the school playing fields, which encircled the red-brick buildings that stood like so many red blocks on an immovable sea of green.

Jack always cycled to school. He thought himself fortunate to be able to do so, to avoid the hassle of waiting for buses, forced conversations in queues and the stuffy air generated inside those oblong boxes on wheels. He had long felt that the principal drawback with public transport was the public it served. He was happy, then, to rely on pedal power.

And the trouble with pedal power was the power it required which, this morning, was more noticeably lacking than ever. It was getting harder these days to push those pedals round, despite the easier gears.

Best not to think of it. So Jack was happy to pursue a train of thought that the phrase 'pedal power' might suggest. The word 'power' was the catalyst, and it led him to Acton's dictum: 'All power tends to corrupt, and absolute power corrupts absolutely.' *How true*, thought Jack. *How true, and in all walks of life*. Teachers and parents, lovers and colleagues, friends and relations are all subject to the same beast, not simply politicians and military dictators. He might have pursued the subject further had it not been for the school gates, which were now unbearably in sight.

* *

Jack stood gazing bleary-eyed out of the staffroom window, thoughtfully scratching one side of his bearded face with one hand and fumbling with the other in his trouser pocket for a paper handkerchief that wasn't there.

'Still out there, is he?' asked Patel, sidling up and nodding beyond the window. Zanjik Patel – like Jack in his late forties, short, clean-shaven, with a slight build and sharp facial features – taught mathematics and always seemed on the ball, Monday Mornings or not. Patel's eyes were perhaps his most remarkable feature: round, shiny, black, intelligent protrusions in a face darkened by his Indian heritage; in another life he might have been a guru.

'Dunno,' Jack grunted. This was his first lie of the day. He loathed himself for it, but couldn't help himself either. He certainly did know he was there. In fact, he had taken pains precisely to avoid the old fellow who had taken to standing at or around the school gates. On sighting the old man at a comfortable distance, Jack had purposely cycled round the back streets, letting himself into the school grounds at the rear entrance. Inconvenient, but safe.

Patel knew, too. He wasn't asking for information, just confirming what he knew already, to make conversation. In fact, everyone knew. True, there was the odd morning when the old fellow didn't turn up; but when he did turn up everyone was bound to notice the fact.

The fact that he was so noticeable was of course the core of the matter. Had the fellow been less remarkable, he would hardly have become a conversation piece. Had he known it, the old man was doing the staff at Morley Comprehensive a profound service, for ordinarily they had little or nothing to talk about at all. After years of teaching together in the same establishment, even their small talk had been exploited way beyond its sell-by date and failed to provide even a modicum of relief from the nausea of their daily round, while the usual jokes and quips were as stale as old bread; besides, it was such a relief not to have to talk about something threatening, such as visits arranged under the auspices of official inspectorates, which were enough to put the fear of God into teachers already hard-pressed; indeed, the imminent prospect of an inspection was perhaps the only time when an appeal to God seemed an eminently reasonable recourse – no other occasion, save perhaps shuffling off of one's own mortal coil, being deemed equally advisable.

The appearance of the old fellow at the school gates was therefore a welcome diversion for the staff at Morley Comprehensive. Their ingratitude was such, however, that the conversation invariably turned on how to avoid him or how to get rid of him; with the possible exception of Monday Mornings, when it was better to pretend that he didn't exist at all.

Even Watkins, the Head, had condescended to pop into the staffroom to alert everyone to what he affectionately referred to as 'our little problem'. He, Watkins, had come, he said, to welcome everyone back after the mid-winter recess, but he was curiously at pains to stress the importance of preserving an image of respectability for the school. Everyone could easily guess what was coming next. 'Our little problem,' he announced in avuncular tones, 'is in hand.' Jack looked at Patel, and Patel looked down at his shoes. Watkins, seriously balding, of slightly above average height, immaculately dressed, portly and in his late fifties, enjoyed speaking in more stentorian tones whenever he had a larger audience.

Afterwards, Jack and Patel agreed how reminiscent it all was of the time when afternoon lessons were interrupted by the ranting and raving of a former patient of the local mental hospital, recently allowed to return to the care of the community, as he paraded up and down some streets, too close to some of the classrooms to be unheard: defamatory expletives had exploded in the afternoon air like firecrackers for the best part of an hour; most of this was incomprehensible at a distance, but the general drift was unmistakable. It happened more than once during Jack's history lessons with the Upper Sixth, providing him with an opportunity to make jibes at the government's expense. 'Another disaffected Tory' or 'Another disaffected Labourite', he would say, because, as far as Jack was concerned, all politicians of whatever persuasion could be tarred with the same brush; such remarks would prompt giggles from some, but not all, of his students. Jack's 'disaffected Tory' or 'disaffected Labourite' had been deinstitutionalised on the pretext that community care would do him infinitely more good, while at the same time benefiting the public purse. Watkins had dutifully complained to the police, and, after a slow start, the disaffected gentleman simply disappeared from the scene, together with his loud protestations about all and sundry. Watkins congratulated the police on the effective, if somewhat tardy, deliverance from embarrassment, ignorant of the fact that the poor, deranged soul had instead been caught under the wheels of a double-decker bus, and had consequently given up the ghost; his protestations therefore necessarily ceased, perhaps now having been delivered into the hands of a much higher authority, thus conveniently saving both institutional and community care, not to mention Morley Comprehensive, from further responsibility.

Watkins therefore congratulated himself, inwardly of course, on his own track record with regard to little problems of this nature. And so, briefly included in his 'Welcome back' talk to the staff of Morley Comprehensive were words of realism tempered by tenderness and understanding, uttered like a love poem with machine-gun punctuation, producing a most effective staccato:

'Most unfortunate. Of course! Having to see these poor people out on the streets. Homeless. Destitute. We know all about it! Even so. Even so, it won't do. We have an image to protect. In any case, please remember. It's best left to the proper authorities. So please don't encourage. Pretend he's not there, as it were. Best for him. Best for us. Leave it to those who know best.'

What Watkins said about other matters, Jack couldn't recall.

'I'm rather surprised he hasn't got the police on to this one – like last time,' Patel remarked during the mid-morning break.

'Elusive. Now he's there. Now he's not – and good luck to him,' Jack suggested, cleaning his spectacles. 'Know anything about him?'

Patel slowly shook his head. 'Interesting, though, I must admit.'

Jack grunted in half-hearted agreement.

Another lie. Jack was intrigued to say the very least. To begin with, the old fellow looked quite out of tune with the world in which he lived, as though he were a living, walking, breathing advertisement for something different. He resembled Socrates, or what Jack thought Socrates might have looked like: in his late sixties or early seventies, bald on top, grey-white hair for what remained, matched by a beard of silvery curls, and his blue eyes stared out of a round face with a sallow complexion, weathered but healthy enough; he was stocky and of average height. He wore a kind of woollen tunic, roughly belted at the waist, which came to just above his knees, and under this a pair of white summer trousers which had seen much better and cleaner times; on his feet were simple leather sandals; and over his shoulder hung a large bundle of what appeared to be rags or blankets – no doubt sleeping gear for the bitterly cold nights which now loomed ahead. His arms, bare from the elbows down, were strong and muscular, again reminiscent of Socrates who was, Jack had read, no pushover in his youth and could hold his own on those long, military marches of his soldiering days; and that old Greek was endowed with a constitution that could drink much younger Greeks under the table and leave himself standing, while his dialectical adversaries succumbed to the fruit of the vine, collapsing one after another in a swoon, while he himself was left sufficiently sober to conclude the argument bereft of all sensible opposition.

Jack and Sally had brought back a statuette of Socrates from the island of Xykanthos, a figure, crudely made, but which was remarkably like the old fellow loitering round the school gates. This very ordinary souvenir, mass produced from a kind of coppery lead, had assumed a place of very little honour on the bedroom windowsill, hidden behind the curtain. Recently and unaccountably, Jack had placed it in front of the curtain and given it a dust or two.

Jack fumbled with his briefcase. 'And what is on the pedagogic menu today?' Patel asked, smiling.

Jack liked Patel, perhaps because his small talk pretended to be no bigger than it was. '*Cromwell and the New Model Army* – yet again!' said Jack, suddenly bursting into life and snatching up his briefcase. You simply had to burst into life if you were not to be swallowed whole by the Monday Morning Syndrome and disappear forever into one of those black holes that have become so numerous since their astrophysical discovery.

Patel smiled.

Jack couldn't remember how many times he'd taught *Cromwell and the New Model Army,* and he had wondered for some time now what it was he was actually teaching, or why he was teaching it. It was as though he stood outside himself, listening to himself speak – a disconcerting experience – and he wondered about the words that came out of his mouth and where they were heading. If he taught facts, they weren't like Patel's mathematical facts. The facts of geometry, for instance, were clean, tidy and irrefutable. You could actually prove that two angles were equal, and if someone didn't catch on, the fault wasn't in the proof. Dates and names in history were a bit like that – but then, dates and names weren't the real stuff of history, just the pegs on which the real stuff of it hung, and they certainly weren't Jack's priority. The problem was to decide just what that priority was. Take the names and the dates out of history and what remained, the real stuff and substance of it all, made him feel uncomfortable. Didn't the study of history really have to do with moral lessons, moral truths, moral *priorities*? If not, why bother at all? But the supreme difficulty seemed to be getting people to draw the same moral conclusions and then sticking to them afterwards. And that meant drawing the same conclusions as Jack – and since they didn't draw the same conclusions as Jack, or drew them but failed to stick to them, or failed to stick to them often enough, the study of history seemed too arbitrary, far too subjective, with far too many loose ends. This whole subject had occupied him now and again as he cycled to and from school and refused to let him be; it was one of those trains of thought that tended to stick burr-like when pedal power was failing: through the stop-starts of traffic congestion, cold rain, strong winds and, of course, Monday Mornings. No, in geometry there just couldn't be any loose ends. Loose ends simply weren't allowed in geometry! Which perhaps explained Jack's parting remark to Patel that morning as he beetled off to teach those kids *Cromwell and the New Model Army*: 'You're better off with maths!'

Patel raised his eyebrows, and then smiled his customary sweet smile. The Monday Morning Syndrome didn't stand a chance when he was about, such a comfort to all and sundry was he, such a balm – how could anyone even begin to guess that all this sweetness was just a facade which masked the turmoil within? You had to be clever – even to the extent of outwitting your best friends, even those with whom you felt the closest affinity.

Still smiling, he and Jack whisked themselves off to their respective classrooms. For, unlike in halcyon days gone by – days when school inspections were more welcomed than feared, when red tape was manageable and examinations taken by all in much more comfortable stride, when teachers were universally respected and students were generally receptive – there were now no morning assemblies to provide a comforting buffer-zone between staffroom and classroom, no space to think, to unwind, with a hymn or two in praise of a loving God followed by The School Song, all of which provided some kind of solace to the godly and the ungodly alike. The school song was entitled 'Towards the Light'; but the newer members of staff were ignorant of its existence, and the older members were hard put to remember the words, or even how the tune went. Jack felt cheated out of his inheritance. For he remembered his own schooldays, when the school song, of a different melody but similar sentiment, was sung every morning without fail at the end of the morning assembly; he remembered how kids sat cross-legged at the front of the assembly hall in their first year, graduating towards the back of the hall in succeeding years, until they finally achieved the accolade of Sixth Form Prefecture and were perched on chairs, no less, at the very back of the hall, from which elevation they might, like birds of prey or Egyptian kings, survey their juniors.

Egypt had fallen, sacrificed on the altar of ethnic diversity. For Christian worship contained within itself the possibility of cultural affront and its own eventual demise.

*   *

During those pedal-pushing days, becoming now progressively harder in his late forties, Jack's memories fell upon him like playful elves jumping out from behind the bushes he cycled past. He had thought of setting some of his memories down on paper, but he had never got round to it; and in any case, he was not sure whether he wanted to call them *his* memories, as though he possessed them. On the contrary, they seemed to possess him, like demons; the best that could be said of them was that they were gentle giants that kept tugging at his elbow. They meant nothing, but would not let him go. Jack himself had been a school prefect and was therefore looked up to by all the juniors; but he had been respected by his peers, too. He remembered that.

He also remembered how he had one day spoken about what he called *The Spiral of Consciousness*. When asked what he meant by it, he could not say; all he could say was that it must mean something because it meant so much to him; that it would not seem so important unless it meant *something*. His peers, and even one or two of the teachers who had overheard him, thought he might well mean something by it and that what he meant might well be important. But since nothing more could be said about it, the subject, if indeed it was a subject, was passed over in silence. Jack was nevertheless respected; his stock had risen, but precisely why, no one, Jack included, could possibly say.

It was all very silly, of course – this stuff about *The Spiral of Consciousness*. But silly things like this happen in schooldays and are forgotten, or, if not forgotten, recalled with smiles of disbelief that they could have happened at all.

And yet, for all that, thought Jack, there might be something in it after all. There is a downward spiral, and there is an upward spiral. No doubt he had meant the latter. Consciousness, then, up towards what? What on earth could it mean, if, indeed, it meant anything on earth? It was all very obscure, and not a little childish. But nor could it be avoided – as though it was something that begged to be considered. Why, after all, should one be afraid of obscurity? Jack remembered something he'd read: *Do not be afraid of the dark, for darkness may be the source of illumination.* He repeated it to himself as though this piece of advice might become clearer through sheer repetition; it did not. He hoped such ideas were not a sign of early onset senility.

He would say nothing to Sally of his pedal-pushing thoughts.

2
A Sense of Foreboding

At the end of that school day, like the end of all school days, staff and pupils wound their way home wearily – the staff with a modicum of discretion, lest the speed of their exit be seen and interpreted as a lack of dedication – all glad to be free, if only for a few twilight hours until the bells of obligation chimed again. Patel trundled off to his semi-detached, insensitively situated at the threshold of a motorway, where he was destined to spend yet another barren evening, later to be lulled to sleep by the repeated and not altogether distant roar of articulated lorries making their way through deserts of darkness to God knows where. Jack turned the key in the door of his fully-detached, a grade up from Patel's semi; an upgrade made possible by the combined incomes of himself and his wife, Sally, who now, as assistant manager, no less, of the branch of a major department store, enjoyed a salary just as healthy, if not more so, than his own, not forgetting her in-store prestige and her out-store self-esteem, a prestige and esteem denied to Jack as a mere teacher of history, for he was not even a departmental head, in a lacklustre comprehensive.

Sally had achieved her position fairly recently, and there was every chance that she would do even better, having been suspected of possessing latent qualities requisite for even further advancement: grit, determination, absolute commitment, an ability to ruthlessly pursue targets chosen by her superiors at head office, an air of authority and, last but by no means least, a strong desire to seek self-development in her chosen theatre of employment. Admirable qualities. Had they existed, Sally would have challenged glass ceilings with a sledgehammer; but there was little need to resort to such draconian measures. 'The sky's the limit!' an official from head office had said during her interview, and she took this to mean that elevation to manager, and even regional manager, was not an impossibility. Thus encouraged, she was unstoppable. But her recent promotion did come with a price-tag: she had been warned that the step from staff supervisor to assistant manager was more a leap than a transition, and one that required what the revered Mr Alex Clark at head office was pleased to call 'the crossing of the Rubicon'. He made it sound like a divine baptism, and it was not difficult for her to find the proposition irresistible. As staff supervisor, she had demonstrated a sufficient number of the requisite qualities to be earmarked for promotion, and when it was offered she naturally accepted with the alacrity and the enthusiasm which head office had expected. 'I'm confident that you have in you the ability to make tough decisions and to see them through,' Clark had said – which was praise indeed. Convinced that such confidence did not grow on trees, Sally was delighted. It was no longer a man's world, if it ever had been. Though it should be remarked that her delight was to stand in stark contrast to the tears of disbelief of those whose redundancies at local level were to be announced in the lead-up to the mid-winter recess; since the party atmosphere of the recess had lessened over the last decade nor so, there being precious little to celebrate, people bought one another fewer presents; December being simply another month in the calendar, demand had declined, and since demand was down, some jobs had to go. There had been a time when the contrary was markedly the case and more employees had been taken on for the December Rush, as it was called. But that was in the past. Now, cuts, of *all* kinds, were the order of the day.

Sally was therefore a no-nonsense woman, and she wanted to bring to her domestic affairs the same rigour that was evidenced in her dealings with colleagues and subordinates. But although the strains of material ambition had by now shown themselves clearly in her personality, they had not yet much dented her feminine allure. Her face was intelligent and expressive, her brown hair and blue eyes showing the least signs of strain; her figure was still attractive, and when she allowed her hair to fall around her shoulders, released from the discipline of the tight bun-like knot in which it was tied at work, Jack was sufficiently responsive to keep the physical side of the marriage alive, though not perhaps kicking.

*   *

At the end of this back-to-school Monday in the second week of January, Jack found himself at home in the bathroom with a pair of scissors, contorting his features this way and that in the attempt to achieve perfection in the thankless and never-ending task of trimming his beard.

'So, anyway, it's time we had a good talk to him about it.' Sally was shouting from the bottom of the staircase. 'Jack… are you listening?'

'Hmm? Yes! Yes, right!' Jack shouted back, repeating these words to himself in a sardonic whisper.

'Maybe tonight's a good time. Don't you think?' Sally went on.

'Oh, God!' Jack mumbled to himself.

'Yes?' Sally shouted.

'Yes!' Jack shouted back.

'You see, the trouble is…' Sally had now climbed the stairs and was poking her head round the bathroom door. '…trouble is, he doesn't seem able to make up his mind! Honestly, He just hasn't a clue what he wants to do. I've tried to speak to him, but I can't seem to get through. *You* should have a go. Maybe he'll listen to his father – yes?'

'Can't put an old head on young shoulders,' Jack mumbled, giving up on his beard.

'Yes, well, we've got to do something. You know what he said this morning? Philosophy! He said he wants to do philosophy at A-level and then…'

'Hold on – I thought you said he hadn't made up his mind!'

'Oh, come on! Wanting to do something with no future in it is hardly making up your mind. He needs something solid. I mean, economics, business studies. 'Course, I don't mind if he does medicine or law – I mean something with a future. If I'd had the opportunities young people have now…'

'You haven't done so badly,' Jack said.

'…goodness knows what I'd have achieved by now,' Sally went on, regardless.

'Do you know what philosophy *is*?' Jack dared ask.

'No, I don't. Do *you*?' Sally intended the question rhetorically, and Jack preferred to treat it as such.

'Well, we could ask Pete, couldn't we?'

'Look, Peter just doesn't know what he wants. We've got to help him. Life's much more complicated than it used to be,' said Sally.

'Is it?'

'What do you mean "*Is it*?" Of course it is! Much more!'

'Didn't have Sixth Form colleges in my day. We stayed in the same school, and we just went on if we could; we made our choices, and things sort of fell into place. Sometimes things went well, sometimes they didn't. You can't guarantee anything,' Jack said with a shrug.

'Fell into place? Yes, or *not*!'

Her riposte contained an innuendo which Jack didn't care to pick up on. She knew he wasn't happy with his lot in life – he'd tried to argue it out before, more than once – but he'd been silenced by the recommendation that those who can't put up had better shut up. He'd tried to reshape his destiny, but destiny just wouldn't be messed with, and everything he touched had turned to stone – or so he'd argued. But he wasn't arguing any more, and especially not tonight.

'Anyway, we've got to go to the open evenings, starting tomorrow. Peter'll come with us, of course.'

'Damn – at this rate I'll be late!' She was right, much more of this banter and she'd better not bother going at all. Things were to be prepared before she could make an important social evening with administrative colleagues, an evening which, luckily for Jack, husbands were not invited to attend. Dinner for Jack and Peter had to be prepared, and then she had to make up and get herself ready… Therefore, the subject of open evenings and Peter's future had to be dropped for the time being.

The prospect of attending open evenings at local Sixth Form colleges appealed as little to Jack as they did to Peter himself. But it seemed like an edict from on high that they not only be visited, but also duly weighed and decided upon without further ado. A-level subjects would also be selected and the proverbial die cast. But Jack's feelings were, as always, ambivalent. After all, was it not entirely acceptable that Sally should express anxieties about Peter's future? Was it not merely a natural extension of motherly love? Commendably natural and naturally commendable. In so many matters, Sally could be somewhat overbearing, frustrating, irritating. Yes, life with her was not always easy. But Jack knew that, without her, life would be impossible.

*   *

With such consoling thoughts, Jack was left alone in the bedroom while Sally left for the kitchen to slam some stuff into the microwave. The subject of Peter's future would no doubt be pursued on her return from the social evening, although, with luck, a late return might preclude it, granting both Jack and Peter a welcome stay of execution, though not a reprieve.

Jack's nightly routine, in so far as it could be kept up, included a response to stress, which he had picked up from a booklet entitled *Stress Management for Teachers*. According to this slim and sympathetic, though not altogether enlightening, tome:

> *The typical staffroom is full of people suffering from different kinds of stress. However, teachers rarely realise what damage stress is doing to them. It is all very well teachers being asked to shoulder the responsibility for what happens to their pupils; but teachers have a duty to look after themselves, too. If they fail to look after themselves, they will hardly be in a position to look after anybody else. Here, as elsewhere, prevention is better than cure: it is better to avoid stress than to deal with its effects once the rot has set in. Everyone agrees that teaching is stressful, but there is much that teachers can do to control it and lead more enjoyable lives.*

The vaguely patronising tone of this piece of wisdom was not lost on Jack. It seemed abundantly clear to him that stress was *damaging*, not at all clear that teachers were at all *responsible* for mitigating its effects, and at least doubtful whether anything *substantial* could be done about it. But it was remarkable how much people could achieve by stating the obvious and understating its importance; he was reminded of those qualities which someone had suggested were the makings of a first-class politician, namely an infinite talent for trivialising the momentous and complicating the obvious.

However, Jack was determined to stop the rot setting in. Every night he would trim his beard if he thought it needed trimming, since he preferred to keep it as short as possible, and, according to the booklet on stress management, one ought to do those little things that make one feel more at ease with oneself and the world. Next, he would lie down on his bed, listening to a CD of the sweet strains of seventeenth-century lute music by John Dowland, and sixteenth-century music for viols – to most of which he found it impossible to relate; but at least it was relaxing and was capable of transporting him to another world, if not another galaxy, which is precisely what he wanted it to do. The trick, again according to the precious booklet, was to empty one's mind of all troublesome thoughts (which, in Jack's case, meant almost all thoughts) and simply concentrate on the sounds emitted by the instruments. It is doubtful whether the author of the booklet had precisely this music in mind; perhaps the classic rendering of 'La Mere', accompanied by waves softly lashing against rocks and accompanied by the occasional and distant screams of seagulls, would have been the recommended choice; but Jack prided himself on wanting to be different, and in this case, at least, succeeded admirably. Jack took the advice about 'getting away from it all' quite seriously when he chose *alter music* for his magic carpet – for this stuff would transport him into a netherworld of nothingness, which is precisely where he wanted to be. But then, he was a historian, and it was thus that he justified his choice of musical ambrosia.

When his musical mantras at last faded and the CD ended, Jack continued to lie on his bed, thinking how strikingly and absurdly true it was to speak as the booklet did of the stress to be found in the average staffroom. For many it was like a constant toothache from a tooth that defied extraction and, in consequence, simply had to be put up with. Teachers were constantly on trial, constantly having to prove themselves – on a daily basis, class after class, lesson after lesson, term after term, year after year; and if this were not enough, formal inspections completed this never-ending panoply of stress with intimidation and threats, though, of course, no one would have used such words, for inspections were to be welcomed as exercises in the maintenance of standards – and who would or could possibly argue against the maintenance of standards? – and as opportunities for self-development.

Good old Patel was a case in point. His Monday Morning smile was not to be relied upon. His serenity was more apparent than real. He had only this time last year undergone heart surgery and had been off work for three months in consequence. Stress seemed to have been the operative word, if the pun may be forgiven; certainly, Patel's cardiac embarrassment had been attributed in part to the stresses and strains attendant upon the loss of his wife, a small, quiet, delicate creature who had died rather as she lived – gently and on the wings of a whisper. It was sadly ironic that Patel had turned to his teaching career for succour, for comfort and relief, only to find there even more stress, and that in considerable abundance. Jack decided that Patel must be of a kind destined to die a coronary death, incapable as he was of living at ease, determined as he was to live on a tightrope of his own solitary imaginings. For Patel was now alone and had to bear his own thoughts; his memories, too, bitter-sweet and heavy as lead.

Then there was Gladys Kennerly, whose lessons in human biology might have been expected to relieve the stresses and strains of this mortal coil by drawing her attention to life's vicissitudes and frailties, thus forcing upon her imagination the brevity of life and the necessity of living it to the full; in short, the necessity to put things in perspective, as the cliché has it, and become impervious, or more impervious than most, to the stresses to which her colleagues were by comparison more susceptible. But such thinking is, of course, naive. Suffice to say, things don't work like that. No, not at all. She would be the first in the staffroom to grab the daily paper, the one containing a horoscopes page, under the pretext, which none of the more acute members of staff were taken in by, of skimming through the entire edition for news of world and state; however stuck for time she was, the paper never left her hands before she had surreptitiously read and inwardly digested her daily prediction, world and state notwithstanding. Yet, had anyone asked, she would have denied her interest in fortune-telling with a contemptuous laugh and shrugged the whole thing off. She was, after all, a scientist, and scientists don't go in for such stuff, for horoscopes are no more than pseudoscience. Such was the potency of stress from which the intelligent and the know-betters sought relief. In her early fifties, but still quite youthful in appearance and not at all unattractive, who is to say whether she would have fared better or worse had she ever married – with or without issue?

Such was the train of Jack's thoughts, his thinking still softened and guided by the music that had transported him elsewhere, when Sally breezed into the bedroom and sat at the dressing-table. Jack's transportation had implied a return ticket.

'One thing to be said for the Japanese system of education,' she said, touching up her eyelashes, 'the kids there know what they want and they go for it. Leave our kids standing!'

They had watched a television documentary on the Japanese system of education, extolling the fierce competition in their high schools and the 'examination hell' that went with it.

'But even the parents complain their kids miss out on their childhood,' sighed Jack, quoting the programme.

'Oh, rubbish! At least they know where they're going. We're a backwater compared with Japan. We ought to get our act together.'

'You don't think they should question their destination?'

'Must you listen to that stuff?' Sally nodded towards the CD player. Jack was accustomed to having his questions answered with a question. 'Dinner's in the microwave. Really must dash – see you in a couple of hours – and be good!'

Good? Don't have much choice in the matter, he thought, as he heard Sally closing the front door behind her downstairs. She meant that she didn't want to return home to find Jack with whisky on his breath. She was worried about his secret drinking. She was concerned about the effect on his health. But Jack was a reformed character; not that he had been a heavy drinker; on the contrary, one or two singles of malt would be enough to flatten him out on the sofa. Nowadays he preferred to doze whenever he had the chance. And this was his chance. He had to shake his head a little and reposition himself on the bed, for the simple business of Sally's entrance, her remarks about Japan, and her exit, had ruffled his feathers. He needed to start the music all over again and allow it to transport him back to where he was. After all, tomorrow was another day of grind, and tomorrow evening, entailing as it did those ridiculous open evenings, followed then or soon enough after by his weekly visit to his mother, would give him little opportunity this week to unwind. It would, on the contrary, demand all of him and more; now was the time to gird his loins and recharge his batteries. The idea was to feel the *Life Force*, as the booklet on stress management put it, surging gently but inexorably through his body, like an electric current: steady, powerful, all-conquering.

This *Life Force* was, however, something of a misnomer, for, within seconds, Jack was fast asleep, an occurrence that the little booklet had expressly outlawed as being not in the least conducive to true stress management, since, presumably, sleep implied a total absence of self-control. Meanwhile, the Elizabethan viols played merely to the air, which was both unappreciative and invulnerable to the effects of stress, while Jack's snoring provided a most unsavoury form of accompaniment.

*   *

For all that, sleep was perhaps the best form of escape available for Jack. For he was assailed by a sense of foreboding which, try as he might, he found it impossible to account for. It came to him at odd times. And in odd ways. The sounds of the younger children playing in the school playground at break times would haunt him and fill him with this sense of foreboding, as though the nonchalant sounds they made, their laughter and their incomprehensible banter were somehow reminiscent of their adult counterparts who, wrapped up in their routines and the worries that went with them, were oblivious to the disasters that lay ahead and were therefore incapable of putting up any kind of defence against them. It was all very silly really, and entirely incomprehensible.

Nor was this sense of foreboding new. It had returned after a long period of time. The first instances, as far as he could remember, had occurred when, as a child and as a young teenager, he had walked the green hills not far from home. He had walked alone, over the hills, those rich, green hills, the grass feeling like a soft, thick carpet, a carpet of welcome; the only sounds were the sounds of sheep and skylarks; all was peaceful; God was in his Heaven and all was right with the world.

But not for long. For then the sky would darken and the winds would begin to shake the branches on the outlying trees and hiss through the longer grass, and the sheep would find some dark hiding places and the music of the larks would cease. God was no longer in his Heaven, and all was not right with the world. The hills had suddenly lost their former beauty, their tranquillity, and nothing could assuage Jack's sensation of forthcoming destruction, his sense of looming tragedy, his fear of winds that would blow vengefully and ruthlessly, inexorably blotting out in their path all forms of life, his fear of icy blasts and unforgiving tempests eradicating all resistance. These were winds of loneliness and despair, memories of half-forgotten times and half-remembered faces, memories of all that you once were and are now no more. How could a being, half-boy, half-man, feel such things? And what did they mean? What could they *possibly* mean? And how could any being feel such things and yet endure?

And why had it returned – this sense of foreboding?

This was something he could mention to no one. Not to Sally. If he could not understand it himself, what hope did she have? Besides, he was not likely to get a fair hearing, so thin her patience had worn; she was too full of certainty. Not even to Patel, who needed to receive support, not give it, having enough troubles of his own. And not to his mother, cocooned in her own world; he was a man now and could look after himself, and he should be able to conduct his own analyses, what with his education and all; besides, the days had long since passed when he and she were capable of real heart-to-heart conversations.

A Bible, inherited from his father, was kept in his bedside drawer. He opened it at random from time to time, hoping to find some soothing words, something he might relate to. The best so far was an extract from Paul's letter in *Philippians*, Chapter 4, verse 4:

> *Rejoice in the Lord always: again I say, Rejoice. Let your forbearance be known unto all men. The Lord is at hand. In nothing be anxious; but in everything by prayer and supplication with thanksgiving let your requests be made known to God. And the peace of God, which passes all understanding, shall guard your hearts and your thoughts in Christ Jesus. Finally, brethren, whatever things are true, whatever things are honourable, whatever things are just, whatever things are pure, whatever things are lovely, whatever things are of good report;*

if there is any virtue, and if there is any praise, think on these things. The things which you both learned and received and heard and saw in me, these things do: and the God of peace shall be with you.

There was much in this, not to mention the style, to which he could not bring himself to relate; yet there was something there, as there was in the music to which he also could not relate, that he found curiously uplifting. It was somehow to do with *forbearance*; forbearance in a world that had to be borne, if you were not to be overcome by what you had to bear. Whether you wanted to speak in terms of God or not, there was something to be picked out here and preserved, like a ruby from a bed of pebbles. When faced with man's inhumanity to man and the tyranny of death, there might be a heroism in forbearance which outshone the beauty of art and outdid the courage of the bravest of the brave.

Still, the sense of foreboding lived on, undefeated yet, and unexplained. And the peace alluded to in the letter, and for which Jack thought he yearned, was felt not at all.

3
Love in the Dark

The monotony of the following day was, if not exactly mitigated, at least overshadowed by a most unexpected encounter with the old man who had taken to appearing at the gates of Morley Comprehensive.

Mindful of Watkins's infinitely subtle humanistic sentiment that the old man should not be encouraged for his own good, and, incidentally, lest doing do should serve to impair the image of the school, Jack had cycled to the rear entrance. Watkins had not advised staff, much less pupils, to use the rear entrance. It was simply that Jack felt easier doing so. He had never put much store by what Watkins said, but it was just as well not to ruffle his feathers; besides, it was too early in the term, the new year having just been ushered in, to seek a confrontation, tedious prig though Watkins was. At least, that's what Jack whispered to himself inside his mental box.

But he was startled out of these whispers by bumping, almost literally, into the old man himself. A large elm tree stood to one side of the rear gate; the old man sat under it, cross-legged, his back resting against its broad and wrinkled trunk. He had slept under it and had by now rolled up his colourful blankets into a neat pile on which he sat; a plain, grey, woollen bobble hat, whose bobble was in the process of detaching itself and hung loosely to one side, protected his bald head from the frosty early morning sting; the hat itself was lopsided, like a hastily positioned tea cosy. There he sat, sniffing the cold air and rolling a cigarette, which, judging by the care he took, was either an indication that such a comfort was in very short supply, or was the first of the day, or both. It should be remarked that smoking was banned throughout the entire school grounds, and even in the street adjacent to the school's car park; another reason why Watkins would consider the old fellow an undesirable visitor. Watkins was known to have reprimanded a member of staff for walking through the grounds with an unlit cigarette between his fingers; Lord knows what he might have said or done had the cigarette been lit, since this was easily grounds for summary dismissal, if not civil action.

Jack had to think quickly. It was too late to backtrack and head for the main gate. Even before the thought had been expressed in a well-formed sentence, he was greeted by a string of syllables, which he first took to be a vague salutation.

'Priceacuppatea?' said the old man, without so much as looking up; his face expressionless, he continued rolling his cigarette with infinite care.

'Grumf!' Jack replied, still not catching on, and he quickly wheeled his bicycle past him, through the rear gate and into the school yard. The bike shed wasn't far from the gate, and, as he was locking up his bike, he realised that the old man had been asking for money. He looked back; the old man had already shouldered his bundle and was walking away, disappearing into the early morning mist like a disappointed ghost. Jack felt a twinge of guilt, overruled only by the need to take up his briefcase and walk.

The day was punctuated by the thought of that quite unexpected encounter. Jack felt uncomfortable for not having given the old guy some loose change – the price of a cup of tea; his discomfort was perhaps explicable because his failure to help the old man out smacked of miserliness – or was it because he had missed a glorious opportunity of thumbing his nose at Watkins? He had no time to debate the matter, let alone settle it one way or the other.

The day passed with its customary grind, the staffroom as ever a hive of exhausted bees, respect for the queen bee increasingly hard to discern, pleasant obedience to her requirements vastly diminished and diminishing still. Yet, truth to tell, the atmosphere in the staffroom was more than usually gloomy and tense. It was not quite the usual gloom that pervades the halls of those who know only too well that every new year is, at best, no improvement on the one that preceded it. No, there was an additional source of grievance, though one which could not be aired too openly or explicitly except to the most trusted of confidants. Patel, for example, was particularly put out today, and his discomfiture was catching and a source of general sympathy.

Here it might be explained that Patel Senior had removed himself from India not long after 1945, and Patel Junior, then a mere strip of a lad, now seemed to regret that he had done so. A return to India, to the country of his forebears, at least to an India devoid of its caste system and its theological metaphysics, seemed more attractive than ever; or perhaps it would be more accurate to say that the UK was not at this moment as attractive to Patel Junior as it had been to Patel Senior.

'I just hope...' Patel began as he sidled up to Jack, 'I just hope reincarnation is an error. I could not go through all this again. I really could not!' It sounded like a joke, but his earnestness was as clear as his large, round, black eyes. Patel's father, an anglophile *par excellence*, had entertained visions of the UK as a Mecca of opportunities, and the security the country appeared to offer as a Holy Grail. Patel had harboured no such illusions; having received a good education, as distinct from a costly one, he had learned to ask good questions and, what's more, to answer them, too. There were, he concluded, definite limits to the warmth that this noble democracy could provide its immigrants; its hospitality was relative, unreliable and uncertain. Perhaps in no small measure due to the stresses and strains that his personal life had inflicted upon him and the dubious comfort that he now derived from teaching, Patel was in no mood to entertain the truth of the proposition that, for all its faults, the United Kingdom was undoubtedly the most beneficent host on the planet. Unlike his father, Patel Junior not only believed that it was better to travel than to arrive, but that travelling should be done for the most part *incognito*, for the sentiment *vive la difference* was not always a recipe for mutual toleration. Be that as it may, Patel was not the sort to grouse aloud to just anyone. It was a mark of infinite trust that he voiced his feelings to Jack, and this fact was not lost on the latter.

There was a time when Patel had taught mathematics with astonishing verve, but that was when he had been left alone to do the job with which he had been entrusted. In other words, before the monster *Staff Appraisal* had reared its ugly head. The verve with which Patel had taught his subject was inspiring, and it was inspiring because Patel was inspired, and both what was inspiring about his lessons and he who was inspired were inextricably linked with *personality*. But what was monstrous about Staff Appraisal was that it robbed teaching of the personality that was essential to free and individualised expression, for essential to Staff Appraisal was the insistence on box-ticking, which went with an incapacity to question the validity of the boxes that had to be ticked. Eccentricity was anathema to uniformity and conformity, yet it was eccentricity that differentiated one personality from another. Boxes defined norms, and no departure from these norms was permissible. Personality was therefore expunged from the classroom. The fear amongst teachers that boxes may go unticked spelt paralysis, and paralysis and free expression were impossible bedfellows. Personality was no more welcome in teaching than it was in the army, and the boxes that had to be ticked were orders that had to be obeyed. Oh yes, things were different now. Why, it was only last week that Watkins had walked unannounced into the middle of one of Patel's lessons, in his much vaunted fly-on-the-wall capacity, 'Just to see how things are coming along.' Had he been a fly, Patel would have swatted him into the plaster; instead, he nodded politely and smiled unconvincingly. Afterwards, Watkins had called him into his office, gave him a three-page list of boxes to tick, and told him to reflect (yes, the exact word he used was *reflect*) on his lesson and decide what he thought he had done well and what he thought he had done badly, and, having decided what he had done imperfectly, to come up with ideas for self-improvement. And all this in the interests of *Self-Development*, another monster that had taken up residence with *Staff Appraisal*, the pair enjoying a status of perfect, and therefore unquestioned, marital bliss.

Jack was standing by the staffroom window, looking out at the Lawson cypresses which lined the pathway right down to the main gate, when he half-heard Patel make what he thought was some wisecrack about reincarnation. He wasn't listening intently, his thoughts still bent towards the earlier surprise encounter.

'It is just not right,' Patel went on. 'Not right I tell you! I've been teaching for over twenty years now. I have worked well and I have worked hard, only to end up being gawked at by someone – someone who is my junior, and who knows nothing about mathematics, to boot.' He now had Jack's full attention and proceeded to relate the fly-on-the-wall incident in full. 'Does he not realise that a human being is not a fly? As soon as he, or anyone else for that matter, walks into my classroom, the dynamic of it all is lost – like the bottom falling out of a… out of a… well, out of a barrel of apples!' Jack wanted to smile, but Patel's anguish precluded it. 'And to tell me to *reflect*! Me! Me above all people! My life has been a continuous process of reflection. I cannot help myself! It is a kind of mortgage I can never pay off! And he tells me to *reflect*! I will tell you, it is Watkins and his ilk who ought to go in for *reflection*. It might do them a lot of good!'

Patel was machine-gunning Watkins, speaking as he did in that full form, not a subject-verb contraction in sight; the kind of construction that one tends to associate with Indians, who tend to speak better English than the English, and he was possibly doing so in imitation of Patel Senior who would have nothing to do with subject-verb contractions. Patel was in just the mood to assert his heritage – anything to mark him off from Watkins and all he thought Watkins stood for. But in every other respect, he was an English as Jack.

'Yes, Watkins—' Jack started.

'Gawked at! And…' Patel edged a little closer to deliver his main salvo in the strictest possible confidence. '…and by someone who has not had any real classroom experience for the last century and a half!'

Patel was famous for his comic hyperbole, but Jack had learned not to respond to it.

'You should look after yourself,' was all Jack could say.

'It is getting harder to do that!' Patel replied in a loud whisper.

'Tell me about it!' said Jack, ironically, and in an equally loud whisper.

It occurred to Jack, as soon as he had said it, how hollow it was to tell someone to look after himself. What did it mean? What did it mean, short of not drinking, eating or smoking yourself to death? Did it mean anything at all? Or was it just an easy, lazy way of ending a conversation by really saying nothing? You might as well tell someone to pay regular visits to their doctor – which might be offensive, or a recipe for hypochondria and therefore stress.

As if in response to the magic word 'hollow', the door of the staffroom opened sharply, and in walked Davenport, which was enough in itself to put a mighty full stop to any subversive talk.

* *

Roger Davenport had been recently appointed acting deputy head at Morley Comprehensive, a position which he had worked assiduously and insidiously to arrive at. Having arrived, he now coveted not only the permanency of the title, but even the Headship itself. His path towards the top had led through the mires of ingratiation both with the teaching staff and with the upper echelons; he was masterly at playing both ends against the middle, of working one end up against the other with the fervour of a radical, and then simply withdrawing to a safe distance to watch the fireworks, thus appearing the picture of moderation to both sides, the voice of common sense, the fountain of oracular judgement. Jack had encountered many such Machiavellian characters in the well-worn pages of history and could sum them up in a word of two syllables. But because Davenport was so masterly at appearing a genuine friend to all and sundry, so adept at having built around him a reputation for sincerity and respectability, Jack dared not make an adverse remark against him in public lest it be interpreted a classic case of sour grapes – clever and subtle are the ways in which genuine, valid criticism may be rendered toothless. Disingenuousness had thus been so successful in the exercise of its own arts that it was thoroughly protected from public censure. Jack's frustration was, in consequence, immense, but irresolvable. It was something he had somehow to learn to live with, like a hereditary pain in the neck for which there is no cure.

But there was a bit more to it than that.

Davenport taught Latin and religious studies, a combination of disciplines which only helped to heighten the celestial light in which he had basked for some time. He sported a beard which he had allowed to grow long enough to hide the top of his shirt collar, the knot in his tie visible only when he craned his neck skyward, which he was quite frequently wont to do. Though long, his beard was well kept and detracted not a jot from the respectability of his general bearing, but on the contrary enhanced it and aided his designs.

Chief of these was to win the hearts of Watkins, the board of governors, and, if public avowals of faith are to be given any credence, the favour of Almighty God, since he put himself forward as a devout Catholic. His spiritual orthodoxy was matched by what had now become political and economic Catholicism. He believed that primacy should be given to market forces in education as elsewhere, and no doctrine could be better calculated to secure the confidence of Watkins and the hearts and minds of the board of governors; and Watkins, it must be remembered, was the ladder to be climbed and later discarded. Morley might be a comprehensive, and therefore of broadly socialist origins, but socialism had at last been discredited, and even if Davenport had in his youth been affected by the socialist bug, albeit in its milder and less truculent form, there was no doubting now that the virus was to all intents and purposes eradicated and that market forces were generally acknowledged to be the way forward, though it was thought at least expedient to be forever on the alert for spasmodic and fleeting signs of the pestilence, which should be adroitly nipped in the bud. Such was Davenport's frame of mind and that of those with whom he sought to ingratiate himself. As Davenport saw it, there are things which, at a distance, may appear irresistible, but which, on closer inspection, are at best questionable and at worst obnoxious; amongst such things he was heard to include very elderly ladies who dress as overly made-up teenagers, and political creeds which promise betterment, not to say perfection, of the human condition. He would have counted himself a religious, political and economic realist.

Jack and Patel moved away from the window and sat down. Jack wondered what Davenport would look like if he shaved off his beard: perhaps wasted from the nose down, the remaining flesh having overnourished the beard which fed upon it – like a mother drained by her offspring.

'How a classicist can be familiar with, say, the wisdom of Marcus Aurelius and at the same time suck up to Watkins beats me,' Jack muttered to Patel, after Davenport had left the staffroom with as much flourish as he had entered it. 'Watkins thrives on it, of course,' Jack added.

'What? Aurelius, or being sucked up to?' Patel managed a joke.

Jack managed a stifled laugh. 'Yes, but how can a classicist be such a toady?'

'Well, there were enough toadies amongst the ancients, you know. And Aurelius was happy enough to persecute Christians – are you forgetting, my friend?'

'Yeah, right,' Jack nodded.

'I thought I could trust him, you know,' Patel said, in a low voice and looking round. 'Watkins, I mean.' They had the staffroom to themselves now. 'I did not imagine how petty he could be. How shallow. After all these years. How people can change. I remember what an obliging colleague he used to be. Very pleasant. Power corrupts, alright!'

If rights are to be earned as distinct from merely conferred, a proposition Patel had never seriously questioned, he now believed himself to have earned the right to be left alone; the right to be trusted; the right to have his opinions respected; the right to live and work with his opinions provided they did not rock the boat unnecessarily, let alone sink it; the right to speak his mind without fear of reprisal. It all seemed simple enough, and these rights had, as it were, been strangely consecrated by his bereavement and his coronary problems. In any case, he was growing older, he was at least two years Watkins's senior, and it was a time when doubts concerning such rights simply couldn't be tolerated. His late wife, Misbah, would have had something to say about all these stresses and strains if only she could raise her head and look about her. Ah, Misbah! Their marriage had been childless, and although it is said that children cement a marriage, no couple could have been closer than Patel and Misbah; joined together through matrimony, they became as one through habit and custom, one understanding the other in the absence of words, such that the phrase 'Zanjik and Misbah' sounded almost like an ancient mantra, sacred and unalterable, solid and unshakeable – until death decreed otherwise.

The fly-on-the-wall episode was bad enough, but if Patel had thought Watkins a trustworthy overseer, friend as well as monitor, the first shock came when Watkins ticked him off, publicly and in no uncertain terms, for being five minutes late for one of Watkins's *Strategy Group Brainstorming Sessions*, a meeting convened to discuss ways and means of increasing 'educational productivity' on a much reduced budget. Such issues were the very lifeblood of Watkins and Davenport, who could not therefore comprehend the degree of unconcern which they believed to be implied by any lateness whatsoever; they approached the question of school budgets with the obsessive commitment commonly observed in crossword fanatics. After some harsh words from Watkins, Patel felt like a schoolboy reprimanded for some prank, and he shrank into an empty chair in the front row, having been obliged to run a gauntlet (in fact, more apparent than real) of reproachful stares and adverse whisperings. Jack, who had observed everything, had dated his own loathing of Watkins from precisely this time. The revelation was, of course, worse for Patel. Watkins had shown his true colours at last, a black narcissus fully in bloom. As for Davenport, who had nodded in grim acquiescence during Watkins's short tirade, he had held no such surprises.

Yes, it was worrying to witness his colleague Patel in such distress. But there was more to come, for tomorrow was Wednesday, and Wednesday evenings held stresses of another kind.

*　*

And so, the following evening, exhausted though he was, Jack made his weekly call at 92 Cutters Way, to spend a dutiful hour with his mother. She lived in a one-bedroomed, well-furnished flat, everything spick and san, sparkling and shiny. She opened the door for him just as he reached the threshold, as she was wont to do, having looked out for him coming, thus obviating the need to press the doorbell. The open door spread some little light into the darkness of the hallway, as Jack fumbled with the lock and chain of his bicycle; his mother seldom used the porch light, mindful of the electricity bill. 'Saw you coming,' she said – as she always did.

Her visits to Jack's family were infrequent and cold, for she and Sally did not get on, and since they were both made of the sternest and most inflexible of materials, Jack had just about given up on his attempts at arbitration and conciliation and remained piggy-in-the-middle. He was now trying, with less than total success, to live with a cold war in which the postures of the opposing forces were frozen solid and therefore immoveable. Being a middle-man faced with the thankless and impossible task of appeasing both sides at one and the same time, the stresses and strains of life were not confined to the changing requirements of his occupation and the sense of foreboding aforementioned.

His mother welcomed his visits, if only to have him all to herself and without competition – as Sally would have said, and what Sally said went uncontested. Look forward as she might to his weekly visits, this did not imply that she lived like a lonely old woman, all by herself in the gloom of her over-furnished sitting room. Very far from it. Though in her early seventies, she looked twenty years younger and was considered quite a catch by more than a handful of the local retired males, who would seek her out in turn and in fits and starts. She kept herself, like her flat, awesomely polished and extremely well upholstered: her hair dyed black as jet, her hands beautifully manicured; and her facial wrinkles, though extant where naturally expected, were not so obvious to the casual eye, lavishly treated as they were to all the cosmetics and artifices that human ingenuity could devise. Company, and the *male* company she vastly preferred, was therefore always at hand; indeed, so much so, that it was the quieter hours that she particularly coveted, that she might, as it were, 'gather herself' and keep her flat ship-shape. After four luckless marriages, all prospective suitors were kept in their place and carefully scrutinised, for she did not truly intend to marry for a fifth time; and who could blame her? Daily callers were one thing, a marriage commitment quite another; suitors tended therefore to be kept at arm's length and somewhat on a string.

All were kept in their place, and Wednesday evenings were reserved for Jack, who was expected to visit the royal apartments like the dutiful son he was, and since he was an only child that duty could in any case devolve on no other to the same degree. Duty it was and very little pleasure.

Having locked his bicycle, Jack entered the hallway and pecked her lightly on the cheek, a peck that was customarily unreturned. He closed the door on the cold and foggy darkness behind him and entered the living room. Of all the table lamps scattered thereabouts, only one illumined the darkness.

'How on earth can you sit in this darkness?'

'Wait a minute,' she said as she fumbled with another lamp. 'There, right now?'

'Better, yes.'

This was the kind and extent of the winter conversational preamble he had come to expect. Conversations between Jack and his mother were invariably set pieces with only minor variations, like pieces of music played by ear. They resembled mechanisms with a winter and a summer setting.

The living room was furnished with dark wooden side tables and a large sideboard, the carpet was heavily and darkly patterned, and the curtains at the windows followed suit with dark floral designs. Two or three coffee tables were replete with large glass ashtrays which no one was permitted to use since smoking indoors was strictly forbidden; scattered about were various vases and a variety of *objets d'art*, which were accident traps for small children, and partly explained why Pete had always been an infrequent and highly nervous visitor in his infant days.

Truth to tell, children just weren't welcome lest they disturb the floral-patterned cushions, which had to be puffed up again, scratch the reproduction mahogany sideboard or side tables, or demand biscuits and scatter the crumbs. Little hands couldn't be trusted to hold china plates steady – *china* plates, mind you, and not the disposable rubbish people use for picnics; nothing but the best for Jack's mother, and therefore it was important that nothing bad should happen to the best of things. Rather than risk scratches or any depletion to her set of Royal Dalton, Jack's mother decided to forgo the frequent visits of grandchildren; not that Pete had been unruly as a small child; on the contrary, he had, if anything, been extraordinarily timid and reserved. But children are children, and boys will be boys; so, better safe than sorry.

'How's Peter?' she asked.

'Fine! Just fine.' Jack knew it was pointless to give anything but the most cursory of replies to the most perfunctory of questions.

'I can't stand winter. I don't mind autumn. Spring's my favourite,' she went on, skipping summer. 'I just can't abide these long, dark winter nights.'

'Right.'

'And I have to be careful to lock all my windows at night. I go round them all, you know. Scared stiff! When George brings me home, he always waits to see if I'm safe inside. "Mind you lock all those windows," he says.' George, his mother's latest suitor, was, like all the others, most solicitous about her wellbeing. 'Of course, he's offered to stay the night with me – yes, he'd do it in a flash. But I said no. He knows I like my independence.'

'Yes, you can't be too careful these days, Mum. Make sure they're all locked.'

'Doing all right at school then, is he?'

'Pete? Oh, yes. Yes, he is.'

'I'll have to get my washer seen to. Making one hell of a noise. George says it shouldn't do that. Less than a year old. Still under guarantee, though – thank goodness.'

What appeared as subjects of conversational banality were in fact a serious of 'openers', which Jack after all those years had become adroit at detecting. Reference to the long, dark nights of winter might on another occasion have been the opener, and perhaps it would be next week's opener. But the opener this week was reference to the malfunctioning washing machine. 'Openers' consisted of windows of opportunity, as it were, to speak endlessly and repeatedly about her past; on such occasions, the ability to play the role of good listener required a level of patience and endurance that was positively saintly.

'Yes, I remember taking in washing – after you left me to go to university. I was on my own then. Yes, I took in some washing, and I used to send you a couple of pounds every so often, when I could afford it – had to live from hand to mouth in those days. No joke. Did it all by hand, you know. No automatic washing machines in those days. All by hand!'

Jack listened in the half-light, afraid to close his eyes for even an instant lest he fall asleep. With the hard listening went the gentle, knowing, sympathetic nods, for he knew very well that every word his mother spoke was unquestionably true. Hers were not the pleasant reminiscences of days gone by; they resembled moans and groans of pain, and it was part of Jack's weekly duty to share them all – no movement of hand or foot or eye, no word of mouth, could be suffered to break her train of spoken thoughts; for it was his business to share her pain, however stretched he felt on the rack of her former hardships and present loneliness; for, suitors apart, she suffered the loneliness that the weight of memory brings in its train, and Jack felt helpless in the face of it.

'All by hand! I wouldn't have had to do it. But your father left me without a penny. You know that, don't you? Except the few hundred insurance, and that paid for his funeral. Not blaming him, of course. But that's how it was. Just how it was. I had to struggle. Had to struggle! And this generation doesn't know what it's about – what with their fancy jobs, and their cars – everybody has a car now – and all their fitted kitchens – all their mod cons…'

Every word true – true and as heavy as lead. The wheel of the rack was given once more turn.

Jack was the only offspring of her first marriage, and that marriage had been a curious match, Jack's father being fourteen years her senior, with first-hand experience of the killing fields of war, first wounded at Dunkirk and then back into the fray from El Alamein to D-Day. He would sit quietly in an armchair or on a hard wooden chair in the garden shed, reading his Bible; he had come from a religious background, his father having been a Baptist lay preacher. But it was his experience of the killing fields that had turned Jack's father into an avid reader of Scripture; perhaps he had hoped to find answers there, or at least the kind of forbearance that Jack himself had read about at random. And so, he would sit and read; and meanwhile his young wife, with experience of nothing beyond her own backyard, would sit opposite him in their small living room, doubtless dreaming of a better life than this, a life of travel, of dancing, of laughter, of gaiety – dreaming, in short, of *life*, of *living,* as distinct from mere existence. Her husband was no doubt glad simply to be alive. But she wanted to live. His object now was to try to make some sense of all the carnage he had seen, while hers was still to see, and to feel the joy of being.

When baby Jack came along, she might at times have thought of him as an extra nail in the marital coffin, a further link in the chains which bound her to a sedentary husband and a life of domestic confinement, an appeal to her youthful proclivities roundly denied.

'For the sake of her nerves – purely for the sake of her nerves,' or so the family doctor was quoted as saying, she should go out with some friends at least one evening a week. And Jack's father, being broad-minded, exceptionally trusting, and deeply solicitous about his wife's state of mind, had agreed. Where there's no trust, there's no marriage, his father used to say. So it was arranged that Jack would be looked after by his father or by his grandparents whenever his mother took her evenings out for the sake of her nerves.

It was during one of these beneficial evenings that Jack's father died of a massive heart attack – a coronary thrombosis, according to the death certificate. Jack was alone with him when he died; about two weeks before Jack's tenth birthday, in November, in the season of Goodwill to All Men – all men, that is, apart from Jack's father. Jack, helpless and beside himself with anxiety and grief, actually saw his father die in his armchair by the coal fire, not taken quietly on the wings of sleep, but in the sharpest pain, his lips crimson as they dripped with blood; Jack looked on, dumbfounded, until he could look no more; then out he ran into the streets having jumped the garden hedge, shouting for help, though there was no help for it now. The night smelt and tasted of death, and that sensation lingered on in Jack's ineradicable store of memories. When his mother returned home that night, she fainted on hearing the news. She and young Jack lay awake in each other's arms through the night, vowing never to part – it was the only way to survive till morning and beyond.

After some years, she married again. But Jack's stepfather died of cancer of the pancreas a year before Jack went off to university; his mother nursed him at home rather than let him die in hospital. He left her with nothing but a pension, and she could not hold done a job 'on account of my nerves'. Time and again, Jack had to listen to this history, a tedious and painful narration. He remembered his stepfather and his sufferings only too well. But he was not allowed to forget the 'sacrifices' his mother had made to give him a university education.

Listening was painful, not simply because it was tedious and Jack was already exhausted, but, again, because every word was *true*. Such was the gruelling experience of Wednesday evenings at 92 Cutters Way.

On this particular Wednesday, however, his mother's narration ended with one of her favourite phrases: 'Well, my conscience is clear! Yes, my conscience is clear.'

That phrase might, in turn, have been another opener into yet another narration.

Jack was spared on this occasion, and the subject of his mother's marital experiences was closed. But only for the present. It was not unknown for his mother to do a chronological *tour de force,* and include her last two marriages for good measure, the first of which ended in divorce on the grounds, properly and justly decided in her favour, of mental and emotional cruelty; the second of which ended in the death of the kindly octogenarian who had been devoted to her – terminated, therefore, by Nature herself, without rancour and simply in accordance with the laws of the human condition. Out of all four husbands, therefore, only one had truly stepped out of line and treated her badly, each one showing her undying devotion and respect; in fact, in this last case, the match was so botched, and so short-lived, that one wonders whether the marriage had, in any spiritual sense, existed at all – anyhow, it was best forgotten, and relegated to the purely mythical.

It was thanks to the kindly octogenarian that his mother's financial fortunes had taken a turn for the better. This, together the last and very short-lived liaison, had no doubt helped her to decide that enough was enough. Permanent liaisons were finally out. There were to be no more attempts at marital bliss, and she was now content to play the part of sufficiently affluent, one cannot say wealthy, dowager, habitually recounting her past trials and tribulations and playing non-condescending host to her many flattering male admirers.

When Peter was a youngster, Jack would take him to see her, believing that she actually wanted to see him. Children, however, are more perceptive. Finally realising that she had no real interest in seeing her grandson, Jack eventually gave up trying to persuade Peter to go with him. Peter's visits faded out, without comment, let alone protest, from his grandmother. She would give Jack some pocket money to pass on to him, perhaps believing herself to have amply fulfilled her grandmotherly duties in so doing. Peter was relieved not to have to go. And so, everyone was the happier.

Her son fared no better than her grandson. Worse even, since Jack not only received no pocket money, but was regularly taunted by the suggestion that there might be a fortune coming to him 'one day' in the form of an inheritance: there was the flat to pass on, together with funds in the form of investments made by the kindly octogenarian. Perhaps she intended this reference to 'one day' to function as a carrot which would lead Jack by the nose closer towards her, and away from Sally. Sally, to whom his mother wanted to leave nothing, was the fly in the ointment. Whatever came to Jack would come also to Sally, and that was the sticking point. It did not bear thinking about; little wonder his mother declined to elucidate, beyond the meagre but tantalising reference to things coming Jack's way 'one day'. One thing was certain: they would not come his way until his mother was ready, namely when, as she put it, 'my eyes are closed'; he would get nothing sooner; for if Sally were ever to become an unintended beneficiary, the less Mrs Barker knew about it, the better.

Meanwhile, clean, pristine and loveless was his mother's embrace; like her living room, and as sterile as a crematorium. One hour a session on those Wednesday evenings was all Jack could take, after which he was mightily glad to have a home of his own to go to, and his Elizabethan viols would help sustain him until the next visit.

*   *

He looked at his watch, which he could barely see in the gloom, and got up to go.

'And how are *you* keeping?' she suddenly asked.

'Well, as a matter of fact, I'm going to the hospital for a kind of kidney scan, and er…'

'Oh, yes? Ah well, these things are sent to try us, as they say,' she interrupted. Jack remembered the rule about perfunctory questions and cursory replies, and said no more.

'You know,' she went on, 'I can't understand why you don't learn to drive. You have a car, don't you? And *she* drives. Ridiculous! And then you wouldn't have to cycle here.'

'Sally, yes. Well, I don't like cars much. I much prefer to cycle,' he said, making his way into the hallway.

She got up and rearranged the cushion Jack had been sitting on and brushed the seat with the flat of her hand to remove the creases, before following him into the hallway.

'I could've made you a cup of tea,' she said apologetically, as Jack rummaged in his pockets for his cycle clips.

'Oh, doesn't matter,' he said, giving her a parting peck on the cheek. 'See you next week, Mum,' he said. 'Oh, and phone if you need anything.'

'Give my love to Peter,' she said from the dark hallway.

Jack cycled away in the darkness, and without the slightest intention of giving his mother's love to Peter. It was just a phrase, and would mean as much to Peter as it meant to him, and as much to Jack as it meant to his mother. He had learned that already; some lessons were too painful to bear. And as for all that stuff about learning to drive – it was probably a dig at his manhood or a slight against Sally, or both. So sad. So painful. So damned unnecessary.

*　*

As he cycled away, he recalled the occasions when he'd tried to get his mother away from herself, away from her past – to bring her to understand that there was a whole world outside her front door, outside herself; that the television news of famine, of murder, of cruelty and disease was anything but chimerical. But she no longer watched the television news, nor had she ever read newspapers. In any case, on such occasions he would be told that he was being 'too deep', and she made it sound like a form of juvenile delinquency. 'You're too deep, Jack, that's your trouble.' And, without further ado, she'd get right back to talking about herself with one of her customary openers, principally about her need for company, though strictly on her own terms, and for a bit of luck while she still had time to enjoy it.

Jack and his mother were like the opposite poles of a horseshoe magnet: forever in opposition, yet forever bound together, as they had sworn to be that fateful night in November. They were, you might say, cast in the same mould and imprisoned together on the same arc of being, and only the fires of death could break them asunder; and even death might not be capable of breaking that bond, perhaps even in death they would be welded together inseparably and hurled through the cosmos for all eternity. If love was there, it was lurking somewhere in the shadows, afraid, perhaps, or too inhibited, to stand in the light.

Was it that life and its unfairness had destroyed her capacity for love, or, if not her capacity, her ability to express it? Jack felt too close to her to make much sense of any of it. He needed to stand back – or rather, to get home through the darkness to another world, a not altogether better one, but at least different from the one he had left at 92 Cutters Way.

And so he cycled on with feelings mixed of abhorrence and pity, of abhorrence and love. No doubt, there was love. Had he not read somewhere that a mother is an individual significant by her individuality? Despite the coldness, perhaps envy, perhaps jealousy, that resided at 92 Cutters Way, still there was love, and that love was mutual. Whatever her faults, he loved her still, as sons should love their mothers, and deeper even than that, for they had shared pain, and shared now the weight of memory. And was it not Robert Louis Stevenson who'd said that love is not blind but merely chooses to ignore? Jack chose to ignore. And was it not Shakespeare who'd said that love alters not when it alteration finds? And life and time had altered many things since the innocence of his youth and the hopes his young mother had entertained.

Apart from all this, he suspected that something was medically wrong, and developments some years later may have proved his suspicions well founded. She developed Alzheimer's Disease, and perhaps the coldness she had expressed at 92 Cutters Way was its very early beginnings. Who was to tell? Who was ever to know? But Jack preferred to seek solace in some vague pathology. And to have suggested at the time that she should perhaps seek medical advice would have been to invite a disastrous response, so volcanic was she, so susceptible to instant and lasting eruption; it would have called forth a display of disquietude compared with which the screeching of all the harpies of hell would be none other than the dulcet sounds of gentle maids singing sweetly of the burgeoning blossoms of spring.

As he cycled into his own driveway, the thought struck him that pain does not necessarily make us stronger, but progressively weaker. 'Poor angel,' he whispered to himself. 'Poor, poor, angel' – because he had known the best of her, and the best of her was unforgettable; her performances at 92 Cutters Way were the worst of her, but the best of her had saved her from all possible censure. She could do no wrong.

4

Jack's Rubicon: First Sighting

It was the Friday of the following week when Jack had his second and far more significant encounter with the old man at the gate.

Until then no one had seen hide or hair of him, and references to him began to be made in the past tense. He had become the subject of stock jokes and staffroom merriment. One story was that he had crept into an end-of-term carol concert at St Mary's Junior School and sat in the back row amongst the doting parents. His presence had become glaringly obvious during the pupils' onstage rendering of 'O Come All Ye Faithful', when the old fellow apparently became overexcited, rocked to and fro in his seat, tapped his feet in time with the seasonal ditty, gesticulated with his hands and finally joined in, disrupting somewhat the performance onstage, causing some consternation amongst the supervisory staff and engendering not a little parental anxiety. Believing him to be more tipsy than the occasion could allow, the police were called to eject him, in the event unnecessarily, since, by the time they arrived, he had crept away peacefully into the frosty night, presumably with the final strains of 'O Come All Ye Faithful' still ringing in his hairy ears. In accordance with the laws of Chinese Whispers, the narrative had been embroidered by the time it finally reached Morley Comprehensive, but it was in all its essentials correct. Jack, like everyone else, was amused by the anecdote and found himself laughing with the others, though his amusement was mitigated by the fact that he still felt a twinge of guilt for not having given the old fellow the price of a cup of tea. Jack half wished he could bump into him again to make good the omission.

Early on the Friday morning in question, Jack's half-wish was granted in full, though not at all with the consequences he had expected.

Jack was cycling towards the rear entrance, faintly self-satisfied in the knowledge that he was rebelliously taking an unorthodox route with unprecedented persistence, when the scene loomed up before him, like a vision in some mystical romance. There was the old man, sitting on his bundle, his back against the old elm, and rolling a cigarette with the concentration of a seamstress dedicated to perfection. There was nothing about the man that would support the anecdote that had entertained everyone in the staffroom; it was hard to imagine him gesticulating, or tapping his feet, or rocking to and fro in some kind of tipsy euphoria. His eyelids were heavy, his eyes deep set in their sockets, and not even the whisper of amusement played about his lips. Everything about him belied the comic narrative, which Jack quickly surmised had more than its fair share of fictional content. There was something oddly unfair about the embellishment, though what was unjust about it he was not yet in a position to say. Perhaps it had to do with the sadness in the old man's eyes.

Jack had been mentally rehearsing his first moves ever since the initial encounter. He would press the price of a cup of tea (better, two, or even three cups of tea) into the old man's hand with a benevolent smile and a sympathetic nod, thus amply salving his conscience and giving the day a very good start. Not a word need be spoken between them; but an example would be set, and Jack's contrition applauded, if ever so lightly, by an unseen benevolent God. With something like this in mind, Jack dismounted and approached him.

'Funny about trees,' said the old man, still looking down at the cigarette he had just finished rolling between his fingers, and then moistening the end with his tongue. Jack was caught on the hop. He opened his mouth, but nothing came out.

'Yes, indeed, funny about trees,' the old man repeated, looking up into Jack's face and looking down again. 'Leaves fall, like people, but the trees go on – leaves and trees, people and life, don't you think?' He spoke in what may be best, though unsatisfactorily, described as a 'neutral' accent; that he was British was certain, and that he was English was probable; but that left many questions. Jack smiled and some sound came from his throat – something between a laugh and a cough. The old man lit his cigarette with a cheap lighter.

This wasn't the script Jack had written for himself, but perhaps some of it, the most important part of it, might still be redeemed. He leant over to press a ten-pound note into the palm of the old man's hand, hoping then to move off quickly. He didn't get the chance. The old man drew back his hand as though the note were contaminated with a deadly poison, and Jack just managed to catch it before it fell to the ground.

'Er… no thanks,' said the old man, quite genially.

Jack just stood there, trying hard to smile.

'No, don't need it – not today, anyway. Thanks all the same, and all that,' the old man said.

The old man seemed so much in earnest that Jack felt he could do nothing but return the note to his pocket, while the old fellow drew leisurely on his cigarette, blowing the smoke up into the cold air of the morning.

It was just then that something quite extraordinary happened, something quite incongruous with the Jack that everyone, including Jack himself, knew. Jack surprised himself out of all recognition by uttering words so unscripted as to have been quite unimaginable even seconds before.

'How about a drink later on, then – in The King's Head, just round the corner? See you there about four. Right?' The words were out in a torrent before Jack could stop himself, and then he sped away almost as the last word was out of his mouth, not stopping to confirm the arrangement with the old man, and giving him no time to react.

It was absurd, of course. But it was unambiguously done and could not be taken back! What would Sally say? What Sally would say was nobody's business. The whole thing was outrageous. But then, it must be said that Jack, in common with many, was impressed by the unusual. He had quickly calculated that the old man was either a lunatic or a prophet, and had banked on the latter. Yes, Jack was impressionable, alright; but that was not the same as being *moveable*; but Jack had actually made a move – he had acted on the basis of his impressions of the unusual. He had actually *done* something, if saying can be said to be *doing*. And there was no *un*doing. For all that, he felt his words had curiously freed him from something that had bound him; but feeling is one thing, and articulation is another; had you asked him to elucidate, the task was as yet beyond him.

The old man, quite unruffled by the speed and unanswerability of the invitation, simply continued smoking, not even bothering to look

Jack in the face. Not of course that he had much chance to say yea or nay, for Jack was off like a rocket. It was all over in a flash, just like so many momentous events in the history of mediocrity.

Momentous it certainly was – at least for Jack. Certainly highly irregular. So much so that one is bound to offer some explanation. In the first place, he was feeling particularly down. These days he felt, to use his own word, 'heavy'; and, on locking up his bicycle in the cold mornings on the threshold of the school buildings, he felt as though it would be as much as he could do to stagger home again at the end of the day, to fade away and die in familiar and friendly surroundings, the strains of Elizabethan viols playing softly in the background, a requiem on a life anything but well spent. In short, he was a spent bullet. The beginning of the day, the beginning of every day, had about it the tired, heavy feel of the end of a hard, long march, but a march to nowhere; and since it was a march to nowhere, the consolation that he had at least achieved his destination was denied him. There was no doubt about it: the days were getting heavier and heavier, like the lid of an enormous leaden box descending inexorably, and slowly, slowly, getting heavier as it did so. Jack felt like one already pronounced dead who, with upstretched arms, was trying in vain to halt the lid in its descent, as it began to exclude all remaining vestiges of light and life. He had tried to explain this to Sally, though not in so many words. But her response was repeatedly: 'If you go on *saying* you're tired, you'll *be* tired! I work even harder than you do, and I know we've just got to get on with things – I mean, come on, that's life!' And just about there, the matter was customarily dropped.

There were indications of inexorability in the classroom, even during lessons; chief of which was the feeling of being wrapped in a blanket of déjà vu, closely applied with the feeling of standing outside himself, seeing himself perform, hearing himself speak – as though he were both speaker and listener, doer and watcher, listening to himself say and watching himself do what he had said and done for the umpteenth time. The effects of this were physical, too: on one occasion he actually swayed a little; just a little more and he might have blacked out in front of the whole class. What would his pupils have thought. And the Devil alone knows what Roger Davenport would have made of it for his own ends! Jack even convinced himself that the experience of standing outside oneself as listener and observer could kill, that it could actually induce your own death if you allowed it to, if you let it take over completely. He could not allow it to. Not yet, anyway. Not until he had proved himself; not until he had lived – and, whatever that meant, if it meant anything at all, was more than a little way off and would not come about anytime soon.

Apart from the early morning encounter with the old man, the day passed uneventfully, except that Davenport had announced that a trainee teacher, a Miss Amanda Fairfax, would be spending the following week at Morley Comprehensive to observe classes. Davenport delivered this bewitching piece of information with his customary benignity, remarking how the staff, collectively and individually, had the solemn duty of inspiring those who would succeed them – namely, future generations of teachers. Jack, having no time for Davenport, turned away in controlled disgust; but he was not to know just how important this apparently uninspiring snippet of information was to become.

* *

Late afternoon, Jack remembered his arrangement with the old man, but decided that it was too one-sided to be described as such and was more like a suggestion. Jack himself had formed the habit of slipping into The King's Head on Friday afternoons on his way home, and he did not believe that the old man would take his suggestion seriously. He was not, therefore, surprised to find the bar empty save for one or two regulars. The surprise, not to say shock, came with a tap on the shoulder as he was in the process of depositing his overcoat and briefcase on a chair at a table in the darkest corner of the premises. He turned round to find the old man smiling and nodding behind him. He could do nothing but smile in return.

'What'll you have?' Jack asked, taking a quick look round and trying to sound pleasantly nonchalant.

'Same as you,' said the old man, quietly.

'Right!' Jack proceeded to order two pints of brown ale, which the barmaid poured while at the same time giving furtive looks into the dark corner where the old man had settled, having placed his bundle carefully beside him.

The routine way in which all this was done belied the fact that it was perhaps one of the most extraordinary events in Jack's life to date. Big things can come in small packages, extraordinary things in the most ordinary of circumstances.

The old man gave a slight nod of thanks as Jack placed the glass in front of him and sat down.

'Alf,' said the old man, after taking a sip.

'Sorry?'

'Alf, my name. And you are…?'

'Oh, right. Yes. Jack. I'm Jack. Pleased to meet you.'

The old man smiled. 'Teacher, are you?'

'Yeah, that's right. History.'

'You're a missionary, then.'

'Missionary?'

'Yes, well, teaching history is quite an undertaking. A responsibility.'

'Well, education is a responsibility.'

'Yes. You know, when I was a young man, I was educated, too. I'm not sure what's happened since. In my day – I don't know what they do now – the vice chancellor conferred degrees with the formula – what was it now? – ah, yes, *Auctoritate mihi comessa, admitto te ad gradum Baccalaurei in Artibus in nomine Patris et Figlii et Spiritus Sancti*, and we felt proud, as though we'd been given a kind of divine qualification, almost like priests who were no longer novices but were now ready to go out into the world and help others to understand. A kind of divine mission. But as I say, I don't know what's happened since. I guess the idea of a mission is as dead as the dodo, like the Latin it was expressed in.' Alf took a large mouthful of brown ale.

'Like God,' ventured Jack, with a nonchalant shrug and a 'Humpf!'

'Ah, that depends. Depends on who or what your God is. I like to think mine is still alive and kicking.'

It was as though Alf had been thinking aloud, hardly aware of Jack's presence – he might as well have been ruminating under the elm tree. As for Jack, the shocks were coming thick and fast. The old man was obviously not what he had at first seemed; he was not a poor old duffer with a head full of nothing. He knew some Latin, which reminded Jack of Davenport; but he was nothing like Davenport, they differed like chalk and cheese. Alf spoke with a gravity and sincerity that was unmistakeable; Davenport might quote Latin to impress and befuddle, but Alf quoted Latin to say something that obviously came from the heart, something about… well, it wasn't immediately clear to Jack what his point was, except that it had something to do with the value of education, but this was something that Jack had to think about at greater leisure; things were happening thick and fast right now, and they tended to cloud his immediate judgement. Come to think of it, it was hard to imagine Davenport speaking as Alf did early that morning about leaves and trees and people and life – and that ought to have given him a hint that Alf was more than he seemed. Yes, Latin or no Latin, Alf was no Davenport, and Davenport was no Alf. Thank God.

The silence was broken by Jack asking a question which seemed trite as soon as it was formed: 'Do you actually sleep outdoors, then?'

'Yes, and then sometimes in a shed. He has a wooden shed in his garden – the vicar, I mean. I can use that. But I like the outdoors. I can dream better outdoors.'

'Dream?'

'I'm a dreamer. I dream in the day and I dream at night. If I'm lucky. Someone said a wise man seldom sleeps deeply and, when he does, dreams advisedly. But I dream all the time – so maybe I'm not a very wise man. Anyway, dreaming is good. It gets lonely, especially at dusk and at night, and then you begin to think life is much too long and is better ended. Dreaming gets you away from that. No, it's healthy to dream.'

'Tell me a dream – one of your dreams.'

'Well, recently I dreamed I was in a room of ghosts. You see, I'd invited them there myself – ghosts of friends, people I'd known. I must admit, my friends amongst the dead vastly outnumber my friends amongst the living. Anyway, I wanted to thank them all for being what they were. And I wanted to apologise to them, too, for not being better than I was… And then everything sort of slipped and I was talking to future generations, and I was apologising to them because the world is no better than it is, no better than it will be, no better than it ever will be. You see? Rubbish, yes? Well, that's dreams for you. But they get you away from the beginning of the world – while the nice dreams last, at least.'

'The beginning, or the end?'

'The beginning. We are still at the beginning – even if it all should end now.'

Jack was puzzled, and took an easier route. 'Well, I dream sometimes, too. And I can never make sense of them,' he said.

'Tell me one of your dreams.'

'Well, honestly, I can't remember. No, I er…' Jack stopped and stared into his half-empty glass. Alf smiled benignly.

After a moment's further silence, Jack drained his glass. 'Well, I must be going,' he said.

'Must?' Alf said.

'My wife, Sally – you see, I need to get home before she does. She…'

'Are you afraid of losing her?'

This question was the final shock in this series of broadsides.

'Afraid? Losing? No, of course not. It's just that she doesn't like me to be late, especially on Fridays, and…'

'You'd better be off, then,' Alf said. 'Sorry I can't return the favour.'

With a nod and a smile, Jack was off like a rocket, leaving Alf to finish his drink and vanish into the evening, which was fast approaching, as it does on those short winter days.

*   *

It has to be said that Alf's last question hit home somewhere deep and dark and otherwise impenetrable. Afraid of losing Sally? Did he mean, afraid that Sally might walk out? Ridiculous. Absurd. In fact, Jack was more than a little annoyed with Alf, and his annoyance inevitably set off a train of thought that was by no means unique. Alf almost spoke poetry in prose and was fascinating to listen to. But this last question wouldn't do. No, it wouldn't do at all.

The problem was all about fear.

As a boy, Jack would be goaded by his mates to sit on what was variously described as The Devil's Chair, Satan's Throne, or even The

Devil's Leap. It was a rocky protrusion with an immediate drop of about one hundred and fifty feet into the valley below. To get to it, you needed to walk over flat, wooded land, and then, suddenly, there it was, The Devil's Chair; they dared each other to take turns to sit in the chair, knowing that one slip would be their last. 'Go on, Jack!' But Jack could never bring himself to do it, and he preferred to suffer the goading and the name-calling. But what would by sensible adults be regarded as a wise course, was in the mind of a child a posture of cowardice.

Nor did it stop at The Devil's Chair. Jack's father had wanted to teach him to swim, but Jack was afraid of the water, afraid of sinking down into its dark, cold limitless depths, without air and light. 'Don't worry, I've got you,' his father said, holding Jack's head in the palm of his hand. 'When I let go, you'll float nice and easy, and I'm right here beside you.' But it was no good. Jack scrambled as fast as he could out of the water and onto dry land where it was dry and safe.

So what was the point of that rusty old sword that stood in the corner of what passed for Jack's study? It was an old, blunt regimental dress sword that had been given to Jack in his early teens by a family friend. It was considered harmless, and young Jack was so taken with it that he was given it with the proviso that he should take care of it. The blade was pitted with age, being at least fifty years old even before Jack had it, but the scrolling patterns could still be clearly seen near the top, and it was presented to him in a rusty scabbard. It had had a clean now and then, but for years had been neglected and now stood in that dark, forgotten corner of his study. Jack would look up occasionally from his desk and make out its outline, as it stood there in its forlorn state, since its poor condition precluded it from a position on one of the walls. Jack hadn't even considered the possibility of asking Sally what she would think of it as an item of decoration, for she would have ruled it out of court in no uncertain terms. In fact, that dark corner preserved it, for on more than one occasion she had referred to 'that rusty old thing'; given more prominence, ever so slight, and she'd have thrown it out without his knowledge.

But although the old thing had no real function, it had, in Jack's mind, and even as a boy, some kind of symbolic significance. It would have been delightful had something been written on the blade;

something like, *Draw me not without cause, return me not without honour.* Unfortunately, such sentiments were left entirely to Jack's young imagination. Yet, as he grew older, and even to this day, the sword was a symbol of something worthy. Perhaps one day the symbolism would become clearer, as though it was something that Jack had yet to discover and that, until discovered, his worthiness to own the sword was unproved. Fanciful nonsense, of course, and the product of a juvenile imagination. Yet juvenility has its uses and is not necessarily limited to juveniles. Thus it was that the sword remained an item in Jack's consideration. Somehow or other he had to earn it and had not yet done so; it was waiting to be wielded, by his hand and no other. Meanwhile, it stood in state, and every time Jack's eye fell upon it, he felt strangely, unaccountably inadequate.

As for being afraid of The Devil's Chair and of drowning, it had to be admitted that Jack had made some strides already. After all, he had trespassed against the edict of Watkins, for it must be remembered that when Watkins offered advice to his staff it was immediately and correctly interpreted as an edict; he had openly spoken to Alf, offered him money, invited him for a drink, and, worst of all, had made good the invitation and bought him a pint of brown ale. He had, in other words, done a great deal to *encourage* Alf, which is precisely what Watkins had advised against, and it was not at all wise to go against his advice. If Watkins or his sidekick Davenport got even just a whiff of this, Jack might find himself in very hot water. Fear remained a problem and seemed well-grounded, for fear of Watkins was bound up with fear of consequences: fear of losing his job, fear of losing his home, of losing his family, of losing Sally; layer upon layer of consequential fear, culminating in fear of ending up alone – as though any of us were not alone anyway, even with all those things we believe we possess.

With this in mind, would Jack meet Alf again, or did he have very good reason to avoid him all the more and to wish him gone, if not from the world, at least far from the vicinity of Morley Comprehensive? Plain and simple. But not quite so simple. True, Alf had annoyed Jack with his reference to fear. The still waters of Jack's being had been stirred and were murkier than ever before. On the other hand, it is sometimes wisely said that where there is no pain, there is no gain. And there was no doubt in Jack's mind that despite the liberties taken by the old man, an invisible thread ran between them – some kind of connection, perhaps yet too slender, too obscure, to be called 'kindred spirit', but something was there nevertheless.

As far as true friendship was concerned, Jack knew only too well how rare this really was. Why, one of young Jack's own teachers had long ago told the class, 'If you can find one true friend in life, you should count yourselves extremely lucky.' How true his words had proved, and Jack had never forgotten them. But how *could* he forget them? After all, it was one of life's tiresome, persistent lessons. In Morley Comprehensive you had constantly to watch your back, never letting down your guard, for whenever you did so, there was always someone there to deliver a blow that knocked you off your feet; one disappointment after another – yes, so tiresome, this back-biting, this one-upmanship, this relentless drive to be first in the queue for honours and praise, this insane desire to be kept in the good books of the mighty and the not-so-mighty and those who were successfully striving to be mightier than they deserved; yes, you had to run a marathon simply to keep still – yes, extremely tiresome. But the truth was, Jack had finally learned to distinguish between colleague and friend; the distinction, not always obvious, had been forced upon him by persistent repetition: in rare times of success and, more frequently, in times of distress, when congratulation and support might reasonably be expected, they were only grudgingly rendered, if rendered at all. Colleagues, even of long standing, were rarely true friends. Colleagues might exist within a spectrum of amiability. Some were unfailingly amiable and all were amiable on occasion. Even a colleague who was consistently hail-fellow-well-met was often amongst the least willing to give support to someone who was in dire need of it; and betrayal or indifference could be seen in their eyes, or in the smile that faded too quickly as they passed you in the corridor. Yes, friendship was another creature altogether. This was a hard but inescapable lesson, especially for the naive and the uninitiated. Well, you could hardly expect much more when that spectrum of amiability was deeply rooted in an unyielding context of envy, jealously and fear and the resulting evils of resentment, back-biting, clique-forming and one-upmanship; no, this was not exactly a soil conducive to the flowering of genuine friendship and selfless regard for your colleagues; nor was it a context in which finer examples of human conduct might readily be set to pupils who were clearly subjected to it and influenced by it. The rarity of true friendship was therefore a hard but inescapable lesson for the naive and the uninitiated. So much so, that Jack had taken the trouble to commit to memory several verses of an ancient Buddhist poem he had found in the Upanishads, and, in particular, the lines:

Friends who seek naught are scarce today.
Fare lonely as rhinoceros.

– lines which were invariably brought to mind whenever the name of that solitary creature came up or whenever he felt particularly isolated and hard done-by. Just as he remembered his mother's neat distinction between acquaintances and friends, and her regular insistence that of the former she had many, while the latter she could count on the fingers of one hand.

Though, counting himself a reasonable man, he was prepared to concede that everyone had problems, and that they were invariably so bewitched by preoccupation that they were incapable of taking those little actions for others that might have rendered the world a happier place for all and sundry.

But he was forgetting Patel. At least there was Patel. Patel was not like the others. Patel could be trusted. Patel was as close as a colleague could get to being a friend – which was not close enough to satisfy Jack, but was rather more than being a mere colleague.

5

A Phoenix Ruffles its Feathers

The following Monday, therefore, Jack related to Patel the essence of his meeting with Alf. Patel's astonishment was compounded by Jack's failure to ask Alf the simplest and most obvious of questions about Alf's background, and how it was that a man of his apparent erudition could possibly end up like that. All Jack could say was that the old man had taken him aback, that he hadn't even expected him to turn up at The King's Head at all, let alone share a table with him, let alone talk in the way he did with such authority and insight. Jack was too polite to even attempt to dig into the man's past; after all, it was not really any of his business; it wasn't the kind of question one asked, because it was the kind of information that is either given without asking, or not at all. It wasn't tendered, and so that was that.

Jack did not, understandably, tell Patel how discomforted he had felt with Alf's allusion to fear; Jack hadn't wanted to prolong the meeting, in any case, and wanted to get away, but he might have been persuaded to stay a little longer had Alf not made that allusion – as it was, the allusion had clinched it, and he had felt there was nothing for it but to bring the assignation to an abrupt end. Perhaps even closer to the truth was that Jack wanted, unconsciously, to preserve the mystique surrounding the old fellow; after a certain point, the less he knew about him the better; enough had been said to establish and nourish that mystique – why spoil it with gratuitous biography? But this, of course, was not something that Jack could put to Patel, or even to himself.

Fear was the subject of Jack's train of thought as he routinely cycled to school that Monday morning, hoping and praying, with every revolution of the pedals, that he would not see Alf anywhere in the vicinity – a prayer, incidentally, that was answered, for Alf was nowhere to be seen. But as for fear, he reasoned, it was fear that kept everyone in a state of submission to people like Watkins and his adjutant. Admiration and respect could never produce such anxiety, such fear of consequences, such awkwardness. Moreover, there was none of that Berchtesgaden optimism which raised the spirits of Hitler's minions in the early days of the war. No one felt uplifted by Watkins, not any more, except perhaps those who could be caught young, like Amanda Fairfax. It was only a question of time before everyone wised up to Watkins and Davenport; the path to enlightenment might be convoluted, but it led nowhere else. When Amanda was divested of all her youthful innocence, she would be just like the rest of them; she would finally arrive at a destination she had never really wanted. What was that joke? An optimist is a pessimist with no work experience. Not so much a joke as a profound indictment of the frailties of human nature, the frailties principally of people like Watkins and Davenport who spoiled it for everyone else by abusing the power they had, or thought they had, over others, the right they assumed they had to patronise others and bend them to their wills; and the frailties of everyone else for giving in to them so easily.

The bleakness of Jack's reasoning was aided and abetted by none other than Watkins himself when, before lessons that very morning, he entered the staffroom to introduce Amanda Fairfax to the staff.

'We are a happy family here, Miss Fairfax, as you can see. But we are also a family with a mission – a *mission*, Miss Fairfax,' Watkins repeated, with solemn emphasis.

Jack was dumbstruck. Did he hear correctly? Did Watkins use the word 'mission'? Uncanny! That was the very word Alf had used himself. How was that possible? Well, fact is sometimes stranger than fiction. As these words left Watkins's lips, Davenport's eyes swept round the small sea of faces like a radar beam, alert to the slightest breach of loyalty should someone fail to nod or grunt approvingly – preferably nod *and* grunt, in deferential support. Patel and Gladys, amongst others, managed to pass, or foil, Davenport's radar. Jack, however, still dumbstruck, was lost in thoughts of his own, and consequently blotted his copybook, a mental note of which was taken by the adjutant for future reference.

'...and that, Miss Fairfax, is what the teaching profession is really all about,' Watkins went on. 'We are preparing young people for the life in front of them. What could be nobler and grander than that? Yes, teaching's a mission if ever there was one! Well, I'll leave you now in very capable hands.' With that, and with further nods and grunts, he and Davenport left the staffroom, leaving Amanda with the firm impression that they were in perfect control of something like a divine mission and had not a moment more to lose in the commission of that Holy Design.

'Well,' said Amanda, rather sheepishly, 'what an act to follow!'

'I think you mean, what an act!' said Jack, leaning back nonchalantly in his chair ad heaving a cynical sigh, while Patel simply shrugged his shoulders and smiled, with the gentle resignation of the wise.

'You see…' Jack got up, opened the staffroom door, poked his head round it and closed it again. 'You see, what I mean is, all this stuff about teaching being a mission is just… Well, the trouble with Watkins is, he thinks it's a mission *already*, when it *isn't*! I mean it *should* be a mission, but…'

'What is it, then?' Gladys was interested. She'd never seen Jack so moved before.

'Alright. Right now it's no more than a way of producing automata – just as it's always been, so that we can all, generation after generation… so that we can all go on being just the same. Sameness. It's all about sameness! It's not about being a bit better than we are. No, it's all about being the same. Oh, and it's fear, too. Kids are taught to fear failing exams. We really teach fear – and we're so good at it. After that, they're ready for the life ahead – because then they fear their bosses. We teach young people how to be afraid.'

'Rubbish!' Gladys muttered.

'No, really,' Jack went on. 'We actually teach them how to be afraid. You can't call that a "mission" – just the opposite! There's nothing holy in fear and submission, is there? Nothing enriching, anyway. Nothing creative. Nothing positive.'

'You are painting a bleak picture, Jack,' Patel put in.

'Yes, I know! Exactly! Because that's how it is. The same old mediocrity, that's what we teach. The same old form, and form is not the same as mission. Well, *is* it? I mean, people like Watkins think that if you succeed in producing *respectable, sensible* people, who toe all the old lines – well, he thinks that's the same as producing good, morally better people. Well, it's not the same at all. You see, we congratulate ourselves if we don't produce little criminals. But the fact is, our sights are low, miserably low. No, conformity isn't the same as improvement. Right now, education is a preparation for life, but it should be a preparation for a *better* life! Not the same old *status quo*. The whole point is—'

'Well,' Gladys interrupted, 'if we can stop brats like young Carter getting any worse, we can pat ourselves on the back, I think.'

'That is a good point, Jack,' said Patel, and left it at that. The truth is, Patel thought this kind of talk a very risky business, which explained why his eyes had shifted between Jack and the staffroom door ever since Jack began holding forth. Gladys could be trusted. But Amanda was an unknown quantity. Who knew what she might let drop to Watkins or Davenport in an unguarded moment or in some misguided or unfortunate attempt to impress the hierarchy, even if she could be trusted not to tell tales. After all, as Watkins and Davenport saw it, the function of the teaching staff was to teach, plain and simple; it was not to discuss the philosophy of education.

But Jack hadn't finished.

'You see, I'd rather Watkins say it *ought* to be a mission. Then we could get down to questions about how to make it one. We could start asking questions! Questions about what we ought to be doing to justify us called it a mission. Problem is, he's thinks it's been settled already, and to everybody's satisfaction. That's just arrogance, plain arrogance. It's contempt, as well – as though what he thinks is what all of us should think.'

'Jack, when he talks about a mission, he just means it's a job, that's all,' said Patel.

'Well, yes. But that's just it. It shouldn't be just one job amongst others. It's—'

'He might say you're in the *wrong* job, Jack!' Gladys smiled, perhaps to soften her rejoinder. 'Well, I mean, if you haven't yet got round to answering those questions you're talking about.'

'Right. Well, maybe I became a teacher so I could *ask* them.' Jack looked at Amanda. 'What about you, Amanda? Have you decided what it's all about?'

'Well, I don't know. But questions and theories don't seem to mean much when you're in the classroom trying to teach something.' Amanda was more ready to listen than participate in debate, but Gladys and Patel liked what she said. 'Exactly,' said Gladys; and Patel just smiled and nodded in approval. 'I know it's a bit of a generalisation,' Amanda, feeling encouraged, went on, 'but education *is* a preparation for life, isn't it?' There were further signals of approval from Patel and Gladys.

'What!' Jack exploded. 'Teaching young kids how to be afraid? And teaching them a life of selfish mediocrity? The whole point is, we should be teaching them a love of learning, because that's the way to make them special, I mean, better than they are, so that society can be better than it is, not the same as it is now and has always been. If we can do that, more of them will go to university, and then university will be less a factory for producing people for jobs and more a place of improvement – you know, a place where they can read good books and improve the quality of their minds, and not just be confined to job-preparation. If you can improve the quality of their minds, as questioning, critical people, you'll improve the quality of democracy as well, because they'll be better able to understand issues and make more informed choices. You'll make them better people! That's the whole point. No, as things now stand, it begs questions about the kind of life we should be preparing them for. If education's a preparation for a life of fear and mediocrity, it shouldn't be allowed – as Alf would say.'

'Alf?' asked Gladys.

'That is Jack's mentor,' Patel explained jokingly. If Patel thought of Alf as a joke, he was no joke to Jack. Alf had managed, in a very short space of time, and of course with Jack's help, to weave around himself a mystique and an aura of respect that the philosophers of old might have envied. Jack was therefore stony faced when Patel said this.

Patel had managed to let slip something Jack would have preferred to keep between them and under wraps. But the proverbial cat was out, and now it was Jack's cue to put both Gladys and Amanda in the picture concerning the short session in The King's Head and what had preceded it. Gladys was at least happy to be able to put a name to what Watkins had referred to as 'our little problem', though she shared Patel's frustration at Jack's inability to furnish a biography, however threadbare. As for Amanda, she was both amused and fascinated by the tale of the weird character who had, until this very moment, taken up part-time residence at the gates of Morley Comprehensive.

'Anyway, it turned out to be a more enlightening experience than you'd get with Watkins or his lapdog, I can tell you,' said Jack.

'But you mean you actually sat with him in the pub?' Gladys asked incredulously.

*　*

Amanda was mightily impressed, and Jack sensed it. Patel sensed it, too. But Patel was impressed by a bolder, more forthright, and altogether more articulate Jack, whose eloquence seemed to emanate from some undefined yet not unenviable source. No matter whether what Jack said was right or not, or even made much sense or not; no, what interested Patel was that he should say it at all, and that he should be so forthright and colourful in his language in front of Gladys, and in front of a young and impressionable stranger. Was Jack a new man? Or was it all just a flash in the pan?

Even if only a flash, it managed to illuminate the classroom, too. That very afternoon Jack began the lesson seated at his desk in front of 4C, with young Harris, who had assumed his usual posture of earnest attentiveness in the middle of the middle row; if not quite yet teacher's pet, Harris believed himself to have at least taken off in that direction. Jack made out that he couldn't remember what he had been talking about in the previous lesson, and this was not merely a pedagogical device designed to test the collective memory of the group – it was more a wilful ploy.

'Perhaps Harris can help me, hey Harris? What momentous issues were we addressing last time we met.'

'Yessir!' Harris sat up straight, poised to take advantage of any opportunity to shine.

'Well?'

'The trials, I mean trial, of Charles I... and his execution in January 1649, when—'

'Yes, thank you Harris.' Jack was curt. 'The very mention of the name Harris, ladies and gentlemen, is like punching a command key on a computer keyboard. I'm sure you've all noticed it, have you not? Harris even corrects his own errors; he's a kind of built-in word-check.' There were some giggles here and there. Harris smiled faintly, as though he was perplexed by the suddenness and force of an unexpected confrontation. 'Can you go further and tell me what I actually said, Harris? Now, ladies and gentlemen, notice that I'm pressing the data request button!' More giggles. 'Well, go on!'

'At his execution… at his execution, the king wore two shirts so he wouldn't shiver with the cold and give everyone the idea he was afraid.'

'Well, thank you again, Harris, for that mind-blowing piece of information. Press exit button and switch off at mains.' No giggles this time. Feeling thoroughly deflated and humiliated, poor Harris visibly shrank into his seat, having been used as the butt of a joke, and failing to receive the complimentary response he had initially expected. The silence that pervaded the classroom suggested that his classmates were unusually sympathetic.

The tone and direction of Jack's remarks were completely out of character, so much so that Harris was not the only one to speculate about Jack's drinking habits, although Jack had never previously given occasion for any doubts whatsoever on the matter. But the oddity of his behaviour begged the question; no answer was obviously forthcoming, and break-time chats amongst the pupils turned on alcohol abuse and domestic upset, and even a possible causal relationship between the two.

Jack had always been unfailingly polite, quiet in manner and fair, and had never knowingly joked at anyone's expense. He had never been so relentlessly curt, and especially not with a model pupil like Harris. As for his forthright expression of opinion earlier in the staffroom, this too was out of character; for Jack was much more the secret observer and the silent sufferer, keeping his thoughts and his indispositions very much to himself; he would keep his mouth shut rather than speak his mind, let alone speak with fire and gall. He had shocked himself; and, as if in compensation or in penance, the rest of the lesson with 4C had been conducted in more pleasant, not to say appeasing tones. He could not fail to realise that his behaviour towards young Harris was arguably inconsistent with his claim that pupils should be encouraged to adopt a love of learning rather than a fear of failing exams; he had belittled Harris, who was at a tender age, and he had risked putting him off completely, rather as the innocent, as well as the guilty, are hardened by imprisonment.

But some damage had been done, and several attempts to establish friendly eye-contact with Harris were not reciprocated, principally because Harris was smarting for having been reproached for being a good pupil; smarting, and not a little confused.

However and to all appearances, the rest of the week proceeded, and came to a close, uneventfully.

*　　*

At the end of the school day the following Monday, Jack heard from Gladys that Patel was in a spot. According to Carter's father, Patel had lost his temper with Carter Junior during the last lesson the previous Friday afternoon, and struck him. Patel said he'd only poked Carter in the lapel with his finger and Carter had lost his balance and fallen backwards over his shoulder-bag, which had fallen to the floor behind him. Luckily for Patel, Carter had a reputation for misbehaving. But then, nothing quite like this, involving Carter, had ever happened before, and it was more than enough to cause Carter Senior to see red and make a blustering entrance into Watkins's study first thing Monday morning, demanding audience, explanation and justice, the intervening weekend having done very little to cool his temper. It all figured. Jack thought he'd heard some raised voices coming from the direction of Watkins's study earlier that day, and it hadn't sounded like Watkins, either. Patel had kept well out of sight. Jack had not seen him all day and had wondered whether he might not be sick and had taken the day off. He took another look round, but Patel was nowhere to be seen.

With Gladys's account ringing in his ears, Jack made his way home. He would have a relaxing evening and catch up with Patel the next day.

*　　*

Later that evening Jack wasn't able to chill out properly, try as he might. First, there were thoughts of Patel. If Patel had only poked Carter in his lapel, he'd still be in trouble. It wasn't allowed to touch pupils in any shape or form, and even Jack's own behaviour, though only verbal, had been deeply questionable – treating Harris like that might easily be construed as a form of abuse. The more he worried about Patel, the more he began to worry about himself.

In a half-hearted attempt to place his thoughts elsewhere, Jack reached for a slim volume which had been unopened and gathering dust on his bookshelf for years. He had found it years ago in a second-hand bookshop, and then forgotten that he had it. It was a translation of something vaguely philosophical by an Alexandre LeForge, an obscure French author of the 1920s. Jack settled back in his armchair and randomly flicked through the pages, stopping here and there, with no apparent intention of seriously reading it. But, soon, Jack was fully engaged. Jack was a selective reader, choosy about the books he read, but, with a book like this, he was selective about which chunks to chew on. The first chunk which appealed to him was:

> The full realisation that we all have our time, and no more or less than our time, is as fecund as sexual intercourse with the person of our dreams; but the offspring of such a realisation is the question: Then what am I to do with the time I am allotted? And the answer may take us in either of two directions: we might abandon ourselves to a life of pleasure, if this is possible, or, if it is not, to a life of mediocrity, gracelessly or gracefully awaiting our final departure; or else, we might seek to make a positive difference to the world which we must, whether we will or no, abandon; this latter requires the kind of selfless courage that is not given to all and often carries with it the very abandonment we would rather not seek. Christ and Socrates were not the only ones who possessed such a courage; many like them still remain nameless and unknown, but the only reward they ever seek is that men should treat each other better than they do or ever have done. That every man has his time is a momentous sentence which I tremble to write; each word falls from my pen like lead.

No piece of prose could have held Jack's attention so well, for it was held as in a vice. His eyes eventually became unstuck and glanced elsewhere, and were then glued to:

We are each of us a developing constant. We are and are not what we once were when we were born; we are and are not the child that ran through the fields; we are and are not the teenager who was frightened by shadows. We develop. We change. 'We' represents the constant, but the rest is flux. The rest is development. But the crucial question is: In what direction does this development turn? Is it for the better? Or is it for the worse? Do we go up, or do we go down? And how much is this direction a question of circumstance, and how much is it a question of choice? How far is our own fate in our own hands, and for how long will we blame the gods for our own deficiencies?

This was more than enough to set Jack's brain racing. It reminded him of something that he could not immediately recollect. But it did not take long for the penny to drop. Development? Direction? Up? Down? Why, it sounded for all the world like *a spiral of consciousness*. The very spiral of consciousness that Jack had himself spoken about when a mere schoolboy; spoken about and wondered about; and it had taken all this time, and someone he had never met called LeForge, unknown, forgotten, long since dead, to help him understand what he himself had seen though only through a glass darkly. You had just one life, and your fate was in your own hands – if only you had the courage it takes to send that development spiralling skyward!

Things were, in Jack's mind, beginning to come together. He read on.

As for help from God, I can only say that what passes between me and my God is not so much a prayer as a smile, a wordless sign of recognition, hopefully of approval. God is someone to smile at from time to time. No more than this.

Instead of replacing the book on the bookshelf, Jack wrapped it gently in a small brown envelope and placed it securely in the bottom drawer of his desk.

6
From Bad to Worse

Patel was nowhere to be seen before lessons next morning. Jack arrived unusually late, but he was in the staffroom long enough to discern that factions were already developing: pro-Patel, anti-Patel, and plain indifference. As he was hurriedly making his way to his classroom, he caught a glimpse of Patel in his own; so at least Patel was in school and could be caught up with later.

En route to the staffroom for the mid-morning break, Jack's attention was drawn to the boiler room, the door of which was slightly ajar.

'Pssst! Pssst! Jack! Jaacck! Here! Quick!'

'Zanjik!'

The door opened wide enough for Patel to beckon nervously; he grabbed Jack's sleeve, yanked him inside, and spoke in a strained whisper, as though the massive central-heating boilers might have been amply bugged. Jack was stunned, like a rabbit caught in the glare of an arc-light.

'Sorry to catch you like this, Jack. I cannot speak freely out there. I saw Davenport go into the staffroom. I just wanted to tell you – it is all a frame-up. Really.'

'What?' Jack whispered, incredulously.

'Look. They want to get rid of me. That is the bottom line. *Believe* me! They have been waiting for the first big chance, and they think they have found it. Yes! Yes!'

'*They*?!'

'Need you ask? Watkins! Davenport! I... I just wanted to ask you, Jack. You see, I know, I know very well, it is difficult for you, but could you tell me if you hear anything? Could you, dear Jack, could you be my eyes and ears?'

'Well...' Jack started. Poor Patel, what was there to say?

'You see, they are saying that I struck young Carter, and of course I did not! I did not, Jack! You believe me, yes!'

'For goodness sake, Zanjik, you've really got to pull yourself together.'

'But there is talk – behind my back.'

'Look, you're distraught. You're really in no fit state to go back to class. What if I tell them you've just gone down with something? And then you can go home and sort yourself out a bit – yes?'

'What? No. No, absolutely not! That is just playing into their hands. I am fine. And I shall stay fine.' He tried to sound more himself, as he cleared his throat and adjusted the knot of his tie. 'There, you see? Now, just be my eyes and ears, Jack – if you will,' he said, as he gripped Jack's shoulders.

'Right.'

'Yes?'

'Yes! Right!' Jack repeated, emphatically. Poor Patel needed every reassurance. There was nothing more Jack could do or say, at that time and in that place.

Jack opened the door of the boiler room and, looking furtively left and right, made his exit, followed shortly by Patel. Jack made for the staffroom for a coffee, wishing he could get something stronger, and was joined there by Patel moments later, and knowing looks were exchanged between them.

There was no further communication between them that day, but Patel was firmly in Jack's mind. Patel was neither drunk nor mad, but behaving as he did, and using the boiler room as his HQ, was less rocking the boat than rocking a flimsy raft – good teachers, superlative teachers, had been sent out to grass on far less compelling grounds. There were the problems that you started with, and then there were responses to those problems that simply created further problems, and Patel was in grave danger of compounding a felony, or an alleged felony, and, in consequence, digging his own grave.

Jack said as much to Gladys, as they made their way out through the corridors at the end of the day. 'You know, he's playing right into their hands. Good God! He's got me talking like him already! Trouble is,' Jack went on, and stopping, getting as close to Gladys as decorum would allow and needlessly lowering his voice to the merest whisper, 'Watkins and his ilk encourage a them-and-us phobia – he must be one of the most unapproachable, uncommunicative, self-righteous prats I've ever had the misfortune to know – his so-called "mission" would turn saints off Scripture.' Gladys nodded approvingly.

Patel had confided in Jack and sought his help. Jack himself felt stronger for his having done so, as though the office of guardian had vested in him some authority hitherto unknown; though he was uncertain how far this authority extended and just how it was to be exercised. It was not too hard to imagine how a case against Patel might be drawn up: the loss of his wife, his illness, this business with young Carter, and, if he was not very careful, his own response to all this – these things could be adduced to recommend his dismissal or early retirement, and the latter would be perceived by Patel as a polite version of the former, and either would almost certainly plunge him headlong into oblivion. Somehow, God knows how, the storm had to be weathered, and Jack had been placed at the helm of a vulnerable ship. Should something be done? Or was it simply a matter of drawing in the sails and trusting to better weather? These were stormy waters, no doubt about it.

* *

With such thoughts buzzing in his head like angry bees, Jack made his way in the dusk through homeward-bound crowds late that afternoon in Morley town centre, having locked his bicycle to a set of railings. He was en route to a music shop to buy a collection of medieval monastic chants to add to his collection of anti-stress CDs when he was suddenly jolted out of one world and into another. For trundling along directly towards him, his bundle humped on his back and his sandals flip-flopping, was none other than Alf, who at last gave him a smile of recognition. Jack stopped dead in his tracks. Had he seen Alf's approach from a distance, he might have changed direction or pretended not to see him. As it was, he was about to be presented with a simple twist of fate.

'Alf! What a surprise!' said Jack, taken aback, extending his hand, which Alf shook warmly. 'Where've you been hiding? I'm really glad I've bumped into you at last.' Jack was not, of course, glad, only stunned, and therefore needed to resort to cliché.

'Where've I been? I can fairly say *nowhere*,' said Alf with a grin, relieving himself momentarily of his bundle, which he placed on the pavement beside him, to the aggravation of passers-by.

What happened next was as much a shock to Jack then as it was to Sally to whom it was related later. But rather like a chess player who is stuck for the next move and stuck for time, but who has to move something somewhere, words which would in less hurried circumstances have been considered, even by Jack, too rash and injudicious to be at all credible, found unambiguous and unmistakeable expression.

'You see, I've been wanting to invite you round to my place – meet my wife, have a drink and a chat, a bite to eat, maybe.' The words were out and could not be retrieved. Were they simply the result of misjudgement, or did they have a source in something that had suddenly taken off skyward? Jack had no time to consider whether they were his words or a missive from a deeper, stranger self. 'Say... er... seven thirty, this coming Friday evening,' he went on, quickly scribbling his address on a piece of paper which he shoved unceremoniously into Alf's hand. 'Great! Well, must dash,' and Jack was away at a rate of knots. The damage, if this was indeed damaging, was done. The speed at which Jack sped away might well have been an expression of distaste and astonishment for what he had done. It was one thing, and bad enough many would say, to invite Alf to The King's Head, but to invite him home was going far too far. But the words, the invitation – the whole thing had come out in one vast, flowing torrent, with a kind of inevitability of its own. What Sally would say to see Alf standing at the door, complete with bundle, and what she would think to see him sitting in their living room, was just too discomforting to contemplate. It was natural therefore that Jack would endeavour to place the prospect of Alf's visit in the outermost recesses of his mind; besides, it was only Tuesday, and Friday seemed a long way off – long enough for Alf to forget altogether, or to have second thoughts, or to lose the piece of paper with Jack's address. Alf had come to the pub, and Jack hadn't expected that – but this time it was different, or so Jack kept telling himself, as he headed straight for his bicycle, giving the music shop a miss. Meanwhile, Alf made off, without a thought in the world, much less with an anxious one, holding his bundle in position with one hand and clutching a piece of paper in his pocket with the other.

*   *

But time waits for no man and would make no exception for Jack. Friday came round soon enough, and it was not the customary preface to a couple of days of relaxation, but a very mixed blessing, for Alf might just take up the invitation, and Sally had not yet been told. Nothing further, or nothing Jack knew about, had happened to or concerning Patel, and the only thing to have passed between them was the occasional knowing glance; all was quiet on that front, at least for now. No, the only outstanding problem was the prospect of Alf's visit, and that of making the possibility known to Sally, who would need to be carefully prepared for the shock. Jack broached the subject with some trepidation early Friday morning, when Sally was making a packed lunch for Pete. He left out reference to Alf's bundle and his propensity to roll cigarettes; he emphasised the possibility as distinct from the probability of Alf's visit, and he suggested that, should push come to shove, he and Alf could resort to Jack's study and remain there for the duration of his visit – a mere hour or two. 'Well, he wouldn't be coming for dinner,' said Jack. 'I should jolly well hope not!' said Sally. 'He's weird, but very clean,' Jack insisted. 'I should hope so!' Sally returned. But the subject was dropped after a few explosive phrases: 'You must be kidding!', 'You can't possibly be serious!', 'Why on earth…?', 'What on earth made you…?' Jack had known that any attempt at justification was bound to be a test of nerves; as it was, he felt lucky to get away with a series of reprimands and the promise that, should Alf materialise, it would most certainly be a one-off.

'If he comes, I hope you know how to entertain him – because I certainly won't feel much like it.'

'No, he's a fascinating guy. You'll like him – if he bothers to come at all, that is. He'd love to meet you, I know.'

'He's *your* friend, Jack. You got yourself into this, so you have to see to it.'

'Well, I wouldn't call him a friend exactly…'

'Whatever! Oh, and by the way, please keep him off alcohol – it's safer.'

They tended to invite people round on Friday evenings, when they invited people round at all, since they had Saturdays and Sundays to recover from the unsettling experience. Invitations were few and far between; Sally sometimes felt so exhausted on Friday evenings that it was difficult to contemplate anything more energetic than curling up in front of the television with a gin and tonic; Jack had almost given up watching television and preferred to unwind upstairs to the accompaniment of Elizabethan viols. And when she was not exhausted and incapable, entertaining still entailed extraordinary effort. Invitations had, therefore, to be worth all the preparation and all the sacrifice they entailed.

Jack refused to believe that Alf would actually take up the invitation; Sally had a premonition that her evening was about to be ruined. Jack was wrong. Sally was not altogether right.

Shortly before eight o'clock, when Jack was beginning to seriously entertain the comforting thought that Alf definitely wasn't coming, the doorbell rang. Alf stood there, complete with bundle. After depositing his bundle in the hallway, he was ushered by Jack into the living room and invited to sit down on an armchair which Sally had previously covered with a patterned dust sheet of sorts. Sally came downstairs and they were introduced. The usual polite and clichéd exchanges took place. Sally was determined to leave Jack and Alf to their own devices as soon as possible; the stress and strain of conversation would therefore be short-lived and she could afford to be courteous and inquisitive. She explained something about her job and something about Pete and her hopes for him. Alf listened attentively; Jack, meanwhile, was hoping against all hope that Alf would not reach into his pockets for tobacco and rolling paper; he needn't have worried, for Alf never smoked the whole time and seemed to have no intention of doing so.

As these customary exchanges were taking place, Sally noticed Alf's eyes, which, although deeply set, were a penetrating blue and seemed to see right through you, as though no thought could be hidden from scrutiny. She also noticed his clothes and his hands. Jack was right. He was definitely weird. But he did seem quite clean.

'And what about you, er… Alf? We don't know much about you.' Sally seemed to stammer, as though she was venturing into unexplored territory and might step on a thorn or two.

'Me? Ah, well, some people are born to be nothing – and if they try to be something, they become less than nothing. Anyway, that's me – I am nothing. No, nothing at all. Really, I have nothing to say.' Alf smiled genially, and Sally detected a distinct sparkle in those remarkable, blue eyes.

'Ohh…' Sally began, in a tone of sympathetic denial, as if to jokingly admonish Alf for being so bashful.

'No. It's good. It's perfectly good to be nothing. Because that's freedom. True freedom. And when you're free you can begin to live. I live, and generally people don't live. Ask yourself, how many people truly live? Most of us die without ever having lived.'

'Ohh,' Sally began again, this time in a tone suggesting that she understood, which she did not.

'I've made myself obscure, which was my intention. My apologies.'

Sally sensed that Alf wasn't prepared to be forthcoming about himself, and reverted back to herself.

'Well, anyway, we, Jack and me, we must count our blessings. We have a nice house and good jobs. I know we're very lucky.'

'What do you mean by that?' Alf asked – rather curtly, Sally thought afterwards.

'I'm sorry?'

'You said you were *lucky*. What did you mean when you said that?'

'Well…' she began, obviously taken aback, embarrassed and uncomfortable.

'Well! I suggest,' said Jack, getting up, 'Alf and I should go into my study and have a chat there for a while. How about that? And then you can get on with things, Sally. Right?'

It was like the appearance of cavalry on the crest of the hill. Sally could almost hear the bugle. She was so relieved, but managed to resist the temptation to kiss Jack there and then. The ordeal was over.

'Good idea!' she said. 'I'll bring you some tea and biscuits – and then er… I'll get on with things.'

A short time afterwards, Sally took some refreshments into the study. She almost closed the study door behind her on the way back out, but left it just a little ajar; then she paused to catch something of what those two must be talking about. She stood motionless outside the study door and, between the tinkles of spoons in cups, heard Alf say things weird and somehow discomforting.

'...it's like being in no man's land, crawling over corpses, soon to be one yourself and not realising it. You don't realise it, because you think you're something when you're not – when all the time you're really living in a kind of shadow world, a world of make-believe, and in that world you're one of the shadow people. I said "living" – but that's not really living, just make-believe... do you see?'

Sally wondered whether she'd heard correctly. What rubbish was this? And it was morbid rubbish, too. Captivating, maybe – like Alf's blue eyes. But rubbish all the same. How could Jack listen to stuff like that? Surely it made as little sense to him as it did to her. She moved quietly away from the door; she went upstairs, taking with her a gin and tonic. She could relax after all. The evening wasn't an entire waste. And if it was a waste for Jack, well he had only himself to blame. The whole event was a ridiculous, ill-advised, injudicious one-off, and one that was never, never ever, to be repeated. She decided to turn in and have an early night, leaving Jack and that strange fellow together in the study. She was glad to hear Alf leaving about an hour and a half later. She felt a strong urge to sleep by now. Jack was still in the study, presumably listening to his anti-stress music in an attempt to relieve himself of the mumbo jumbo Alf had been spouting. She knew that the next morning she would need to busy herself in the study, removing the crumbs from the small Persian carpet, almost certainly deposited carelessly by Alf and left as an unwholesome reminder of his advent.

*   *

True, Jack had remained in the study after seeing Alf out, but it was not the Elizabethan viols that had filled his head. Instead, Jack was full of ideas; ideas which took the form of questions: when Alf spoke about the realisation that you are nothing, could this realisation be what was meant by 'consciousness' in the phrase 'spiral of consciousness'? The consciousness that we are really nothing? And did this consciousness imply freedom, as Alf said? And was this freedom a freedom from the paralysis that fears engenders – the kind of freedom which is the very root of courage? The courage that was needed to wield the sword, at least the symbolic wielding of the symbolic sword? Was this night a night of enlightenment? Was this the night when the meaning of his own phrase, coined by him in his schooldays, was finally revealed, as though by some mystical or magical design? Was this the night he had been waiting for all his life? Was this night destined? Was his encounter with Alf at the school gates predetermined? And who, exactly, was Alf anyway? Jack even entertained the idea that Alf was the reincarnation of Socrates. After all, wasn't it Socrates who wanted his sons to be admonished if they thought they were of some account when they were not, and wasn't Alf saying much the same when he said the trouble was our thinking ourselves something when we are nothing. It was all mixed up – confused and confusing. Whether Alf and Socrates were saying the same thing wasn't at all clear. But was Alf the reincarnation of Socrates? Of course not! Nonsense! Nonsense or not, the very idea served to rejuvenate the mystique which, in Jack's mind, had surrounded Alf from the very outset. Sally might say, as she subsequently made a point of saying repeatedly, that the only thing worthy of admiration was the colour of his eyes. Yet Jack felt instinctively that she had been impressed with a certain charisma that Alf seemed to exude; Sally would never admit to that, but he felt sure that it was the same charisma he had himself felt from the very first sighting, and one that was confirmed by subsequent experience.

It was getting on for midnight, and Sally was fast asleep, aided and abetted by her gin and tonic, when Jack reasoned that, behind the mystique, and vastly more important, Alf seemed to have something to say about people who couldn't appreciate the stuff and substance of life – those he called Shadow People; they were incapable of understanding the value of life, because they couldn't grasp the reality of death.

'If only they really knew,' Alf had said, 'if only they really knew they were going to die, that they could take nothing with them and that nothing awaited them, they'd get their priorities sorted out, because death's the great leveller – the cure-all for conceit, for arrogance, for fear, for cowardice. Instead, they are preoccupied with job security, mortgages, promotion, status, keeping-up-with-the-Joneses, when the only thing you can ever own is your own integrity and sense of decency. They're so bound up with the trappings of life, they forget what's really important. And you know the strangest thing? Many of them are stupid enough to pray to God for the trappings – as if such stuff could be of any interest to Him. Strip away all the trappings, and we are *nothing*. Nothing at all. When we see we are nothing, life can begin – as it did for Lear in the storm…'

That was Alf's cue to produce a piece of paper from his pocket which he called his 'poem', consisting of several stanzas, though he read out only one of them:

And if you knew your time is short,
Really knew it, and not just by rote,
You would see more, hear more, taste more, listen more,
Above all, love more, and so be loved,
And in this way live more too,
For love's sake, and before it is too late.

Alf refused to read the rest, returned the paper to his pocket, and said he must be going. Jack took his refusal to be an expression of artistic modesty and was impressed more than ever. No, whoever, whatever, he was, Alf was no old duffer.

So it was that Jack awoke next morning to Sally's wrath, the hoover roaring away revengefully downstairs.

'What did you find to talk about for hours on end, anyway?'

'It wasn't hours on end,' said Jack, meekly.

Ideally, Jack would have tried to explain Alf's reference to Shadow People, but Alf's name, whether or not the man himself possessed undeniable charisma, was taboo. Sally would have asked the same old question: why he was a teacher at all if he felt about things the way he did? It was better for the question to remain unprovoked, like a sleeping dog. Jack dared not tell her that teaching in the present state of things was no better than digging holes in the ground which were filled in again at night. Teaching mere dates and digging unwanted holes enjoyed the same status; both were ways of paying the bills and keeping the wolf from the door – which was necessary. The problem was, it was not sufficient; more, much more, should be expected if life were to be meaningful; but he had difficulty, as always, explaining what exactly that sufficiency amounted to. Jack was wearied by his own doubts and the unthinkable thought that Pete's hard work and performance at school meant no more than his own ability to pay the bills and keep the wolf from the door – wheels were turning, but meaninglessly, without engaging anything; meaninglessly, that is, if you were looking for something else, something deeper. It was so stressful – the pretence that the wheel was actually covering ground, when all along it simply stayed put.

But there never seemed to be a time or a place to discuss Jack's version of the insanity of an insane world. Which is why the verbal exchanges between him and Sally continually bobbed and weaved and skirted the issues, as though they were each testing the other's defences, seeking out the lay of the land before committing their forces, as yet unsure whether to mount a full assault upon a subject that might well prove simply impenetrable.

7

Simplicity Itself

'The staffroom's so depressing these days! You don't want to go in, and once you're in, you come out suicidal,' Jack said, as he handed Amanda her martini and sat down beside her. 'Mind you, I wouldn't make a habit of lunchtime drinking – but once in a blue moon, it's no bad thing, don't you think?'

Jack had suggested a quick lunchtime drink, and Amanda had accept demurely. Today her hair was disbanded and fell forward around her young, fresh face.

She smiled her sweet smile and sipped her martini. They had a table all to themselves in a corner of the room. 'Watkins tripped in this morning beaming from ear to ear, said "ning" once or twice and left.'

'Ning?!'

'"Good Morning."' Amanda giggled.

'So you see, you can't even get depressed in peace. Wonder what he's dreaming up next. He's forever dreaming things up.'

Amanda giggled again. 'Poor man,' she said.

'Hmm?'

'Well, nobody has much to say for him, do they?'

'That's hardly surprising – oh, it's all the pretence, pomposity, duplicity – the leadership thing, the old *Fuehrerprinzip* at work. Got all his priorities wrong.'

'See what I mean?' Amanda giggled once more. 'I bet he's harmless enough, though. Maybe he's got to be like that – it goes with the job.'

'If it goes with the job, the job's not worth it,' said Jack. 'It's not really a bit of harmless fun. People are under a lot of pressure, and he's responsible for most of it.'

'He's under pressure, too, isn't he?'

'He shouldn't pass it on. But he's not just under pressure – he *creates* it. Leaders should build bridges, not stand on their dignity. Leadership is a vastly overrated quality, anyway. No, don't try to defend him. He's a Shadow Man.'

'A what?'

'A Shadow Man – Alf's term for people who are sort of dead to the important things in life.'

'Oh, yes, you said you'd tell me all about it.' Amanda perked up. 'So how did it go?'

Jack was in buoyant mood, ready to embellish and entertain, even if this meant bending the truth and resorting to absolute falsehood – even if this meant putting things into people's mouths that were never there and converting them into a clownish version of the real thing. The effect of young and attractive female company was quite astonishing – intoxicating, even; and not a little revealing. Jack might be a teacher of history, but, for once at any rate, veracity was on vacation.

'Marvellous! Fascinating! Yes, we enjoyed every minute of it. Sally would say something simple, and that'd start him off. She's say something like, "It's Saturday tomorrow, so we won't have to rush about," and Alf would have something to say, like, "The way I see it, you don't have to rush about at any time. The trouble with people is, they spend their time doing what they don't want to do – they decide to go with the tide, then they blame the tide for it and call it necessity. They just end up being resentful."' To accompany this embellishment, Jack rolled his head from side to side and squinted, though Alf was devoid of such mannerisms. He was good at it. He wanted to make Amanda laugh, and he certainly succeeded.

'No, but really, he's quite right, isn't he?' she said, through her giggles.

'The way I see it...' Jack began, rolling his head from side to side again and squinting like someone demented and seriously myopic – but the effect was disappointing second time round, and he became serious. 'Well, of course he's right! That's not the point though, is it? It's what to do about it – that's the problem.'

'Hmm. Anyway, go on.'

'Well, it didn't take him long to get to education. He went on about cooperation *versus* competition – you know, kids sweating over exams and where does it all get them? Teaching them to do better than the next guy, and so on.' In fact, it was Jack, not Alf, who had, in the study, raised the question of education; and Jack who had distinguished between cooperation and competition, favouring the former and denouncing the latter. But right now it didn't seem to matter who had said what. Jack had found a hook to hang his thoughts on, an outlet for the bees in his bonnet, and he was determined to make the most of it.

'Hmm. He's a bit of a philosopher,' Amanda said.

'Shush! Dirty word!' said Jack, in a mock whisper. 'But yes, it really got me thinking. What am I doing if I can't teach what I want in the way I want to teach it. I don't want to teach conformity with the status quo, but I'm damned if I don't. So maybe I should think more about what I'm doing and what I ought to be doing. Should I be teaching at all? I don't know.'

'Did he say that?'

'Yes – well, not in so many words. You know, it reminds me of the time Pete was working on an essay about education. He asked me to help him, and I said I was still working on that one myself. Sally heard me and gave me a right ticking off later. "What's the point of having kids if you're not prepared to help them get on?" she said. Well, I was working on that one, too. But I couldn't say it. Anyway, I thought I *was* helping him – by being honest, and getting him to ask for himself. "What's the point of having kids if you can't be honest with them?" I said.' (Actually, he hadn't said that at all. He wouldn't have dared. Perhaps not now, either.) 'You know, Alf might have an answer for that one – something to do with providing fodder for mediocrity.'

'Hmm.' Amanda looked thoughtful, but said nothing.

'He writes poetry too!'

'Alf? Really!'

'Yes, versatile, isn't he? Philosopher and poet. Oh, that reminds me!' Jack dug into his inside pocket. 'These are the lyrics I was telling you about – you know, the Elizabethan song.' He unfolded the paper and handed it to Amanda. 'Keep it if you like.' She scanned it quickly.

What is our life? a play of passion,
Our mirth, the music of division,
Our mothers' wombs the tiring houses be,

Where we are dressed for this short comedy,
Heaven the sharp, judicious spectator is
That sits and marks still who doth act amiss,
Our graves that hide us from the searching sun
Are like drawn curtains when the play is done.
Thus march we playing to our latest rest,
Only we die in earnest, that's no jest.

She liked it, and Jack offered to bring her the CD.

'Better still,' he found himself saying, 'we can go out for a drink one evening, er… I'll bring Sally along, and you can come back to ours and listen to it there. Bring your boyfriend, too – if you like.'

'Without *him*, please! We split up. Your wife, Sally, she likes this kind of music, too?'

'Loves it! Anyway, he must be crazy – your boyfriend.'

Amanda smiled and glanced at her watch. 'Oops! We'd better be getting back.'

'Speed is inimical to appreciation, and "life in the fast lane" is a contradiction in terms,' said Jack, rolling his head from side to side.

'Alf again?' Amanda laughed.

'The very man,' said Jack, knocking back the last dregs of bitter and getting up.

They threaded their way through the small crowd which had by then assembled round the bar. Jack watched her as she pushed her way through. Once outside, he lightly held his hand around her waist as they waited for a space to cross in the traffic. It looked like the act of a friendly chaperone, but this chaperone wished to tighten his grip, if only he could. Jack was considerably older than Amanda, but this close to her and the years rolled away; the prospect hazily dawned before him that he might yet make up for lost time. Electricity, not blood, coursed through the arm that guided her through the traffic, though whether the current was strong enough to take effect only time would tell.

*   *

Early next morning Patel requested a few words with Jack in the boiler room. He had been avoiding the staffroom, keeping pretty much to himself in his classroom, especially during the breaks.

'We must stop meeting like this,' said Jack, attempting a joke, which was unappreciated.

'Have you heard anything?' asked Patel in a loud whisper, despite the fact that he was alone with Jack and entirely out of earshot.

'Heard anything? Well, no. No, not at all.'

'You're sure? Absolutely sure? You are not hiding anything from me?'

'Look, I really haven't heard anything.'

'Hmm.'

Patel was in no mood to take reassurance. It was bizarre. The more Jack denied having heard anything, the more dissatisfied Patel seemed.

'But you shouldn't hive yourself off from the staffroom,' Jack said, trying to establish sensible common ground between them.

'But, if you do hear anything – remember?'

'Yes, yes. Of course!' Jack said, with a sigh.

It really was getting too much. Communicating with Patel was a chore – it was one-sided and uncomfortably surrealistic. Jack was glad to get away from him. Patel's biggest problem, he thought, was fast becoming Patel himself; not only that, Patel was like a vortex, dragging everyone down who ventured, and suffered, to get close to him.

Jack felt the power of the vortex again the following morning. Patel stopped him in the corridor and led him into his empty classroom.

'Watkins wants to observe me – first thing Friday morning!' Poor Patel opened his arms wide in a mixed expression of consternation and disbelief. 'It is one more step along a downward path. I told you! I told you it would happen!'

'Look, it's alright. Nothing alarming in that. Just routine. Just part of his thing about teacher support – his latest hobby horse.' Jack, like most other staff members, didn't give any credence to all that stuff about teacher support. He regarded it as so much hogwash. What possible good could come of Watkins sitting at the back of classrooms? No, it was a question of policing, pure and simple; and it all looked good on paper during the regular visits of the inspectorate. But this was not the time to go into all that. He had to put things in the best possible light for Patel's sake, even if that meant leading him up the garden path. Jack had always expressed cynicism, in private, concerning any initiative Watkins put forward. He was therefore being inconsistent, hoping Patel wouldn't call to mind everything he had previously said on the subject of observations, especially the bit about 'policing, pure and simple'. He needn't have worried. Patel wasn't listening.

'He is looking for faults. Looking for something to strengthen his case. A weakness. An Achilles heel. I feel like some sort of performing monkey.'

'Nonsense! An experienced teacher like yourself has absolutely nothing to fear. You can teach all of us a thing or two! And Watkins stands to benefit the most!'

'But that is just what I mean! Yes, I *am* experienced. Therefore, I do not deserve to be treated as though I were incompetent.' It was like a proof in mathematics that could support conflicting conclusions – and therefore no proof at all; but Patel had convinced himself that he was a target of scrutiny.

'Everything will be fine. Just fine,' said Jack soothingly, tapping Patel lightly on the shoulder and walking away. Patel was going through a bad patch and was insisting on the most negative interpretation of every event in his sad life. Not, of course, that his interpretation was entirely wrong. On the contrary. Watkins had made a telling remark about experienced teachers. 'You can be highly experienced in doing the wrong things,' he had said. Jack thought the remark unjustifiably cynical and caustic. It felt as though Watkins was suddenly finding grounds for questioning the *person* inside the teacher, and Jack had not been alone in disliking it, and in disliking Watkins all the more for it.

* *

'When Patel's wife died, he was shattered – I mean more, far more, than you might have expected – completely devastated,' Jack explained to Amanda as they stood together in Jack's classroom at the end of the day. She watched him putting unmarked essays into his briefcase. 'Yes, so after burying her, he buried himself. He made the mistake of thinking that stress and overwork are the best antidote to grief – as though teaching with more gusto than ever before could help keep him sane – you know, a kind of anchor when all around you is falling apart. It might, just might, have worked, too. But then Watkins came along, and Davenport, and they seemed to bring with them all this crap about treating education like some kind of profit-making conglomerate, as though business criteria… Well, you know.' He stopped and glanced at Amanda. Unlike Patel, she hung on to his every word. He smiled. She smiled back, and he clunked his briefcase shut.

'You could have a word with Watkins. Put him in the picture.'

'Hmm?'

'Well, just explain a bit about Patel. What he's gone through. Tell him what you've just told me. I'm sure he'll understand. I get what you say, but he can't be a total monster.'.

'Oh, come on.'

'Yes, but it's worth a try, though – isn't it? It can't do any harm, and it might help Patel a bit. Watkins can't be as bad as you're painting him. Anyway, appeal to his better nature. He'd see Patel in a different light and—'

'Yes, well, I'll sleep on it.'

Right then, Jack had no more intention of tackling Watkins than he had the north face of the Eiger. Amanda's faith in human nature was as fresh as her complexion; such faith was invigorating, but no sound basis on which to proceed with a Shadow Man. On the other hand, things with Patel were unlikely to improve. On reflexion, it might just be possible to smooth the ground for him a little. Left as it was, the situation could only spell disaster. And was Jack not the helmsman in these rough waters? Didn't Patel look to him for support? Wasn't that what true friendship was? The likes of Watkins and Davenport wouldn't do the same for anyone else. But Jack was different; he aspired to be more than a mere Shadow Man.

* *

Which explains why, the following afternoon, Jack found himself seated uncomfortably before Watkins's large metallic desk. The elbows of The Master rested upon its cold surface, as he cupped his hands, tapped his fingertips together and frowned. Jack tried to articulate his concern for Patel, but it didn't sound at all as it did when he had spoken to Amanda the previous day. He felt awkward and, at least to his own ears, sounded awkward, too, like a small boy trying to give an unconvincing account of himself. Perhaps the large metallic desk had something to do with it, not to mention Watkins's body language, which seemed to Jack decidedly off-putting. After listening to Jack for what seemed, to Watkins, an age, he leaned back in his metallic office chair, uncapped his hands and placed them behind his head, a movement which was taken by Jack to mean that he had already said too much. All he had said so far was that Patel had been overdoing it since his wife had passed on, that grief compounded by stress was taking its toll, that it might possibly be a good idea to adopt a softly-softly approach and that, if at all possible, the strictest confidentiality should be observed. Jack would have gone on to add that perhaps, if it were within the realms of possibility, the planned observation might be dropped or at least postponed – but Watkins's body language seemed to be telling him that this was a bridge too far, and the possibility was therefore not mentioned. When Jack came to the end of a rather halting appeal, the immediate response it occasioned from Watkins was, 'Yes, I hear you, Jack.'

The phrase 'I hear you' was one of a series of devices Watkins had picked up from a weekend course he had attended entitled *Management Techniques in Education*; such lexical curiosities irritated Jack immensely, but all he could do was grin and bear them. Equally irritating was the fact that Watkins addressed him by his first name; had it been a mark of genuine companionship and amiability, as might be expected between friends, it would have been welcomed with open arms; but since it was instead an expression of false intimacy, designed to engender a false sense of security, and yet another device that Watkins had derived from his management course, its use was naturally suspect and a further source of irritation; the exchange of first names, rather than suggesting equality, sounded belittling and one-sided. Watkins preferred to be addressed as 'Mr Watkins', especially when pupils were present, and it seemed uncomfortable to address him as 'George', even when they were not; therefore the invitation to address him by his first name was seldom if ever taken up. No wonder Jack felt like a pupil curiously coming to the defence of another.

After his 'Yes, I hear you, Jack' there was an unsettling pause, as though Watkins were waiting for managerial, as distinct from divine, inspiration.

'I had not realised the problem was so acute,' said Watkins, slowly and with gravity, managing to make this sound like a revelation about Patel's criminal propensities. He unclasped his hands from behind his neck and placed them on the desk, proceeding to drum the surface with his fingers. 'No!' his arm shot up and he wagged his index finger in the air like someone about to pronounce a moral lesson. 'I have it in mind to observe one of his lessons tomorrow, and I'm more determined than ever to do so. I think I owe it to the school, don't you, Jack?'

Jack was alarmed. 'Well, what I think, you see, is that... well, it's quite simple, really, he just tries too hard, and the stress...' Jack hated himself for stumbling, but he wasn't permitted to stumble for long.

'Simple, did you say, Jack? Oh, I don't know. Few things in life are *simple*. And as for stress, well that's a natural and inevitable feature of life, of life on this planet at any rate, and we must just learn to cope with it. No, I prefer to take the view that someone in his – indeed, *our* – sort of position ought to seek medical advice and, to put it bluntly, jolly well sort himself out – for his own good and for the good of all those who manage to pull their own weight in an increasingly demanding profession. Should a parent complain about a member of staff, it reflects badly on all of us – *that* is what I should call 'simple', Mr Barker! After all, nowadays education is more like a business than ever before. It's dog eat dog. We have standards to uphold and inspectorates on our tails.'

Watkins obviously enjoyed delivering these droplets of dubious sagacity; and he did so with such confidence and gusto, that Patel did seem about to be roasted alive unless he could somehow manage to turn things right round. Jack took a deep breath, perhaps to calm his temper, perhaps to muster his forces to try Watkins's defence from another angle. But any outflanking manoeuvre was stopped in its tracks before it could even get underway. Watkins stood up, which meant that their exchange of confidences was at an end. 'Thank you for coming to see me. Your doing so will not be forgotten.' Jack felt more than ever like one who had grassed on a friend, landing Patel in even hotter water by inadvertently turning up the heat. Nor was it lost on him that his first name had been replaced by his surname and that Watkins had used no name at all in his parting words. Jack felt deflated and not a little ashamed.

*　*

On his way home, Jack bumped into Old Jacob carrying an empty plastic bucket. Jacob had been tending the school gardens and lawns for years at Morley Comprehensive and long before Jack himself had arrived. Short and scruffy, a white shock of hair on his pear-shaped head, his old tweed jacket miles too long in the sleeve and halfway down the backs of his legs, Jacob was as much part of the place as the cornerstones of the main building, and just as irremovable. He was solid, reliable and, above all and in the best possible sense, simple. Jack had no trouble speaking to Jacob. Words flowed and were a pleasure to utter. But then, Jacob was no threat, either.

'No pleasure cycling backwards and forwards to school these days, Jacob,' said Jack, bringing up his bicycle as Jacob stopped and put down his bucket. 'What with all the pollution and traffic,' Jack explained.

Jacob shook his head, gestured with open arms and smiled. 'State of the world, Mr Barker. State of the world!' Having made this profound observation, Jacob's own droplet of sagacity, he picked up his bucket and, continuing to smile from ear to ear, resumed his course to the school's potting shed with all his customary jauntiness. Jack felt strangely reassured. That simple encounter had done him a power of good. For Old Jacob hadn't a complicated bone in his body, and, just for that, Jack was not alone in loving him.

*　*

There was a special kind of continuity in history. At least Jack thought so as he lay that night listening to Elizabethan songs. He imagined Watkins and Old Jacob dressed in Elizabethan garb: Jacob as a simple cottager, perhaps; Watkins as an overbearing schoolmaster or magistrate; Davenport as a priest convinced of his own salvation. The clothes were different, the faces the same; the faces the same, the clothes different. Clothes are superficial. As he lay there, the dictum 'history repeats itself' took on a new significance. Jack was not certain whether he should feel reassured or depressed. Bound up with all these mental images were Amanda's legs, a divine continuity if ever there was one. The lyrics 'What is our life? A play of passion' were ambiguous, and Amanda had not a little to do with the ambiguity. Jack sighed.

'If you really can't take any more, for goodness sake ask your mother to help you out. She can afford it, can't she?' It was one of Sally's bad nights and Jack wished he hadn't told her anything about his meeting with Watkins. But Sally was tired, too. There was little solace from Jack, and seeing him lying there on the bed, good for nothing, and emitting the regular and by now familiar sigh, was just too much. If he was fed up with teaching, he should get out of it and lean on his mother for financial support while he sorted something else out. It was quite simple, really. But he seemed to think himself too old to change career; he had grown accustomed to a mood of indifference to change. But on Sally's income alone they couldn't possibly hope to continue to live in the manner to which they had grown accustomed. Jack was an only child, and his mother should do the decent thing by him. Yes, it was really quite simple.

We've been through all this before, thought Jack. But the thought was better unexpressed. He preferred to remain silent, listening to the music, which transported him as if by magic to times far distant. If only he could hop into a time machine, taking Amanda and her legs with him.

But time machines were at best unreliable. Instead, he would take his music CDs to school with him from now on and play them in the classroom. After all, he was a history teacher, and the history of music was a valid part of his concern. Yes, that was it! Life without music was dead. So, why not take life to the death that was Morley Comprehensive? What were those words again? 'What is our life? A play of passion.' Jack had already, and surreptitiously, polished off a quarter of a bottle of Sally's favourite whisky (would she know that he'd topped up the bottle with water?) and the lyrics of that Elizabethan song seemed enshrouded now in velvet, as he lay back and sighed himself into sleep, such sighs that were of a sort taken by Sally as sighs of desperation – which, indeed, they were. Ah, sleep! Sleep, perchance to dream.

8

Grand Admiral of the Fleet

The following day, and fifteen minutes before the mid-morning break, Jack began playing one of his CDs of Elizabethan songs accompanied by the lute, on the pretext of creating a fitting historical atmosphere for class 4C as their lesson on Elizabethan maritime exploration came to a close. In reality, he was far more concerned to escape the atmosphere of 4C, the classroom, Morley Comprehensive, Morley and, were it only possible, the entire planet. If only a time machine had been available! True, such a device would not enable him to escape the planet, only to move backwards and forwards. He might move backwards to the reign of Good Queen Bess, not that this period had a great deal to commend it; but he had arrived at a point where a change, *any* change within an ever widening compass of reasonableness, was as good as a rest. In the absence of a time machine, he consoled himself with the thought that it was at least Friday; not, for that matter, that Fridays were really any more to be desired than Mondays; both Mondays and Fridays had after all these years been saturated with their own defining routines, each routine as tedious as the other, so that there was in essence very little to choose between them; by the same token, Saturdays and Sundays yielded little in the way of relaxation and escape; weekdays and weekends merged into one another to form an amorphous lump. But still, if you said it quickly enough, the very word 'Friday' would suggest a feeling of release; the feeling was illusory, perhaps, but it was an illusion hard to relinquish, the harder for being pleasant.

'Quietly now!' he bellowed, as books, papers and pens were stuffed into bags, seconds before the buzzer for break was sounded. He turned up the music, stood at the classroom window and looked out onto the quadrangle, where a fierce wind made sweet wrappings dance into a frenzy. He was listening to the refrain, 'There was a lover and his lass, with a hey and a no, and a nonny, nonny no', wondering how on earth children could be so impervious to the ingeniously harmonious strains of musical simplicity, when, suddenly, a fact even more astonishing came into view. Out there, in the bitter wind, Patel was running across the quadrangle like one possessed. Patel hotfooted it across the quad and disappeared into the building at the far side, perhaps making for the rear exit. Jack blinked, but it was no apparition; Patel's short, thin frame was unmistakeable. Next, Watkins appeared in the quad, looked sharply left and right, and re-entered the building looking mightily perplexed. It was all over in a flash, but there was no disputing that it had happened.

Jack didn't expect to find Patel in the staffroom during break, so wasn't surprised at his not being there. He almost expected a 'Pssst! Pssst!' from the boiler room on passing it, so that his curiosity might at least be satisfied. Jack paused and backtracked and went as far as to open the boiler room door gingerly and peek inside, but no one was there. And when Patel failed to show up by lunchtime, Jack decided to express his concern and ask Watkins, tactfully of course, whether he might possibly be of any help. There were whisperings and half-formed mutterings in the staffroom, so that Jack's solicitude wouldn't seem out of place, especially since he had broached matters with Watkins already; Jack might have a role in dispelling malign gossip and misguided fears.

'Ahem! I don't think it quite appropriate to make any comment at all at this stage. I should be grateful if a discreet silence were observed while the matter is in hand. Thank you very much.' Whenever Watkins cleared his throat before a pronouncement, it signified that someone, somewhere, was about to be put in his place. Having been firmly put in his, Jack backed off and was left with his own thoughts.

Watkins had talked to Davenport at length, and the latter was not such a stickler for discretion, for he soon made the details known to all and sundry. According to Davenport, Watkins had been observing Patel when, near the end of the session, Patel began to stammer uncontrollably and for no apparent reason, causing pupils to stare in wonder and Watkins to shake his head in disbelief. Then, just as suddenly, Patel made an almighty dash for the door. Luckily it happened near the end of the lesson, and until then everything appeared normal; all the more reason why Watkins and pupils should be astonished at his behaviour. It must, therefore, have been only seconds later when Jack saw Patel scurrying across the quad. Unable or unwilling to join in the chase, Watkins had apprised Davenport of the whole episode and told him that he needed to fill in for Patel next lesson; Davenport's composure was disturbed, and his customary cup of camomile tea did little to ameliorate his displeasure at having to stand in for Patel.

'We must do what we can to establish a semblance of normality,' Watkins whispered. 'Just imagine how this would have gone down during an inspection! Not at all well. No, not at all well!'

'Yes, it's a question of perception,' Davenport put in. Watkins nodded his full agreement with a prolonged bout of nodding.

In fact, Patel reappeared after lunch and was actually seen teaching a class, but when Jack tried to catch up with him at the end of the day, he proved elusive. Then Gladys made a suggestion amongst a select number of the staff which at the time seemed quite reasonable: Patel's GP should be discreetly informed of his behaviour and advice should be sought. It was agreed that Jack should take on the task of expressing friendly concern, since, so Gladys said, Dr Rose Blanchard would be more likely to take the matter seriously if the appeal came from a man, and a man who was particularly close to Patel, or as close as anyone at Morley Comprehensive had managed to get. It was not a suggestion that Jack would normally have agreed to, but he allowed himself to be persuaded with surprisingly little effort, and it was agreed that Jack should pay Dr Blanchard a visit that very evening, catching her in her surgery after she had seen her last patient for the day. Gladys said that Patel needed supportive colleagues, particularly in view of the fact that his job might be on the line if help wasn't forthcoming, and that Patel's GP was an obvious source of sound, professional advice. It all sounded so reasonable.

It was only when Jack was waiting in the surgery for all Dr Blanchard's patients to be seen and leave that he began to have serious doubts about the whole idea. After all, GPs were not necessarily the obvious people to speak to. There were GPs and there were GPs. In a recent visit to his own GP, antibiotics had been prescribed for nervous exhaustion and overwork. Jack put his nervous exhaustion down to long-term disillusionment, and how on earth could that be treated? The cure for his kind of disillusionment seemed too heavily dependent on the moral improvement of mankind, and was therefore incurable, obviating the visit to the GP in the first place; and as for exhaustion, what GP could prescribe what was truly needful? Six months off work and a course of forgetfulness. Jack had thrown the antibiotics down the loo and spent an hour or two in The King's Head.

Then again, patient confidentiality had to be observed, and... Just then, the last patient popped out of Dr Blanchard's surgery and left with a cough and a splutter. Jack would leave, too, and as inconspicuously as possible. Too late, for he was seen!

'Yes, can I help you?' said Blanchard, looking round her surgery door into the waiting-room.

'Well, actually, yes – if you have a few moments to spare?'

And that was that. It was like a second visit to Watkins's office.

'So, you're not a patient here? No? No, I thought I didn't recognise you.' Like Sally, she sounded crisp and a no-nonsense woman. Now he knew the whole thing was absurd. But it was too late to back out. 'Oh, never mind – sit down for a moment.'

Jack introduced himself and gave his account of events, prefacing his narrative with, 'It's all very awkward and delicate, but...'

'So, we are talking about Mr Patel, is that right?' She looked at him menacingly, and Jack felt like an idiot.

'Frankly, I'm very worried about him. He's having to cope with a very stressful job, and the fact that his wife—'

'Yes, Mr Barker. But do you come to me as his friend, or do you in some way represent my patient's employers?'

'Not at all!'

'Not at all *what*?'

'This isn't some kind of conspiracy, some attempt to compromise him, or do something nasty behind his back. I'm here as a friend, one of the few friends he's got – it's as simple as that. If he doesn't get help quickly, he stands to lose his job, and that would be disastrous.'

'Disastrous for whom?'

'For Patel, of course!'

'And what do you propose I do about it?'

'Well...'

'I mean, do you think he's in some kind of danger? Do you think he might harm himself? Or do you think someone intends to harm him – in which case, it's really a matter for the police.' She was curt. 'Look, what I'm trying to say is that I can't possibly do anything unless Mr Patel decides to pay me a visit himself. You do understand that, of course?' And then she ended with a reference to patient confidentiality, as if for good measure. 'You do understand, Mr Barker, don't you?'

Of course he did. He had been brought up against the proverbial brick wall at last; he felt ashamed of himself for not having predicted this explicitly, as soon as Gladys suggested the whole thing. What made it worse was the expression of incredulity on Blanchard's face, as if to say that surely an intelligent person would have known in advance that her hands were tied. Another implication of that expression, at least as Jack understood it, was that Blanchard remained uncertain of him, as though Jack was possibly a malign agent working on behalf of dark forces and hoping to stir up a medical case against Patel. Blanchard had the annoying habit of tapping her biro on the top of the desk, staring Jack straight in the eye and saying 'Hmmm' in a tone that threw doubt on Jack's moral credentials – or was she humouring him in the hope that men in white coats would burst in at any moment to escort him back to the loony bin; in which case, he could imagine himself shouting, 'It's not me, it's Patel you should be concerned about!'

She led him to the door of her surgery without thanking him for coming. He said goodbye weakly, like someone who'd done wrong, hadn't a leg to stand on, and had been let off lightly. Infinitely worse, he knew he'd asked for it. He couldn't even function as helmsman for Patel without letting the poor fellow down and feeling much the worse for wear for his pains. *What would Alf say?* he wondered. He remembered Alf saying something to the effect that the more good you try to do, the more resistance you will meet. Yes, that was it. You more you try to free yourself from quicksand, the deeper you sink.

On reaching home, he telephoned Patel. There was no answer. He texted him. There was no reply. He spent the evening relaxing with his music, but the more he relaxed, the more militant he became. After all, Blanchard should have shown a gentle concern, to say the least, not an exalted indifference masquerading as professional incredulity and suspicion. He ended his meditations with cynical reflections on the relevance of the Hippocratic Oath to modern medicine. Well, it had to be said: there were GPs and there were GPs. In any case, Jack's expectations, as usual, far exceeded the likelihood of their being met – a fact which he had long attributed to the innocence and naivety of his upbringing.

Late next morning, he called Patel again, this time successfully. Patel was short on words, but insisted that everything was alright, that everything would turn out fine. He sounded wearily optimistic. Jack asked if he might pay him a visit. Patel said he would rather he did not; there was no need and he would see him on Monday. Patel was doing his best to sound convincing; in any case, Jack was more than ready to give him the benefit of the doubt. Jack had had enough – for the moment at least. It could all wait until Monday. Sally overheard the conversation and thought he shouldn't meddle with things that didn't concern him; but she kept her thoughts to herself. Jack said nothing, and Sally didn't raise the subject.

*   *

On Monday morning Patel wanted to close the matter, and decided that it was best ended where it had begun – in the boiler room. He seemed reasonably calm. Patel's account of the extraordinary events of last Friday was that his mind had momentarily wandered during Watkins's observation and failed to return. It was very odd, he said, but he couldn't finish the sentence he'd started; he found himself repeating the first bit, until the spell broke and he felt he had to rush off and be somewhere else, *anywhere else* but there. He couldn't really say why he'd rushed off like that; perhaps it was to save what face he could; perhaps it was to get somewhere where he could think things through. He was at a loss to explain it to his own satisfaction.

'Anyway, I walked for hours Friday night – trying to straighten things out.'

'You've spoken to Watkins?'

'Oh, yes. Last Friday. Before going home – I shall tell you all about it some other time.'

'How about tonight, in The King's Head?'

'Alright.'

Jack had thought Patel was a teetotaller and wouldn't be seen dead in a pub – on principle. But he had agreed readily to meet Jack there that very evening. Life was full of surprises.

*   *

Jack was right, Patel was a teetotaller, and he managed to last out the entire evening with a tomato juice and Worcestershire sauce. Jack's nerves were racked watching him nurse his glass. Listening was worse. They sat at a small table, Patel with his back to the bar, Jack facing it. Patel's glass was cupped in both hands ever so carefully, like a grenade that might go off if released. Jack downed one pint of brown ale after another with as much decorum as he could muster, and his attention was regularly diverted by the young brunette who stood at the bar, making listening harder still. Those two hours with Patel seemed to pass in some twilight world, with Jack repeatedly looking over Patel's shoulder at the girl at the bar while at the same time struggling to appear engrossed in Patel's account of events. Patel didn't seem to notice Jack's distraction, ready as he was to spill the beans of inner turmoil. The central core of Patel's account was his meeting with Watkins late on Friday afternoon.

Watkins had taken him into his office and given him a lecture on the importance of appearances, and of therefore pulling himself together for the sake of the 'ship' as whole. (Watkins's favourite image was of the *Ship of State*, one borrowed unknowingly from the ancient Greeks, and which he customarily applied to Morley Comprehensive.) Watkins was not unaware, Patel reported, of the stresses and strains under which Patel, like everyone else, must labour, but it was up to Patel himself to sort things out and maintain an even keel. It was all a question of personal, as distinct from collective, stress management. He advised Patel to consult his GP; and so strongly did he advise it that it sounded like a condition of his not being recommended for disciplinary action. As Grand Admiral of the Fleet and Captain of the Ship of State, Watkins's job was to command overall operations with optimum efficiency, which implied that each member of the crew must play his part or else be sent ashore. Above all, the flagship did not carry passengers; it was a battleship, geared for the battle of life and unprepared for the sick and the lame; its sole business was to do its job, and its job was solely to manage the business of educating the young. During the whole length of Watkins's extended metaphor, Patel had simply agreed, nodding or shaking his head at all the appropriate places; of course, he was in any case quite powerless to do anything else, even if he had wanted to. He assured Watkins of his utmost efforts in future, in return for which Watkins would do his best to forget, though not fail to record, the little incident of that morning – with the strict proviso that Patel succeeded in sorting himself out. Patel gave every appearance of feeling grateful for not having been keel-hauled on the spot; though, given a liberal interpretation, that is precisely what had happened.

As Patel recounted all this, the thought occurred to Jack that Watkins had come out of this the stronger, Patel decidedly the weaker. Yet again, the precious lifeblood of the humble had filled the cups of the victors to overflowing.

'No. I shall be perfectly alright. I just need time and rest.'

Jack simply nodded, though how Patel could possibly hope for either time or rest while at the same time holding down his job to Watkins's satisfaction was quite mind-boggling.

'There are things I need to come to terms with. Watkins has helped me to see that.'

'Watkins?!'

'Yes. You see, things cannot go on as they are. I understand that clearly now.'

'Well...'

'And I can promise you, Jack, there will be no need to meet in the boiler room from now on.'

Patel hung on to his glass, as if for support. He was entirely straight-faced and almost obscenely in earnest; not even a flicker of a smile on his lips or in his eyes; not a trace of humour, sarcasm or irony about him or in his narrative; just deadpan. Perhaps things would work out, after all. But the odds seemed piled against it. There was no piercing the plastic armour Patel was wearing; Patel would not allow it. Precious little help could be expected from the likes of Watkins, yet

Patel seemed to regard him as a kind of saviour. Almost as someone under painful interrogation might come to love his torturer – no, that was an analogy too far, and Jack reproached himself for it; no, it wasn't that bad.

Patel's narrative and his assurances concluded, he and Jack exchanged some childhood reminiscences, and it was only in this way that the evening might be said to have brought them a little closer. Both were haunted by the past and by the people that had belonged to it. But not simply people.

'There were hills quite close to home,' Jack said, 'the silences of a thousand Sundays crammed into them day and night. I'd run home, scared stiff of the silence, the loneliness of the place, and I'd promise myself never to go back. But, give it a week or so and I'd go back again – only to run home again, vowing never to return!' Jack smiled, but it was clear that it was no joke. Patel sat there, expressionless. Perhaps he hung on to Jack's every word; but it was hard to tell and didn't seem to matter anyway. Jack found it satisfying to say these things, and in the telling he even forgot all about the brunette at the bar. He'd tried once to tell Sally about these things, but she'd laughed it off and changed the subject, giving every indication that she hadn't really been listening – or worse, that she's been listening alright but couldn't care enough to take it seriously; that had wounded Jack deeply, since he really did think himself a haunted man and didn't have a clue how to understand it. Now, here, he could tell Patel and be listened to. Had he found a kindred spirit at last? But surely he and Patel were like chalk and cheese. No, perhaps Patel's presence was purely incidental, and perhaps he wasn't really listening, either. Jack was ruminating out loud, and the beer tasted fine.

9
Alf, forgive me!

Plastic armour or no, Patel really did seem more like his old self next day. There he was in the staffroom, nodding nervously to Gladys, Davenport and Harper. He couldn't have found it easy to make a social comeback after his boiler-room antics, which had gone neither unnoticed nor unremarked, and Jack put his nervousness down to that.

Harper taught physics. He was in his late fifties, and the advancing years seemed to make him more careless. He wasn't the same prim and proper Harper that Jack had known years before, when Jack had just started at Morley and Harper had introduced him amiably and faultlessly to everyone in the staffroom. Harper wouldn't have done then what he did unconsciously and habitually now. For he now ate his boiled-egg sandwiches by tearing manageable chunks off them, losing some of the filling down the sides of his armchair and all too audibly chewing the rest and gulping it down, followed by a quick swig of coffee which he had brought in a large, red thermos flask; no wonder no one ever occupied Harper's armchair but gave it, instead, a wide berth. Jack marvelled that the Harper who had introduced him so mannerly all those years ago seemed quite oblivious to the careless spectacle he made of himself now. Even Gladys, as easy-going as she was and as accustomed to Harper as she was, raised an occasional eyebrow in disgust, or perhaps it was in sympathy, or a mixture of both. Even when Amanda graced the staffroom with the innocence of beauty and the beauty of innocence, Harper conducted himself in just the same way; her presence did nothing to soften his zeal for boiled-egg sandwiches, and he continued to drop crumbs on his trousers, while bits of egg sometimes tarried in the corners of his mouth, reluctant to take the final plunge.

While Amanda politely pretended not to notice Harper's failings, Jack noticed her efforts to remain oblivious. It was too late for Harper. Too late for simple etiquette, let alone idealism. He'd burned out his little bit of candle – or squandered it, more like. He was as much a slave as Patel to the conventional and the mediocre, and this was the way he chose to wallow in his mediocrity, like a slave who enjoyed his confinement. Quite simply, routine had triumphed, and he had given up trying. 'Slaves in their bondage lose everything, even the desire to be free,' Jean Jacques Rousseau had said, and Jack thought it was an observation that should be indelibly written on Harper's forehead, and on countless other foreheads besides; it is noteworthy that he had begun to include himself in this wide circle of the brethren.

Jack was afraid of mediocrity, of atrophy of spirit, of death-in-life. So what if he preferred the music of the Elizabethans? At least it was different. Perhaps that was the whole point; if he could not be different in everything, at least he could be different in that. He had so far made a mess of his attempts to guide Patel's unhappy little vessel through the storms that threatened to sink it, and when he looked around the staffroom he saw little to sweeten what he saw – except the face of Amanda, for there was freshness in it, and youth; and in the freshness of youth, he caught a glimpse of something like hope, a door which might lead into a garden of forgotten delights, something transient perhaps, but certain and wonderful while it lasted. Amanda seemed to like him, and he owed it to himself to follow the path he had already set himself upon.

'Well,' he said, as he and Amanda were walking down the corridor, having left the staffroom together, 'if you're not too busy, Sally and I could meet you tonight for a drink in The King's Head, and then take you back with us and have that musical evening. Hm?' The jaws of a trap were now set. He was nervous, but he had built himself up to it, and now it was done. He almost felt like thanking Harper for it, for the sight of that poor slave to mediocrity and death-in-life had helped to convince him that there was no more time to lose.

'Fine!' she said. There, it was done. Well and truly done.

Since Sally was aware that Jack had already met with Patel, it was easy to tell her that he had arranged to see Patel again that evening for another tête-à-tête. It was entirely convincing. It was natural, even laudable by any standards, that Jack should be taking a sustained interest in a vulnerable colleague, despite Sally's view that he should really leave well alone. So, no questions were asked when Jack left home after a dinner for which he had very little appetite, ostensibly to play the gruelling and apparently thankless role of helmsman in Patel's wretched life.

He was waiting outside The King's Head when Amanda pulled up in the adjacent car park in her little yellow Mini. He walked towards the car as she made to get out. Now he had to sound as convincing to her as he had to Amanda.

'I'm so sorry, Sally couldn't make it! She suffers from migraine and she's having one of her attacks. I didn't have your number, so I couldn't...'

'Oh, poor thing! No, but that's alright. We can forget about it tonight if you like, and—'

'Okay... but we can have a quick drink, can't we. I mean, now we're here. Oh, and I've brought some CDs with me for you to take home. So, shall we? Have a quick drink, I mean?'

The jaws of the trap were moving slowly but inexorably. In no time at all they were settled down with their drinks, the conversation turning first to Patel, for even the afflicted had their uses.

'No, the trouble with Patel is, he's a slave who's come to the end of his chain – it won't stretch any further and it's biting into his flesh, and it won't snap before he does. So, he's on to a loser if he hopes to break away. He just can't do anything else. He's a born teacher. No, I can't imagine him doing anything else, and neither can he. The limits are set *for* him as much as *by* him – if you see what I mean. He's not in control of his own life – unable to choose. He's had it up to here with everything – he's lost his bearings, and there's not a blind thing he can do about it. It's the Rip Van Winkle Syndrome – you know, finding the place you've woken up in isn't half as good as the place you fell asleep in. Devastating! Your whole world's shaken, and you with it. Worse than that is the realisation that you can't do a damned thing about it. Alf's right – slavery is not so much a revived institution as an eternal fact of life. Patel's a victim of circumstances he can't change for the better – and when he finally realises there's no changing them, he hides himself away in mediocrity – just like Harper. But the inner conflict goes on all the same. That's slavery for you!'

Amanda was most attentive during this deluge of cliché. Whether Alf had made that remark about slavery was to be seriously doubted, but naturally she was in no position to know one way or the other. (In fact, it was rather like falsely ascribing to Machiavelli the phrase 'The end justifies the means', which, although something he never actually said, expressed a sentiment he would no doubt have assented to readily enough.) In the same spirit, perhaps Alf would have agreed with the sentiment that slavery was an eternal fact of life. But Jack quoted, or misquoted, him whenever it suited his purpose, whenever it seemed to lend weight to a point he wished to make. Whether all this stuff about Patel was good psychology or not, Amanda was unable to judge; but it certainly sounded sensible enough. Neither did she think to ask herself whether Jack was perhaps talking as much about himself as Patel.

'Have you seen Alf again?' she asked.

'Me? No. No, I haven't.' He took a thoughtful draught of beer. 'You know – one thing Alf and I have in common – we can't make head nor tail of the treadmill. But he jumped off, and I stayed on. That's the difference. Of course, I still go through all the motions, so I'm superficially and publicly sane, while he's supposedly insane, an eccentric, a character, a one-off, a nobody, someone all respectable people pretend not to see – a standing joke amongst social equals. Question is: who's the joker, him or me!'

Amanda laughed. Jack looked at her. She was beautiful. She was too beautiful to be used like this. For he knew he wasn't speaking to her at all, but at her. He was speaking to the glass in front of him, and that had to stop. In any case, it was time for the jaws of the trap to move a little further.

'I'm sorry,' he said, after draining his glass and putting it down on the table forcefully.

'What for?'

'Babbling on and on like this – on and on about other people. And I'm sorry about this evening, too.'

'Not at all. To tell you the truth, I was really looking forward to it,' she smiled and shook her head slowly, as if sympathetically – and there was a kind of beauty in that, Jack thought.

'Well, as I said, I've brought some CDs with me. Take them with you. The lyrics aren't written down – but you can usually make them out.'

'Tell you what! Why don't you come to my place – we can have coffee and listen together and you can help me with the difficult bits. Oh, no – unless you want to get back… I mean, Sally…'

'No, Sally's fine. I mean, when she gets these bouts she takes some strong painkillers and goes to sleep and wakes up feeling much better. She's fast asleep now, I bet. And I wouldn't want to disturb her.'

'Fine then,' said Amanda. 'Let's go!'

The jaws of the trap had certainly moved on a bit, and Jack was most grateful that Amanda had innocently given them an important shove. They left in Amanda's little yellow Mini, Jack mesmerised by the aroma of Amanda's perfume in such a confined space – already a strong foretaste of paradise.

* *

After a short drive, Jack found himself in Amanda's bedsit, listening to one of his own CDs of Elizabethan songs sung to the gentle strains of the lute, the very same sounds that relieved him at home of the stresses of the treadmill. There they sat, drinking coffee and listening to the sound of music; in Amanda's very bedsit, no less; not in the staffroom of Morley Comprehensive, a seat of pretension and false formality, of stale jokes, forced joviality and dry humour, where people tried to be clever and invariably and signally failed, the antechamber of Watkins's great flagship, in the miserable hotchpotch generally and euphemistically referred to as 'routine'. Here he was, with Amanda, whose body was a gift, nothing less than a gift from above. The jaws of the trap were now in place, and all that was needed was to throw the switch and Amanda would be his in that small delightful bed that seemed to beckon in the far corner of her bedsit.

But how exactly was that switch to be thrown? Should he not suddenly confess everything? Confess that he had lied about Sally? That Sally knew nothing about this evening? That she knew nothing of Amanda? That she loathed Elizabethan music – or, indeed, any music that was more remote than the 1960s? Confess that he had planned it all? Confess that he found Amanda irresistible? That she was the only light in the otherwise dark room of his existence? That Amanda was his only hope of rescue from mediocrity and oblivion?

Or should he simply wait for an opportunity to put his arms around her and kiss her? Confessions could come later, if at all. Or perhaps Amanda would make the first move. She had helped him before – she might do so again. Yes, perhaps Amanda, wonderful, beautiful Amanda, would help him out again. If not, he would fall back on confession, and things would hopefully roll on from there to a bed of roses and forgetfulness.

While he sat pondering these options, the music played on and on – the lyrics magically appropriate and needing no translation:

Shall I come sweet love to thee,
When the evening beams are set,
Shall I not excluded be?
Shall I find thee willing yet?

But, paradoxically, the more he pondered, and the more the music played, the more absurd the options he pondered began to appear. He suddenly found himself asking what on earth he was about. He actually began to debate with himself, and such debating had a similar effect on his desires as it has on sleep – it inhibits both. There was no doubt that Amanda was physically desirable – she was beautiful – but then, beauty was also dangerous, devouring and distorting. After all, he was old enough to be her father. He felt old, and his recent attempts to dye the greyness out of his beard seemed more futile than ever. If destiny had intended he and Amanda to be bedded, it would have happened before now, and he would not be there debating it, weighing different courses of action over and over and sickening himself in the process. He began to feel ridiculous. A younger man would have known instinctively what to do and would have done it long before now. That was the trouble with growing older – you gradually lost your instinct and your impulsiveness; that instinct and impulsiveness that got things done, whether the things done were wise or not. You thought everything needed to be calculated down to the last detail, and that ruined everything before it could even get started. If he had failed to steer Patel's boat into calmer waters, he had scuppered his own by putting a gigantic hole in the keel. No, the whole thing was absurd; yes, quite absurd.

There was something else that nagged at him during these sad reflections. Whether a confession came sooner or later, he would need to talk about Sally. He would need to babble on and on again, stirring the waters on which Amanda herself floated like a delicate lily and muddying them. He imagined himself boring her with all his misgivings about his marriage, trying all the time to find something clever to say:

It's a bit like being a pole on a horseshoe magnet – you're apart and in a state of permanent opposition. Yet you're bound to each other on the same arc and unable to break away. Poles apart! There was that party of hers she dragged me to. There I was, trying to talk politely to people I didn't know and didn't want to know. The host scuttled around, trying to introduce and reintroduce you so you wouldn't stand about like a vegetable and spoil the fun. 'Fun,' did I say! 'Jack teaches history' began to sound like a cheap punchline. I asked myself what I was doing there, standing round with a glass of tepid white wine (I hate the stuff!) trying to shout irrelevant questions and answers to her friends above the din. They kept telling me how hard their businesses were hit by economic uncertainties and company taxes, and then in the very next breath they'd tell me all about the extended holiday they were planning in the Caribbean. 'Ever been to the Caribbean, Jack?' Well, I damned well hadn't! Nor was it ever likely I'd go. So I wondered what I was doing talking to this lot. Nothing new about that – but what was new, I blamed Sally for my being there, for putting me where I didn't want to be. Did she know I didn't want to be there? If she didn't, she should've known; if she did know, she obviously didn't care. Either way, Sally was anything but a kindred spirit. From there, it was a short step to the question: What was I doing with Sally in the first place? As Alf would say, 'Ask one good question and you raise a thousand – you just have to follow the logos wherever it may lead.'

Jack was good at rehearsing speeches, not so good at giving them; in any case, this is one he didn't want to make. For one thing, it was a betrayal. He would be talking to a third party about Sally, something he promised himself long ago he would never do. The principle was, what could not be worked out between them, and them alone, could not be worked out at all. At least, that is a promise he now remembered.

I saw my lady weep
And sorrow proud to be advancèd so.
In those fair eyes, in those fair eyes,
Her face was full of woe.
But such a woe, oh, such a woe,
Believe me, that wins more hearts
Than mirth can do with her enticing arts.
Sorrow was there made fair.

The phrase 'enticing arts' pierced him like a dagger. He was himself indulging in the arts of entrapment, and it was a shoddy business; unworthy of him. And what would Alf say? Then he imagined what Amanda herself would say:

'You can't blame Sally altogether, Jack. I mean, if you don't want to be where you are, you can do something about it, can't you?'

But then, she wouldn't sound just like Amanda. Amanda would be transformed from a sex object he was seeking to entrap, and become more like a marriage guidance counsellor, or an analyst dealing gently with a bewildered patient. It would be more than embarrassing. It would be soul-destroying, stripping him of all dignity.

'Can I? Really?' Jack suddenly said, out loud.

'Sorry?' said Amanda, getting up to turn down the volume.

'Oh, I said I'd really best be going. It's getting late. Besides, I think I might be coming down with something.'

'Oh dear, shall I get you something – an aspirin, maybe?'

'Er, no – thanks all the same. In any case, I'd better see how Sally's getting on. She might have woken up and… you know.' With that, he got up and picked up his overcoat, which had lain over the back of his chair. 'You can keep the CDs for a bit, if you like.'

'Thanks.' Now Sally got up and started to put on her coat.

'What are you doing?'

'I'll drive you home.'

'Oh, no. Absolutely not. No, I'd rather walk – it's not that far. And whenever I feel like this, a good walk does me good.' He was quite emphatic.

'Well, alright then – if you insist.'

And that was that. Or, almost that. She put her arms round his neck, as a daughter might embrace her father, and kissed him quickly on the cheek – an action which, however innocently intended, might have sparked Jack into irreversible gear thirty minutes before. As it was, he held her for a few seconds; she smelt and felt like the girls of his youth, lost opportunities even then, and now lost irretrievably. Amanda was firm and fresh and untainted by experience of life and work – the kind of work which produces a resentment that increasingly shows on your face and in your posture and gait. But she also felt to him as a daughter would have felt as he hugged her on her twenty-first. He was not, therefore, turned on by this simple event. He was, however, saddened by it, as though it were a pertinent reminder of where he stood both in Amanda's affections and in life as a whole; a reminder of where he was and what he was. His own movie was well-advanced, and there was no rewind button. Her embrace aged him, and he was glad to be released from it at last. 'Careful, you'll catch something!' Jack said, half-jokingly. And then only a polite smile stood between him and the dark chill of the night.

*   *

He walked home slowly, and had much to think about en route. He had set it all up, set it all in motion, and at a vital stage in the proceedings he had spiked his own guns. The trap had been set and then left un-sprung. If he had let himself down, he had done it on purpose – wilfully, as though he had wanted to be his own worst enemy. What did it all mean? There was, first and foremost, a cynical interpretation: perhaps it was all down to fear; fear that Amanda would have rejected him had he tried to play the game out. Perhaps. Or perhaps he had doubted his ability to play the seducer to the end. True, he had desired her, but then something had happened when the music played on and they both listened in the semi-darkness, while in his head a debate was in progress. What was it that had transformed Amanda from a purely sexual prey into someone unassailable? Was it merely a fear of inadequacy on his part? Or a fear they she would reject him, and a fear of all the consequences that would follow from that?

On the plus side, Jack managed to convince himself that he had at least managed to reject convention and mediocrity. After all, it was neither mediocre nor conventional for a seducer to spike his own guns and purposely ruin the act of seduction. Then again, there had been enough duplicity already, and he needed to make amends; there were just some lengths to which he could not go, and this was one of them. Spiking his own guns had been a last-ditch attempt to halt his descent into hypocrisy. Yes, that was it! How could he possibly denounce people like Watkins and Davenport for duplicity if he practised it himself? Yes, it sounded good; quite plausible. And so, to the possible charge that he had lacked the moral courage to jump into bed with Amanda, Jack could answer that it was sheer gobbledegook to speak of lacking the *moral* courage to do *wrong*. It seemed that in all his reasoning, backward and forward, he had somehow temporarily forgotten that his plan to seduce Amanda was wrong. A brief fling might, in the minds of many, be considered little more than a peccadillo. But you needed moral courage precisely to withstand the temptation to follow suit. Sex between him and Sally might have lost its heat, might have degenerated into one habit amongst others, and finally become largely a thing of the past, but there were things he couldn't do simply to appease his lingering, though weakening, appetite. You could not stand against your true self; like a house divided within itself, you would wither and fade and become – yes, and become one of the Shadow People, and that was death-in-life. The very thought! Beauty and deception could never be good bedfellows; Amanda would have kicked him out of bed when she finally came to see what a Shadow Man he really was: oblivious to hurting Sally, oblivious, too, to her own feelings when the act was done, because physical release is all he wanted, and less, much less, of a man than he had all along pretended to be. No wonder he had failed to play the role of helmsman for Patel; he couldn't even steer his own ship. Sex with Amanda would have been followed by lame excuses and a deluge of apologies, followed in turn by his making a quick exit from her bedsit and his wishing that he could make an even quicker and more final departure from the planet altogether. Alf, of course, would have disapproved profoundly. Surely, Jack was more than one cut above a mere Shadow Man. There were some things you had to endure, lest you became one of the Shadow People.

As he walked along, feeling the sobering chill of the night air, he began to feel fortunate to have escaped the ultimate duplicity in the nick of time. Had he found himself in bed with Amanda, his conscience would have got in the way and spoiled it all, making all that planning and all that desire quite pointless, and worse than pointless. Just like the time he had his first sexual experience with a girl called Laura. She had a kitten which kept jumping playfully onto the bed, pricking the bare soles of their feet with its claws, even in the throes of ejaculation – not quite painful enough to call an immediate halt to proceedings. But certainly off-putting and pleasure-spoiling, for sex had to be perfect if it was worth having at all. True, Amanda had no overactive kitten. But Jack had Alf, instead. And Alf had said no. Alf had helped him. Alf had guided him. Even if the seduction had been successful in conventional terms, the ensuing guilt would have killed him, giving him a conscience one mile deep and ten miles wide. He had never betrayed Sally. Not physically. Not even verbally. He was not about to start now. No, the whole episode had shown him his limitations, the limits of what was possible for him. Doleful Elizabethan love songs would never sound quite the same again. Jack's head was bursting with thoughts he never knew he could form.

He walked on, suddenly wondering how Alf was coping in temperatures like that – bitterly cold and damp as the conditions now were. For Alf was homeless, with nothing but the incalculable weight of bitter-sweet memory to accompany him through the night-time of his life.

'Alf, forgive me,' Jack muttered, as he drew his coat tightly around him.

* *

By the time he reached home it was already late, and Sally and Pete were fast asleep. She had read herself to sleep over one of her gooey novels; Jack carefully put the book to one side, switched off the bedside lamp and climbed into bed. He did not want to wake her, not relishing the thought of having to answer questions, for answers would necessarily be one lie on top of another. He had already built the foundations, but the resulting structure was one he longed to abandon. In any case, tomorrow was another working day; late nights had always been a mistake, having to spend the next day paying for it, and this one would be compounded by a mountain of lies.

It was one of Sally's staff training days, of which she was in charge, and she had to be up bright and early that morning, which is why any interrogation couldn't even achieve first base until the morning, while she washed and dried the dinner plates which had been left the night before.

'How was it with Patel last night, then?' she began.

'Oh, he's er… he's making progress, I think. Just needs some support – a good listener.'

'What did you talk about?'

'Well, it was just a repeat of last time, basically. He told me about his childhood, his parents. And Misbah – you know.'

'Just you and Patel then, was it?'

'Hm? Yes. Of course.'

'What time did you get home. Must've been very late.'

'Hm. I didn't want to disturb you – you were fast asleep.' Actually, she was not, but she did not correct him.

'You couldn't've been in the pub all that time. I thought he didn't like pubs, anyway.'

'He made an exception this time. No, we went back to his place after a while.'

'That's a novelty, too. I thought he didn't like visitors. You must've made an impression!' She paused. 'Patel drove you to his place, did he?'

'No. He doesn't drive. We walked.'

Jack said he had a lot of lesson preparation to do and had to get off early, and since Sally needed to make an early start, the interrogation ended there. Nothing had happened between him and Amanda, but it was vital to maintain the lie. Telling the truth, Jack reasoned, would not simply have been an act of reckless folly, but also one of senseless cruelty, creating a doubt in Sally's mind which would have been impossible to dispel completely. Telling the truth was invidious and would have entailed more lies. How come he had met Amanda and not Patel? Hadn't he specifically arranged to meet Patel, and Patel alone? He could not spill the beans without convicting himself of duplicity and deviousness. No, he had done well to leave matters as they stood. It was in Sally's best interests, not to mention his own. The lie was irremovable.

What he did not know was that Pete, on his way home from a friend's place, had spotted his father and Amanda leaving in her little red Mini which, in the lighted car park, was unmistakeable. He saw Amanda, whom he did not know but who struck him as particularly young and attractive, and his father sitting beside her; he waved to them, but the car passed too quickly and he was unseen, or at any rate unrecognised.

He had naturally reported the incident to his mother, and Sally was intrigued to say the very least. Pete was naturally subjected to a barrage of pertinent questions. What time was this? About 9.30, according to Pete. Just about the time when either Jack was in the pub with Patel or when he and Patel were on their way to Patel's place. Yes, but *walking*, not driving. Did he see anyone else in the car? He was not sure, but he thought there was no one else.

'Why?' Pete asked.

'Oh, nothing! Just one of Dad's colleagues, I suppose.'

Sally spent the whole day thinking about it. Just how the staff training session managed to get underway and finally reach what everybody considered to be a satisfactory and welcome conclusion, she could not say. What for Pete had been made out to be nothing in particular, a trite and unremarkable observation, was for Sally a most worrying development; and the most worrying feature about it was clearly the web of lies that Jack had woven. People lie to conceal – what did he have to conceal? Nothing was said over dinner that could possibly have a welcome bearing on the matter, and the whole thing was passed over in a kind of strained silence. After dinner she was supposed to put together a report of the staff training session, but she spent a good part of the evening staring at a blank piece of paper; after a while she did jot down one or two notes, but this was a pretence. She was actually wondering how to go about things, or whether to go about them at all. She decided on a strategy of wait-and-see. Sally had built a reputation for herself as a no-nonsense woman; she was not the type to allow any water, let alone polluted water, to pass under the bridge unnoticed and un-dealt with. She was sharp and direct with juniors and equals alike; and she believed it right and proper to apply the same standards to her domestic affairs. But first, she wanted to be sure of her facts. Once sure, she would act, and no mistake about it. In the meantime, she could not force Jack into the open with threat or coercion, by, for example, withholding sex, since there had been nothing physical between them, or at least nothing worth mentioning, for goodness knows how long; by the same token, neither could she properly test his affections with a sudden demand for sexual gratification. Diplomatic relations between two countries could be not be broken if they had already, and for quite some time, ceased to exist; nor would they be renewed unless both parties to them really desired to renew them; no, it did not occur to her to make entirely new overtures of love and affection; perhaps because, after all, she was not sufficiently interested. It just felt right to await further developments, one way or the other. And then, should the evidence prove sufficiently damning… Well, she was not one to cross her bridges before she came to them.

It was altogether an awkward, uncomfortable evening, and not at all the kind she had grown accustomed to. It was also important to keep Pete in the dark, for what might, after all, turn out to be nothing in particular. On the other hand, if it proved to be *something* in particular, it was vital that nothing should be allowed to interfere with Pete's studies and the future that Sally was planning to steer him towards, which was anything in this broad, wide world other than something called philosophy.

10

Juggernauts and Schellenberg's Machine Guns

Two weeks later and life at Morley Comprehensive had largely been without incident. Patel no longer seemed particularly nervous, just his quiet, unassuming self. It was Monday, inglorious Monday, made even less attractive, were that possible, by yet another plenary staff meeting called by Watkins for four that afternoon in the recently renovated Conference Room, to discuss the topic 'Systems of Staff Appraisal', which was the subheading of the more general 'Quality Control in Education'. Jack had strongly considered the possibility of a couple of lunchtime drinks in an effort to soften the blow and mitigate the effects, and partly as a protest, partly a personal treat. He was tempted, resisted stoically, and won. Ultimately, he reasoned, whether he resisted temptation or not was neither here nor there. But then, ultimately, everything was neither here nor there; ultimately there was just you and eternity, and then just eternity; and being good or bad at anything, being an alcoholic or being a teetotaller, a one-girl man or a downright fornicator, all came to pretty much the same thing, namely zilch. But it was dangerous to begin a sentence with such a word as 'ultimately'; if you dealt in ultimates, you were in danger of losing all motivation, at least all motivation to do good. But it was unfair: it was gross misconduct to get tipsy in school time, or even to be seen with a bottle, whether one imbibed or not, or to be perceived to be drunk when one was not; yet it was not gross misconduct to organise meetings and enforce attendance when no one but the organisers wished to attend them. Life was grossly unfair, and astonishingly one-sided.

With such depressing thoughts still loitering with intent, Jack found himself sitting next to Patel in the Conference Room, which still smelt nauseously of fresh gloss paint, while Watkins droned on about the need for what he called 'quality control', with Davenport nodding sagely and incomprehensibly at every hackneyed phrase. It might just as well have been Adolf Hitler and Joseph Goebbels, or Heinrich

Himmler and Reinhard Heydrich – the pairings were all pretty much the same to Jack, who was in the habit of imagining people he disliked in Nazi uniforms replete with all the regalia of the SS. Had he known, Patel would have said that that was going too far. Patel did not know what Jack was picturing, and it was just as well for him that he could not peer into Jack's mind, or that what filled it could not be seen by anyone else.

Of course, quality control and staff appraisal were very much 'in' these days; they were 'in' everywhere; indeed, they were so far 'in' that one could only be regarded as perverse in questioning them. Such ideas not only went unquestioned, but, infinitely worse, they had become unquestionable, too. Which perhaps explains why Jack and others had to be content to picture the adherents of such notions in Nazi uniform, but say nothing that could possibly be construed as a questioning attitude. If only dead fish swim with the tide, it was infinitely better to be dead and well and truly kippered than to risk one's job by appearing to be subversive. Which was only right and fair, since, like any other business, the business of education could not possibly tolerate questions of a kind which was perceived to undermine its foundations. There was nothing for it, therefore, but to sit and listen, or at least to sit and *appear* to listen. Jack pretended to listen while inwardly nodding off. He would have liked to line up all the Watkinses and Davenports and give them all a damned good kick in the butt, if only for presuming to know more about – not the 'business' – but the *stuff* of education than the front-line teachers. He wanted to punish them, and to do it now, for when they were dead they couldn't be punished. But even if he did manage to kick them all, and as hard as he possibly could, he wondered what earthly good it could do.

Then he wished he'd had that lunchtime drink and risked young Harris reporting him for gross misconduct, for Harris was still smarting and was perhaps waiting for a chance to hit back. He glanced out of the window and caught a glimpse of Old Jacob hoeing the shrubberies. According to Gladys, Jacob was on his way out. She'd heard it was all about necessary cuts, in an effort to curb expenditure and trim budgets, which was intriguing to say the least, for Jacob earned a pittance anyway. His going was bound to be a minuscule saving, she said; and what would happen to the shrubberies? Left, no doubt, to go to ruin, but this was of little interest to inspectors. Jack would miss Jacob, and for the best of reasons. The place just wouldn't be the same without him. 'It isn't the shrubberies I'm talking about,' he'd said to Gladys. 'Who in their right mind would sacrifice a poor old fellow like Jacob, doing a good job for a pittance and loving every minute of it?' he'd said, forgetting that it wasn't a question of right minds at all, but of pennies, for every penny counted.

The sound of Watkins aggressively clearing his throat brought Jack's attention back to the meeting, just as a sudden, loud, discordant note might reawaken the somnolent during a recital of a tedious concerto. It really did seem interminable. He was now rambling on about self-development for teachers:

'…and in *my* view, not to say in that of all those who care for the future of teaching in this and every similar establishment, or, I might say, in this *business* and every similar *business* – in *my* view, it is vital that people in my position should give the lead and clear the way forward. After all, what teachers want for themselves is precisely what schools should want for teachers…'

Giving the lead? Clearing the way forward? Watkins sounded like a latter-day John the Baptist. Leads should of course be given, and you hoped there was a way forward; but as far as Jack was concerned, the lead was misdirected and the way was backward. Was Watkins trying to say that self-development, whatever that was, was to be *imposed* by him? How could *self*-development ever possibly be an imposition? And was he equating the school with himself and people like himself? If so, he was expressing pretensions towards absolute monarchy, as when Charles I said he could not be tried for crimes against the State, since he was himself the State. No, you never knew where you stood with people like Watkins. His sentences were convoluted and, besides, one never knew how much to contribute to cunning and how much to intellectual incompetence. And if his sentences were expressions of sheer humbug, one was not allowed to say so. As it was, Watkins looked out onto a sea of heads nodding like little toy people with their heads on spring swivels, his radar alert to any signs of dissension, which might consist of a twitch or a sideways glance, or an otherwise imperceptible groan of disbelief or sigh of boredom. Dissension on this occasion was anything but overt. Everyone, including Jack, was looking right back at Watkins, as though hanging onto his every word. It would be more accurate to say that Jack was looking *through* him and saw Jacob beyond, as though Watkins was no more than a window into something other than itself.

If Gladys was right, what was Old Jacob to do with himself? Watkins could formally suggest his staying on. But the recommendation for dismissal had come from Watkins himself. The staff might get up a petition in an effort to retain Jacob, but unanimity amongst the staff, especially an increasingly youthful staff, could hardly be expected; newly or recently appointed staff were more easily manipulated by the hierarchy, were less likely to challenge the authority which had appointed them, and less inclined to take a lenient view of people they hardly knew. No, it was fear. Definitely fear that spiked the springs of rightful action. And if Watkins was unendowed with even a spark of eloquence, he was at least full of self-confidence, full of himself, which made him an impressive speaker, giving off the signal that he was not simply unchallenged but unchallengeable. Yes, he was certainly an impressive speaker, if one could forgive him his propensity towards duplicity and deviousness, his duplicitous and devious nature often revealed in the frequent application of the *Need-to-Know Principle*, a principle which was rigorously applied even on those occasions when the staff had an obvious right to know. Jack had long decided that he should have as little as possible to do with him and that it was best to give him the widest possible berth. Why was Watkins gaping at him now? It was as though he could read his thoughts. Trouble was, people like Watkins seemed to have the luck of the Devil – perhaps because they were his emissaries; everything they touched seemed to turn to gold, and because they had the Midas Touch, they were invariably the envy of others; they were 'successful' in their own eyes, and in the eyes of others, according to a most popular and pervasive conception of success.

Suddenly, chairs began to scrape the floor. Watkins had finished! Glory be! Jack felt like a pupil again, finally released from detention after having been justly lectured and roundly put in his place. He almost felt grateful, as those upon the rack might have felt when the session of indescribable pain comes to an end, albeit a temporary one. There was to be no protest, no demonstration of manhood, no visible resistance. Not even a passive resistance, a kind of Gandhian *satyagraha.* Nothing. Nothing at all, apart from giving Watkins and his ilk the widest possible berth.

*　*

'I just can't understand it!' said Jack, glaring at Gladys. It was now Thursday and the end of a long day, and he and Gladys were unlocking their bicycles in the bicycle shed. Some kind of volcano had erupted. 'It seems just the sort of thing a creep like Davenport would say if he wanted to get Patel out of the way for good – or has he been put up to it? They get rid of Patel, and Davenport ingratiates himself with Watkins at the same time. A masterstroke. No, I just can't believe it – just doesn't make sense – I mean it's completely out of character; doesn't sound like Patel at all!'

'Yes, I know. I know it's far-fetched. But the problem is, it's just *possible,* isn't it? And just the kind of thing people love to gossip about,' said Gladys, as Jack just stood there shaking his head. 'And Patel wasn't in yesterday, was he?'

'Oh, come on, Gladys!'

'Well, that's what I heard. The story is, Davenport was passing Patel's classroom late Tuesday afternoon and—'

'Caught Patel watching a hardcore porn movie. Gladys, can you hear yourself?'

'Davenport said it was after classes, and he poked his head round the door just to ask if he was alright. Patel was intently watching something on the desktop screen. Davenport went in and approached him, and... bingo!'

'Bingo!' echoed Jack, laughing incredulously.

'I know. I know. But there it is. Patel is supposed to have fumbled with the controls when Davenport went in, got confused and couldn't turn the desktop off – just *froze*, apparently! He began to mumble something or other, Davenport said, but gave up and just made a dash for it, leaving everything as it was – computer on, DVD still running! Can you imagine? The embarrassment!'

'Embarrassment? For Patel, or for Davenport?'

'Well, both, of course.'

'Davenport said he had to remove the DVD and dispose if it asap before it got into the wrong hands and…'

'Pupils' hands? What, late on Tuesday afternoon?'

'Well, a pupil might have wanted to see Patel and then found him…'

'Gladys, I find it hard to believe any of this. It sounds like a cock-and-bull story contrived to do Patel down – or at least, Patel has a perfectly good explanation. Either way, it doesn't impress me. It really doesn't. Are you sure Davenport wasn't spinning you a yarn – just for a laugh?'

'He isn't the type.'

'Well, you're right about that, at least. But look, Patel isn't the type to be into that sort of thing. Even if, and I don't believe it, but even if he were into it, why didn't he watch the stuff at home? Why here? Why take such an enormous risk? No, it just doesn't make sense. But that kind of story doesn't have to be true to do the greatest possible harm. Even if he has a perfectly good explanation… I mean, if there is just the smallest grain of truth in a story like this, Patel has managed to let the wolves in through the front door. He might just as well hang a notice round his neck, *Come and Get Me*!'

'Of course, Davenport made as much capital out of it as he could. You know the sort of thing: "I had little option but to report the incident to Mr Watkins. Suppose he'd been caught in the act by one of our pupils? Just think of the effect that might have had – parents involved, and all the rest. No, I couldn't let it pass. In fact, I was doing Patel a service. Though I don't expect any gratitude for it, of course." I mean, stuff like that!'

'What? You mean to say, he thinks Patel owes him something for grassing on him? Good God! I suppose it doesn't occur to him that our precious little pupils know far more about that subject than Patel could ever hope to learn? No, no it wouldn't.'

'What are we going to do, Jack?'

'*We*? *Do*? Look here, Gladys, I don't, I can't, believe any of this garbage. Just can't be Patel. I don't know. I'm going home.'

Jack pedalled away as fast as his weariness would allow – from Gladys, Davenport, Watkins, Morley Comprehensive, and Patel and his alleged misdemeanour. All this was enough to drive the sober to drink, and tipplers to Kingdom Come.

It was a windless evening, and as Jack rode homeward he remembered that yesterday had been a windy day, and he entertained the thought that the howling of the wind had mingled with the baying of wolves out for blood – Patel's blood, evidently. Not that he wanted to doubt what he had already told Gladys. None of it sounded at all like Patel. On the other hand, Jack had for a long time been struck by an irony in life that was bound up with a kind of inevitability. His grandfather had said something about a bullet having your name on it, and if your name's there, there's damned all you can do about it. The cock-and-bull tale he'd heard about Patel was just crazy enough to be true, or to be true enough; and if so, it would be a kind of cosmic setup, with Patel as its target. What was the point of trying to be a helmsman for Patel's poor storm-tossed vessel if it was bound to sink anyway?

On the other hand, it was no use blaming the gods for our own shortcomings. Jack had read Homer's *Odyssey* in translation and had committed to memory the telling lines:

Perverse mankind, whose wills, created free,
Blame all their woes on absolute decree.
All to the dooming gods their guilt translate,
All follies are miscalled the crimes of fate.

It was all very confusing. You just didn't know how far Fate was predetermined and unalterable and how far we were ourselves its authors.

* *

There was no sign of Patel next day, either, which some thought served to confirm guilt and others to indicate little more than plain embarrassment, two interpretations which were not of course mutually exclusive. In any case, the atmosphere in the staffroom was strained and peculiar. People seemed to be talking in gentler tones, more politely, almost in considerate whispers, as though to underline the momentous nature of the event, as though what had happened was big enough to concern everybody, and as though anybody might be implicated at the mere drop of a hat. Naturally, even if Patel could be cleared of intentional impropriety, it really wasn't the sort of thing that could ever be lived down. Guilty or innocent, it was enough to be charged with the offence, which is why the very thought of implication, real or imagined, was enough to disturb everyone's composure. Things like this stuck, especially if pupils themselves got a whiff of it; and how on earth could something like that be kept secret in a place like this, for a school was notorious for rumour, which could spread at Olympic speed, and grow like Chinese Whispers. *Patel doesn't stand an earthly* was a recurrent thought in Jack's tired brain, and one which divested Friday of all its customary attractions.

As if to add insult to injury, Davenport now seemed to walk round the place with an added and unspoken air of authority, suggesting perhaps that he had brought a difficult and delicate situation to light and had dealt with it with astonishing efficiency and competence. He was intensely polite to everyone, like a vicar who had been temporarily appointed an ARP warden in the Blitz.

'Come on, Gladys!' said Jack. 'Nobody could possibly be as sweet as that and mean it. Especially *him*. He's a damned hypocrite. He saw his chance and took it. If Patel walked in now, he would get up and offer to make him a cup of tea, as though butter wouldn't melt. Yes, Patel's the poor guy on Death Row – given a hearty meal before he goes to the chair. Davenport's the one who offers him some refreshment. And guess what? Davenport's the one to pull the switch.'

In Patel's absence, Gladys was the only one Jack felt he could talk to.

'What are we going to do, Jack?' Gladys had asked this question before. This time, Jack pretended he hadn't heard.

'If I told Davenport what I thought of him, he'd condemn me with Patel, or accuse me of disloyalty – and they'd believe him. Such is the hold of the Latinist on the poor, ignorant majority.'

Gladys just shook her head.

There was a lot of giggling in 4C that Friday afternoon, which seemed to have very little to do with Jack's comments on the Restoration of 1660. Perhaps it had nothing to do with the allegations against Patel, either; but in Jack's mind it was otherwise. After all, that kind of gossip was the fastest on the planet. And even Jack was perhaps beginning to imagine connections where there were none. Patel's stand-in possibly knew all about it by now; she had stood in for him before during periods of illness and was therefore not new to Morley Comprehensive. One of the staff could easily have said something, Davenport himself might have dropped more than a hint or two; he had already proved himself to be the soul of indiscretion and it was he who had the job of arranging stand-ins for absent staff.

As Friday drew to an uncomfortable close, Jack really had to address the question Gladys had posed twice already; he felt a need to pre-empt the possibility that she would ask a third time and then be perceived to do nothing. The number three had a religious significance associated with betrayal, and he wanted to avoid its application here.

He might speak to Watkins. But then, so much for the idea of giving him the widest possible berth. Even if he spoke to Watkins, it would have to wait until next week. But so much the better; it would give Patel a bit of time to sort himself out, and give Jack some time to work out what was best to say and how to say it. Better still, he would see Patel over the weekend, whether he liked visitors or not, and then he could get the story from the horse's mouth. Armed with a visit to Patel, and the Truth in his pocket, he would be in a much better position to speak to Watkins if that was the course to be taken. Yes, that's it. He would speak to Patel first and get the whole thing sorted out. And as for inevitability and the dire hand of an unalterable Fate, well, if you believed that, *really* believed it, you might as well jump in the river now and end it all. No, if the course things took could not be altered come what might, life would be unspeakably pointless.

*   *

Zanjik Patel lived at 158 Cherrytree Road, in a house he had been pleased to call 'Bhagavad' (Blessed), after the *Bhagavad Gita* (The Song of the Blessed), a work of philosophical and ethical genius designed to release man from the morally inhibiting web of material entanglement. In the hands of an estate agent who knew his trade, 'Bhagavad' might come across irreligiously as 'A desirably modern semi with the added convenience of main road frontage and immediate access to essential motorway connections.'

It was early Saturday evening, and it took Jack a full twenty minutes to cross the road to the front door – the traffic was that dense and the noise thunderously off-putting. 'Bhagavad' was positioned half a mile from a main motorway access, and was as far removed from a divine release from material entanglement as one could possibly get. Neither were there cherry trees on Cherrytree Road, nor for that matter any trees at all. Grass grew stubbornly here and there at the roadside, putting up a resistance to the concrete excreta of thoroughly modern civilisation – but it was a lost cause, and nothing could come of it.

Jack knocked repeatedly at the front door, and still harder, but without answer. He walked round the side of the house and pushed open a wooden side door, very much on its last hinges, which led onto the rear garden. In the greying light, Jack saw the remains of what might once have been a pretty garden but which was now overgrown and left to fend for itself. He banged on the kitchen door at the rear and shouted. Still no answer. Well, if Patel didn't want visitors, he didn't want visitors; and if he wasn't in, he wasn't in. It was time to give up. He made his way to the front of the house again and was wondering whether to give the front door another try, or whether he should go straight home, or even phone the police just to be on the safe side. Suddenly, the front door opened, and Patel just stood there expressionless, unshaven and decidedly the worse for wear. He said nothing, not even the most perfunctory word of greeting. He opened the door wider, stood to one side, and Jack walked in.

Patel showed him into the living room. 'Bhagavad' was as untidy as Patel was dishevelled. Patel was embarrassed.

'My wife, you see, she was so house-proud,' he said, bending down to remove a book and a pair of spectacles from an armchair so that Jack could sit down. 'It wasn't always like this.' He sat down opposite Jack.

'At first I kept it was she would have wanted it. Well, I tried my best. I exhausted myself cleaning this, polishing that. Afterwards, I would just sit down, look at it all, and weep, just weep. It was the same with the garden, you know. It used to be as pretty as a picture. It was her domain. She took such care. It was her pride and joy. Beautiful flowers. Such beautiful flowers. We would sit in the garden together on warm summer evenings, on our bench under the willow tree right at the back, admiring her handiwork. Every spring she would prepare border plants, and they were a showpiece, every year a showpiece. I had plans to do just the same, so that it would seem that she was back here with me again every spring – she would be present amongst the flowers, yes?' He paused musingly. 'Present amongst the flowers,' he repeated, as if to himself. 'I am going to make some tea.' He suddenly got up and went to the kitchen.

Jack walked to the window which led onto the garden at the rear. There was not quite enough light to see clearly to the rear of the garden, but he could make out the willow tree, surrounded, it seemed, by weeds of all descriptions at its base. The living room was scattered with books on every subject under the sun, from gardening to obscure works in Sanskrit; bookshelves lined the whole of one wall, and Patel had taken books from them and neglected to replace them, as though the effort had proved too much, so that you had to pick your way carefully to get from one side of the room to the other. Eventually, Patel returned with a tray of tea and biscuits. Some of the biscuits were broken, but no apology was forthcoming. He carefully placed the tray on a small coffee table poised between the two armchairs, Jack having picked up some books to make way for it.

'Most people do not know how to make tea – I mean, how to make it properly,' said Patel, sitting down. 'And having made it, they do not know how to drink it. They gulp instead of sip, and they sip when it is too hot, and they burn their tongues. And they are always in a hurry. They spoil it. They spoil everything.' He poured a cup of tea and handed it to Jack. 'Please take milk and sugar as you wish. That is another thing. I really cannot understand this obsession with milk and sugar. They make tea in the teapot and then they disguise it with milk and sugar.'

Jack laughed. Patel's remarks about tea and how to drink it sounded very much like Alf's remarks about life and how to live it. Jack made the connection in the silence that followed, a silence far too pregnant to last long.

'Jack, please understand this,' said Patel, breaking the silence. 'That DVD thing was not mine. I did not put it into the computer. I simply turned the computer on. Perhaps I touched the wrong button. I do not know. It flashed onto the screen. I tried to remove it, but Davenport came in and, well, it was so embarrassing. I did not know what to do or say, and the look on his face was like an accusation. I found myself unable to speak. My only explanation is that perhaps a pupil had inserted it and… But for some reason I could not say this to Davenport at the time. I was paralysed for a moment, and then my only thought was to get away. To get away from it all.'

'You've explained this?'

'Later, yes. To Mr Watkins.'

'Well, that's alright, then.'

'I think Mr Watkins did not believe me – like you, Jack.'

'Me? No! Nonsense! Of course I believe you.'

'But you find my account difficult to believe, do you not?'

'Your account? Er, no. No, not at all. Why should I? In any case, it's hardly a crime, is it?'

'Ask my judges.'

'What did he say – Watkins?'

'He said that I should take a couple of days off – for the matter to cool, he said.'

'And you agreed?' Patel nodded. 'But if you stay away it might be understood as an admission of guilt, of some kind of guilt, as though you're hiding from something, as though you're ashamed of something. I mean, it's the wrong sort of signal – you're sending the wrong sort of signal.'

'No matter. No. I have had enough. I have no wish to return. What is more, I am sure that they have no wish to seek to persuade me. You have been very helpful, Jack – a true friend. But my mind is made up. It is all over now. I am ashamed. That I should have sunk so low – with all that business in the boiler room! So undignified. So foolish. So weak.'

'But you're giving in to them! You're giving up without a—'

'You know,' Patel cut in forcefully. He was now standing by the window which looked onto the access road at the front of the house.

'You know, it was not always like this. It used to be peaceful here. But then the motorway came and this became a major access road, and everything changed as if by magic, a kind of black magic. Oh, what a difference! Suddenly and without warning, it seemed to us then. Yes, suddenly we became an access road and it happened one year and six months to the day before my dear wife passed on. She had a long and hard illness, you know. I looked after her at home, where she wanted to be and where I wanted her to be. It is said that you cannot observe changes in people when you live with them day in and day out. But it is not so. Every day I saw that she was a little worse, a little paler, a little lighter, a little thinner, a little darker under the eyes – every day I noticed something. And as she got worse, so did the noise of the traffic. I often used to blame the noise for her illness, which was very silly, I know. But the noise gave her no real rest. I never forgave them for building that motorway. Once, I carried her to the willow tree so that she might enjoy the sunshine and what was left of her poor flowers. But the noise from the front was too much for her, even at the back of the garden, and I had to carry her back indoors again. That was the last time she saw the willow tree. And one night she passed away, but not in a dignified silence, but with the roars of juggernauts. Where is the dignity in that, I ask you.' Patel's fists were clenched at his sides, but now his shoulders relaxed. 'But it was not always like that. It was once peaceful, and we were happy, though we did not know how happy we were.'

'What will you do now?'

'I shall be fine. There is plenty to do. I can find great comfort in things,' he said, picking up a Bible from the floor. He opened it at a bookmark and read: '"And David said to Solomon his son, Be strong and of good courage: fear not, nor be dismayed: for the Lord God, even my God, will be with thee; he will not fail thee, nor forsake thee…" Yes, I find great comfort in words like that.' Jack smiled and nodded. 'We must endeavour to find comfort wherever we can, my friend Jack,' Patel went on. 'Because we are all on our own, whatever we are told, and whatever we tell ourselves. Parents, wives, children, relatives, friends, yes. But really we are all alone. This is the horrible truth – yet perhaps it is also our strength, if only we know how to use it.' Patel looked ahead blankly. He was talking to himself again.

'I'll call you from time to time,' said Jack.

'Please, no!' said Patel, suddenly jerked back from his flight into self-reflection. 'I always worry who it is, and my phone is usually switched off. No, it is better if I call you. Is that alright?'

Of course it was alright. There was nothing more to say. Jack got up and was shown out. After Patel shut the door, Jack stood outside for a few seconds listening to the roar of the traffic. Saturday or not, it seemed as busy and therefore as noisy as ever, the juggernauts as oblivious to the dying as they were to the thunderous rumbling of their own fearful engines.

Despite Patel's assurances to the contrary, perhaps in view of them, Jack decided that the fellow must be at his wits' end. Patel was a poor, tortured soul, who had done a poor job of hiding the turmoil within. Patel was just fooling himself if he really thought he had plenty to do to keep himself occupied – even if he had the financial means to give up working at the drop of a hat, which by the mere look of things was far more certain. No, the truth had leaked out when, as Jack was leaving, he had asked him to act as a referee in the event that 'something came up'; the relaxed exterior had masked a Mr Micawber within. The poor fellow was at a loss to tackle the life of increased solitude that unemployment would entail, not to mention the circumstances that had brought it about. Patel couldn't be allowed to waste away in that crumbling sarcophagus that he called a house.

Which is why Jack the helmsman came to life again, and why he was now determined to speak once more to Watkins as early as possible the following week, before the judgement against Patel turned to granite. The whole business was quite ridiculous, and the very idea that anyone, particularly a good guy like Patel, should be shunted aside ignominiously for the sake of a sexy piece of plastic, the ownership of which Patel had in any case disclaimed... Well, it just didn't make sense. No practical sense. No moral sense, certainly. No, Jack felt he had to do something, which meant of course that the strategy of giving Watkins the widest possible berth had, for the moment at least, to be abandoned, but in the best possible cause.

* *

The meeting with Watkins started off amicably enough. Jack related his visit to Patel, stressing his belief in Patel's 'innocence'. The whole thing was simply a misunderstanding and stemmed from circumstances he could not have known and could not have helped.

Watkins allowed Jack to run on for a while and then began to tap his fingers on his large metallic desk while eyeing Jack steadily, his eyes half closed, as though he were sizing him up. Watkins's other hand was under the desk and hidden from view. Jack felt uneasy by now and began repeating himself. He remembered something which now flashed across his mind, something about Hitler's Chief of Foreign Intelligence ('Spy'!), Walter Schellenberg, who had an ingenious mechanism built into his desk consisting of two machine guns, the muzzles of which followed the movements of the 'guests' who sat in front of them; Schellenberg could eliminate opposition merely by pushing a button concealed under the top of the desk and within easy reach. Jack had never seen a photograph of Schellenberg; no matter, Watkins could easily fit the bill, and Jack once more found himself imagining the Headmaster of Morley Comprehensive in an immaculate SS uniform. And such imaginings did nothing to stem the tide of Jack's uneasiness.

Jack, conscious now that he was repeating himself, simply stopped. There was a moment's silence, which seemed like an eternity, while Watkins continued to tap his fingers and stare into Jack's face with half-closed eyes.

'Do you feel bitter for some reason, Mr Barker?' Watkins asked the question slowly, seeming to relish every syllable, then he folded his arms and leant forward in his chair, still staring into Jack's eyes.

'Bitter?'

'You see, I have considerable difficulty understanding your true motives. If you really want to speak up for Mr Patel, I find the fact rather disturbing. It must raise questions in my own mind about your own integrity, Mr Barker. Yes! Yes, I speak bluntly, and I think it's better for both of us if I do.'

'I'm sorry, but—' said Jack, shaking his head incredulously.

'Look at the facts,' Watkins interrupted quickly. Jack had had his say and Watkins was determined to have his. 'A member of our staff, I stress the word *our* to indicate the concept of collective responsibility – a member of our staff is caught—'

'*Found*, I think.'

'A member of our staff is *caught* in circumstances that can hardly set the kind of example parents expect of us, and *rightly* expect of us. I remind you that we have a duty of care towards the pupils in our charge. I take the view, and I was hoping that everyone would take the *same* view – I take the view that Mr Patel is letting them down. Indeed, he is letting his colleagues down. That means you, too, Mr Barker. Yet you come to see me in the hope that I might take what you call a sympathetic view! On the contrary, you ought to be as incensed as I am, as incensed as any decent person would be. Oh, I agree, Mr Patel has been on the staff of Morley Comprehensive for a considerable number of years now, and his work here has been creditable; but times change, and so do people, and whatever has happened or has not happened in the past cannot excuse his lapses of late; and it cannot by any stretch of the imagination excuse this latest lapse, because it is one that threatens the very image we wish to project, which is one of the utmost respectability and propriety. No, this kind of behaviour will not do, and it isn't the first time recently that Mr Patel's conduct has been brought to my attention. Nor, I hasten to add, is this the first time you have spoken on his behalf – indeed, you have gone very much out of your way to speak for him, and I might say that you yourself have stepped beyond the bounds of propriety in so doing. You have approached not only myself, but Mr Patel's own GP. Oh, yes! I know all about it. She, Doctor, er...'

'Blanchard,' Jack said, immediately disgusted with himself for unaccountably helping Watkins out.

'Yes. Dr Blanchard called me to see whether you had had my authority to make that visit. Most unorthodox, and extremely embarrassing for me, Dr Blanchard, and indeed for the whole school. What on earth were you thinking of, Mr Barker? You have far exceeded all the natural sympathies one might feel towards a friend and colleague and managed to compromise your own position into the bargain – not to mention my own!'

'I'm sorry now that I did make that visit,' said Jack, after a pause, and as much to himself as to Watkins.

'I beg your pardon?'

'I said I regret making that visit.'

'Regret it? Well, that's something, I suppose. But it doesn't go far enough. Not by a long chalk.' Jack hadn't meant it as an apology, but Watkins didn't give him time to sort it out, even if Jack had been well disposed to try.

'No, as I said earlier, your concern in these matters prompts me to question your own motives. You realise I might easily have refused to see you today, and I might certainly have refused to speak about Mr Patel. But I'm intrigued. Tell me, do you really feel comfortable here, Mr Barker? At Morley Comprehensive?' Watkins got up and both he and Jack walked slowly to the door of the office.

'Well, yes. I do.' Jack felt as though he were betraying something, or someone, and he half-imagined he could hear a cock crow somewhere, deep in some mental recess, or as if there had been yet again a lost opportunity to be himself.

'Hmm,' Watkins's response was slow and highly suggestive of something sinister and mistrusting. 'Well, Mr Barker, I strongly advise you to leave well alone. Mr Patel is not without recourse to adequate representation. I can assure you that everything is in hand and taking its proper course. Mr Patel is himself quite capable of stating his own case and expressing his own preferences. No, think of the school, Mr Barker – think of your colleagues – remember that our responsibilities are *collective* responsibilities – we are all like members of the same government and we have a responsibilities towards each other. You know,' he concluded, placing a hand on Jack's shoulder, 'you know, it's all really a question of the right kind of attitude. *Attitude*, Mr Barker.' Smiling coldly, Watkins opened the door of the office, and closed it again. Jack was on the outside once more.

The explosion in Jack's breast came later, when the blast could affect no one but himself. He blamed himself for being spoken to like – well, like some well-meaning simpleton, or at worst a disgruntled and incompetent advocate. What was it that gave Watkins that kind of power, akin to the power of hypnosis? Watkins had been only two metres away behind that metallic desk of his, but he was actually in a different universe, not even a different planet. They might just as well have spoken two different languages, each of which was unknown to the other; as it was, Jack had no problem with the words when spoken severally – but when they were strung together to make sentences, he couldn't make head or tail of the propositions they expressed; if words were arrows, the words that had passed between them had failed to reach their target, and just fell helplessly to the ground. If only people like Watkins would do their worst in a different universe and leave decent people alone! If only they would contain their narrowness within them and not judge others from within their own limited compass! Watkins was a virus, spreading here and there at will, meeting little or no resistance, like weeds when the gardener turns his back on them. It didn't seem to matter what civilisation put in his way, what obstacles it threw up – Watkins and his ilk would simply jump over them with ease or mockingly throw them aside. Jack had had an interview with Schellenberg, and Schellenberg had pressed his little button and blasted Patel into oblivion, and Jack with him, and all without the merest shadow of conscience. What hope for Patel? Alf would probably say that people like Watkins knew exactly how to use and abuse people, wring the life out of them and throw them away like so many old rags. That's what it was all about – treating people like old rags. And what was galling was that people like Watkins somehow had the power to sound so damned convincing! Yet, however persuasive they were, there was always something *missing*, something vital, something deeper and infinitely more far-reaching than the perceived soundness of their reasoning, something so far removed that it seemed to belong to another universe of thought and feeling; but the problem was that it was hard to articulate this omission, to identify it, to say what it was – just as hard as it was to explain why people may speak the same language and yet fail miserably to communicate anything of real substance. And as for all that stuff about collective responsibility and being in the same government – wasn't it J. B. Priestley who'd said something about a good writer not being a joiner, because a good writer had to preserve his independence of spirit and of mind? But didn't that apply to everyone, not just writers? Didn't everyone have the same right – the right to maintain their independence of spirit and of mind? But if Watkins was right, maybe Jack was in the wrong government.

11

Perhaps in Another Life

The meeting between Jack and Watkins had taken place on Monday afternoon. It was now Tuesday lunchtime, and already on several occasions Jack had passed Watkins or Davenport, sometimes both together, in the corridor and had been unmistakably cold-shouldered. Acting singly, Watkins and Davenport had cultivated a remarkable talent for freezing out dissidents in the ranks, or, as Watkins once put it to Davenport, 'amongst the rabble' – Davenport had smiled knowingly at this phrase, but it was hard to know whether Watkins had meant it. As a team, there was no limit to what they might achieve; they might even succeed in freezing hell over. 'If I was the type to take that sort of thing seriously, I'd have followed Patel into the boiler room long ago,' Jack had remarked, only half-jokingly, to Gladys. Certainly, being sent to Coventry could push someone over a precipice, someone who had either the un-wisdom or the misfortune to be dangling his legs over the edge in the first place.

No one so much as mentioned Patel's name. There were a few references to 'the incident', but as though it was bereft of all real or human content. No one enquired after him. If he who dies is no more than a nine-day wonder, Patel was even less. True, Harper stopped Jack in the corridor and hoped that Patel would be alright in the ever-increasing likelihood that he wouldn't be returning to Morley Comprehensive. He wondered what his intentions were now and said how much he liked him, adding how unfair everything was. Harper spoke in whispers and gave the impression he was in a hurry. Should he perhaps consider giving Patel a solicitous visit? But before Jack could make a considered reply, Harper was excusing himself and dashing down the corridor; the lunch hour had just started, and Harper was doubtless making a beeline for his egg sandwiches, further proof, if further proof were needed, that colleagues, however amiable they might appear, are not necessarily friends and may have far less to them than their words seem to convey, like an oak whose trunk, despite all appearances and expectations, proves hollow.

Late the following afternoon, Jack made his customary pilgrimage to 92 Cutters Way, where he received the customary low-key welcome and, as usual, spent the ensuing one and a half hours listening to his mother cataloguing her personal history, a process that was invariably repetitive and boring, but more or less tolerable depending on Jack's physical and mental state of health. This time, the threshold of tolerance was particularly low, but, as always, it had to be borne. For, after all was said and done, his mother could do no wrong; he must act as though he owed her some incalculable debt, one that could never be paid off and would hang about his neck forever.

He would have liked to tell her all about Patel and Watkins, and about his own dire need to leave Morley Comprehensive, if not forever and a day then at least for a good solid year, while he recuperated and recharged his batteries. He needed time to come to terms with… well, whatever it was he needed to come to terms with, because he could not say precisely what this was. But time is money, and he and Sally hadn't enough savings to tide them over the time he thought he needed, and they couldn't live on Sally's salary alone, and then there was Pete to think about. But it was no use. He had been through all this before, not once, but many times, and it always ended up in the same way – with his mother attacking both him and Sally, and Sally in particular, for, as she put it, 'biting off far more than they could chew'; she would punctuate the attack with the fierce observation that she'd had to struggle with one husband after another to achieve some measure of financial independence, and, she insisted, no one was going to deprive her of her hard-won pennies, not, that is, 'until after my days – and then I won't care who gets it'. She would finish off with a battery of repetitive salvos, which had the curious effect of inducing feelings of unremitting guilt in any poor creature who had dared to raise the subject of financial support in the first place. After such volcanic eruptions, it would take at least another forty-five minutes of patient listening to appease her and cool her fiery bowels. In short, the subject just wasn't worth the hassle involved in bringing it up. So here, as in Morley Comprehensive, what Jack would have liked and what he had to put up with were two entirely different things. It never seriously occurred to him to take the matter to an ugly conclusion and have nothing more to do with her. He preferred to suffer in silence rather than sever that natural bond. For again, his mother could do no wrong.

This particular visit came to a conclusion with his mother holding forth on the advantages of the long summer days over the short, dark days of winter, a discourse she had entered upon every year about this time for as long as he could remember. 'I can't abide these long winter nights. You never know who's on the prowl, especially these days. Sometimes I'm frightened to go out, wondering what I'll find when I get back. I could be trying to get my key in the door, and somebody could come up behind me, and that would be that! Oh, yes, life's changed, alright. You know, I remember your grandmother waiting up for me to get home. Had to be back by nine at the latest! And woe betide me if I wasn't. In those days, it was...'

But it wasn't merely the theme she was repeating; it was the words as well, and, it seemed, in exactly the same order. Jack rubbed his eyes, coughed, cleared his throat, looked at his watch, yawned, and rubbed his eyes again – all to no avail, as she rambled on and on. She would bring matters to an end when she, and no one else, decided to do so, and there was no stopping her until that decision was made. Perhaps she had never been able to put herself in the background; so she pushed herself to the foreground, oblivious to the irony that people who do so frequently find themselves shunted to the rear. But there was no helping it. As she grew older the need to occupy the foreground was increasingly pressing, until she occupied the whole canvas. As far as she was concerned, Patel, Watkins and the whole population of this most uncelestial of globes had little more than a nominal existence; unless, of course, she decided otherwise – until then, all would be chimerical figures, or items in someone else's dream. So it was quite pointless Jack's attempting to have a meaningful exchange about any of them.

On this occasion, it was only by feigning an acute attack of migraine and pretending that he'd been thoughtless enough to leave his medication at home that he managed to extricate himself from this additional source of exhaustion and vexation and tunnel himself out of 92 Cutters Way.

*   *

An hour or so later, he was forking his way through some precooked Chinese noodles he had microwaved for himself and taken to his study. Sally and he had taken to eating separately, which had started with evening meals and gradually included all others. True, to some extent this was the natural result of Sally's unpredictable and sometimes erratic hours of work, often necessitating late evenings and the odd working weekend, leaving Jack and Pete to fend pretty much for themselves; and Pete often did this own thing, distrusting his father's attempts at culinary dexterity.

But there was more to it than that. They were, in fact, all leading separate lives. Sally was keeping a close watch on Jack, when she could spare the time, wondering whether he would trip himself up, perhaps expecting him to, perhaps even hoping that he would. He was under observation, so that no chinks in his armour might go undetected. As for Jack, he kept himself more and more to himself, marking essays, preparing his lessons, devising classroom tests, and otherwise trying to shut everything out – all to the mellow notes of the Elizabethan lute. As for Pete, he had his own room, too, and largely kept to it, preparing for forthcoming exams, and mixing this laudable pursuit with his relish for soft pornography. Sex between Jack and Sally was a thing of the increasingly distant past, and neither of them could have said just when, or, for that matter, why, the cooling process had actually begun. Sex is one thing. But even physical contact had finally managed to elude them; no, there was not so much as hand-holding in bed, let alone out of it; there was not so much as a perfunctory kiss on meeting or departing. Now, when one of them went to bed, the other was already there, not merely feigning sleep, but actually well and truly in the Land of Nod, oblivious to any world but that of the deep, mysterious recesses of cerebral darkness, and quite often snoring with a vengeance. When Alf had asked Jack whether he was afraid of losing his wife, the question seemed to hurt deeply, dropping like a warhead, heavy and destructive and most unwelcome, and so Jack had naturally resented it. If Alf had asked the same question in the circumstances in which Jack now found himself, he would have found it far more intriguing than destructive and far less hurtful, and his resentment would not have been so keen, as though a sharp knife had somehow been blunted.

* *

Jacob doffed his old gardening hat as Jack cycled into school next morning. The very sight of the old fellow sent a wave of pleasure through Jack's tired body. There was more comfort in that rugged, wizened old face than anything that could be produced by all the arts that feminine craft could devise to enhance the natural beauty of woman; there was more comfort in that face than ever could be expected from Jack's mother, Mrs Muriel Barker. But the comfort was short-lived, as Watkins and Davenport, with enviable teamwork, froze Jack out once more as he entered the main building. 'Morning!' Jack said, to himself.

'I know what Alf would say. He'd say, "Don't say I didn't warn you!"' It was the end of the teaching day and Jack was in the history section of the school library, confiding in Amanda, whose last week at Morley Comprehensive was fast coming to an end. They were alone, which was just as well, because he wasn't in the mood for discreet whispers.

'Strange you haven't seen him round recently,' she said.

'Alf? Not really. He could be anywhere. I mean, it's not as though there's anything to keep him round here, is there?'

'No, I suppose not. I hope he's alright, though.'

'You can never tell. It's a mad world. Anything could happen, and frequently does.'

'You're in a good mood!'

'Well, it's the lunacy of things. It gets to you. It's bound to, in the end. Alf would say the world is a big lunatic asylum...' When Jack and Alf had talked together in the study, and Sally had lain upstairs listening to the drone of voices below, Alf had said something about it being an insane world, inhabited largely by the Shadow People, who were mad but invariably clever, and clever but invariably mad. For once, Jack was not putting words into Alf's mouth. 'Yes, and people like Watkins and Davenport—'

'Whose number is legion,' said Amanda, smiling and making light of Jack's intense seriousness.

'—whose number is legion, are among the inmates, though not, he'd hasten to add, amongst the very worst of them.' This time he was putting words into Alf's mouth again, though Alf need not have disagreed. 'And if you decide you have to live with them because there's no escaping them, then you've got to try to humour them to survive. I mean, if you tell a madman with a chopper what you really think of him, you're asking for trouble, aren't you?' This last part was pure Jack.

'He'll chop your head off,' said Amanda, still smiling.

'Yes. It's not that these madmen lack intelligence. It's not that they aren't clever – after all, they amount to something in the asylum, and they wouldn't if they lacked intelligence and weren't clever – or full of guile, I should say. You can expect them to be entirely consistent – no, you'll never catch them out. And you know what they're most consistent about? Their damned insensitivity and lack of compassion!' Jack said – any louder and he would have been shouting.

Amanda looked around to see if anyone had come in, and she was no longer smiling. 'I know, but—' she began.

'But it's a question of being able to abide them, to tolerate them with all their hypocrisy, and to tolerate yourself putting up with them when you should be making some sort of stand. How long can you go on deceiving yourself? Telling yourself that you can stand it when you can't bear it, when you know you shouldn't be putting up with it one minute longer? You see, Alf reached his threshold of tolerance very early on – he just couldn't bring himself to humour the insane, and he actually did something about it! He just upped and left and got right out of it while he still had something left of himself to save.' This, again, was pure Jack.

'Yes, but the trouble is, he had to opt out of *everything*!' Amanda said. 'There was no use trying to find a better place *inside* the asylum, was there? No half measures, right? And then he had to put up with being *called* insane by all those he thought *were* insane!' She squeezed Jack's arm tenderly when she said this. It was the most intelligent thing he'd heard her say, or anyone else say, and he was impressed, not to say stunned. At any rate, he had no immediate answer.

'This is my last week, Jack,' she said, after a short silence.

'I'll miss you,' he said.

'Me too.'

'Let's say goodbye somewhere else. Say, The King's Head, at eight tomorrow night?'

'Tomorrow's Friday, my last day. Yes, if you're sure it's alright.'

'Perfectly. Why wouldn't it be? Yes,' he went on, 'you know, really crazy people, in a real asylum are confined there, limited to a space so they can't do themselves or others any real harm. But in the asylum of life they have a free run, making and administering their own rules, changing the rules just as and when it suits them, punishing the sane merely for questioning them, let alone flouting them. The insane call all the shots, and the sane must come running when called, or suffer the consequences – for themselves and for their dependents. So, those who stay in the asylum, living amongst the insane and taking orders from them – well, those who stay without good cause, when there's not even self-sacrifice for the sake of their dependents to justify it, well they're crazy, too, or soon become so, graduating down to the level of inmates themselves, don't you think?'

'I really am going to miss you,' Amanda chuckled. 'I don't have the foggiest what you're talking about half the time – but you must be the biggest cynic I've ever met, or am ever likely to meet.'

'Scorn not the cynic, for from Heaven he comes and to Heaven he will return! As—'

'As *Alf* would say!' said Amanda, with a chuckle. But Alf had said no such thing.

'Is that what you really think I am – a cynic?'

'A very nice one, though,' said Amanda.

*　*

Next morning, as Jack wheeled his bicycle over the stone bridge that spanned the river in the park, he spotted something familiar. It was before eight and the cold mist was still blanketing the river and curling along its banks, while the occasional flap and quack of ducks splintered the frosty air like arrows of ice on sugar-glass; in the bitter cold, it was small comfort to stand and stare at the beauty of Nature's winter wardrobe. As Jack descended the slope on the far side of the bridge, he couldn't help but notice the figures that huddled together for warmth under its frosted pillars. It was the colour and pattern of Alf's bundle that attracted his attention. Alf was using what remained of it as a pillow while, presumably, the material it had contained served as blankets or sheets – presumably, because Alf had covered himself in a pall of brown cardboard up to his nose and his woollen hat was pulled down over his ears and neck. To be sure, there was not much of him to be seen. But it was Alf, alright. And he was obviously trying to survive what brass monkeys allegedly cannot. Jack stopped and watched him, and, apart from a mild grunt or two and some small movement, he gave every appearance of being asleep, and Jack assumed that he was. He might have ventured to test his assumption. But he did not. He might have given Alf a prod or two and asked if he were alright. But he did not. Why? Perhaps because, unless he had anything to offer him, apart from a prod and a solicitous question, it would have seemed a cruel intrusion. So Alf lay there, and Jack passed him by.

The picture of Alf under his cardboard under the bridge haunted him all day; it was the sort of picture that might return to haunt anyone for the rest of their lives, a persistent, burr-like thorn in the flesh. But it was at least good to know that Alf was still around and in the land of the living. Yet, it seemed entirely incongruous that the guest who had spoken so profoundly, so wisely, in Jack's study should be bunking down under a bridge – the cardboard, and the fact that it was the kind of morning that would have tested the tenacity of an Eskimo, only contributed to what appeared to be a glimpse into the theatre of the absurd. That, and the ensuing fact that Jack's conscience was more than somewhat pricked, produced a bitter mix: perhaps he should have prodded Alf awake, come what might, intrusion or no; even better, perhaps he should have taken the bull by the thorns and boldly yanked Alf out from under that ridiculous pretence of a bed and taken him home, dressed him in his own best clothes and sat him in the most accommodating armchair and treated him as a most honoured guest, or a long-lost and treasured member of the family. The parallels with the philosopher Socrates were not lost on Jack;

he had read Plato's *Apology*, albeit in translation, unlike Davenport, who could read it in the original Greek and yet be unmoved by it as though he were reading a slushy novel – forgettable after the first scant reading. It was hard to imagine Davenport taking the story of Socrates to heart, or anything to heart. Socrates was on trial for his life and they were hell-bent on getting him executed; the court was not amused when Socrates, asked by the court what he thought his punishment ought to be, suggested that he should, instead, be honoured by the State and given a handsome pension for life. The murderous court were not amused, and Socrates was put to death, as they had intended all along. Was it not the same for Alf? Who cared about him? And yet, he had something to say, and he should be given a fair hearing and, if anything, honoured by the society that was, almost literally, freezing him out.

His perceived parallels with Socrates did nothing to assuage Jack's conscience. Was Alf a latter-day Socrates? Perhaps. Perhaps not. But what did seem particularly incongruous that afternoon was his lesson on the growth of parliamentary democracy, a theme which struck him as totally irrelevant; not merely irrelevant, but hollow. But his job was to take the relevance of the theme for granted, and explain it, not to reject it from the curriculum. It was not simply that he wanted to talk about Alf instead of the growth of parliamentary democracy, but that he wanted to set Alf's being under his cardboard under the bridge *against* the growth of parliamentary democracy, as though Alf's condition was proof against the theme! What was it Alf had said about mankind still being in its infancy? Even the best of men were really still crawling around on all fours, and, if true, that would most certainly include Jack himself. And if the best of men were still crawling around on all fours, what did that say about all the rest, whose number was legion? It didn't bear thinking about. There was no doubt that Jack was confused. Equally, there was no doubt that he knew he was confused. It turned out to be a very discomforting day.

Discomforting or not, he gave the class a good lesson; yes, all about the growth of parliamentary democracy, albeit to kids who hadn't been listening – with the exception of young Harris, still smarting, but still determined to outshine everyone else. And Jack hadn't even come close to questioning the theme, let alone condemning it or proving it hollow. It was wonderful to see how far one could go, how much might be achieved, what waters might be stilled, simply by resorting to cliché and custom. In fact, had Watkins or Davenport sat in on the lesson, policing it on the pretext of helping Jack along the road to self-development, they would in all probability given it a five-star rating – privately, while giving it a four- or even three-star rating on paper, just to keep Jack on his toes. At least, they would have found no evidence of dissention or subversion, neither in what he was telling the class, nor in his tone of voice; there was not a hint of sarcasm or cynicism. To all appearances, the sight of Alf early that morning had made no material difference to his performance as a teacher of history.

But Jack had had that feeling again: that feeling of stepping outside himself, listening to himself speak. He had stepped outside himself, broken away from himself, and what he saw and what he heard was of no real comfort. He saw two Jacks, not one. He loathed the one and preferred the other. The one he preferred would have said what he really wanted to say, and then just walked away, like a hero into the sunset, a foetus struggling to break free of the womb, and actually managing it.

Jack Barker was a rational fellow, or so he would have said. One day he glanced at the horoscope section of the newspaper, which Gladys had been scrutinising with the zeal of a scientist on the verge of a momentous discovery, and he belittled the advice given under his own star-sign. '*Study your dreams,*' it had said. '*A dream ignored is like a letter unread.*' In the first place, Jack rarely dreamed at all – a fact he had always lamented, because who in their right minds would give up the chance of living two lives at once, if the dream-world is infinitely better than the world we're stuck with? In the second place, whenever he did dream, he always forgot it on waking. If dreams were like letters, either he received none or the letters he received evaporated in the letter box before he could get his hands on them. Had Jack been an Old Testament figure, God would have experienced considerable difficulty getting through to him.

There was, however, one dream that had got through intact, and only days before his encounter with Alf under the stone bridge, and it had burned itself into his psyche. In his dream he had stood on the shore by a big sea. There was a small boat lopping about in the waves, and someone was in it, apparently beckoning him to come aboard. He wanted to go, and nothing stood between him and the boat. But he couldn't bring himself to traverse the intervening spaces, because the intervening spaces consisted of dark, deep waters. As dreams go, it might have been a classic, as far as he knew, and quite forgettable. But it happened to strike an important chord in Jack's memory. For he remembered that trip to the seaside with his father – that time his father wanted to teach little Jack how to swim, or at least get him more accustomed to the water and less afraid of it. His father had stepped waist-high into the sea and then told little Jack, still on the beach, to come to him, which he did; but when he was told to lie on his back so that his father could cup his head in his hand, little Jack froze with fear. 'Don't worry,' his father said, 'I've got you. You won't sink. I'll take my hands away and you'll float.' But little Jack could not bring himself to believe it, and he cried until his father gave up; they both came out of the sea and dried off, and the swimming lesson was never attempted again. Jack never learned to swim, and he was still afraid of the water, of the deep, dark and seemingly bottomless sea, capable of engulfing ships and their crews, capable of mocking, belittling and devouring even the strongest and the bravest and the best.

His dream seemed to beg the question: Who was the man in the boat?

* *

'Spring's what we need!' said Jacob, as Jack locked up his bicycle in the bike shed that Friday morning. Jacob was standing right behind him, and his voice sounded incorporeal, as though it conveyed a celestial message. 'Yes,' Jack nodded. 'Christ, that's deep!' Jack said to himself and laughed aloud at his own joke.

He laughed a second time at his own joke, when he shared it with Amanda later that evening in The King's Head.

It wasn't a good joke, and neither of them was in the mood to make out that it was. 'You know,' Jack broke the silence, 'if you think of ideas or spirits, and you think our bodies, human bodies, are just vehicles for ideas and spirits – well, you see, I look at old Jacob, and I think it doesn't matter about his body at all. He may be weather-beaten and frail, and he might look absurd in his old jacket – but, you know, he'll do very nicely, all the same. He's like an old coat: much more comfortable than all the newer, expensive stuff; he'll put all the latest fashions and fabrics in the shade. He's something the human race, so long as it remains human, will always come back to – he's something to thank God for, if He's still in His heaven and hasn't bunked off like everyone else; and I suppose He couldn't have bunked off, because then there wouldn't be anyone like Jacob to thank him for, would there? Well, the bodies of Watkins and Davenport don't matter, either – it's what's inside them and peers out of them that matters, because it's what lives inside you that does all the damage, or all the good! In their case, all the damage! Am I being obscure?'

'Yes.'

'Good.'

Amanda hadn't stopped smiling from start to finish. 'I hope things work out for you, Jack,' she said.

'Work out?'

'Well, it's funny. I want to start teaching, and you want to stop. You *do* want out, don't you?'

'I've served my sentence, yes. And my behaviour has been exemplary. But wanting's one thing, doing's another.'

'You're such a good teacher, Jack. Alright, alright – you're fed up with it. But it's not too late to change career! You just need to know what you like doing best.'

'I used to think we're all cut out for something – the trick being to find out what it is before it's too late, but so far I've only found out what it isn't!'

'You're too independent, that's your trouble. You should've gone into business and been your own boss.'

'You must be joking! You haven't been listening to a word I've said all this time!' Amanda smiled again. 'No, really, I'm not morally good enough to be a businessman, especially being my own boss.'

'Now who's joking.'

'Look, what people call business just brings out the very worst in them. So I would have to be more than saintly to avoid becoming just like them, to avoid becoming monstrous. And I'm just not good enough to avoid that!'

'Anyway, it's a pity about Jacob,' said Amanda, changing, or diverting, the subject. 'They're letting him go, aren't they?'

'Oh, that's a nice phrase, Amanda – "letting him go". Very businesslike – as if to suggest it's at his own request! You see what I mean? How can anyone be successful in business without being duplicitous and devious?'

'Who'll look after the shrubberies?'

'The teachers, I suppose,' Jack suggested sarcastically. 'Shrubbery upkeep will become part of the curriculum, or be palmed off as self-development.' He made Amanda laugh.

'You know, when Socrates was accused of corrupting the young and denying the gods and was asked to name his own punishment, he suggested he should be given an honorary pension for his services to the State. Dear old fellow! Dear old Jacob! How they endure, when all the lunatics who've killed them off and put them down have long since perished from the earth – occasional flowers in beds of weeds.'

'That's very poetic,' said Amanda, who wasn't even smiling now. 'But anyway, there's not much in common between Jacob and Socrates, is there?'

'I don't know. I don't know at all. I've heard they've accused him of buying more garden stuff than necessary and pocketing the difference. He denies it – but his denial isn't worth much.'

'What? Pocketing the difference, or the accusation? By the way, Jack', said Amanda, skirting the question, 'what was Davenport talking to you about this afternoon?'

'Oh, that! Yes, well he said he'd been having some complaints – didn't say who made them – about my music, my Elizabethan lute CDs. I'm playing them too loud, apparently.'

'They never say who's made complaints, do they?'

'No. That's part of the game they play. It's called Need-to-Know. It's cat-and-mouse. They keep you guessing. It's all part of the power game.'

*   *

Soon they were getting up and leaving. Jack had made sure he'd done most of the talking. It was the safest thing, short of not meeting Amanda at all. Speaking was like the drums of war – once they stopped, trouble could be expected. The truth was, he was liable to give in to the same lustful desires that had brought Amanda to his attention in the first place. For lust was all it was. He had rationalised this way and that, but the beast within was merely napping and Jack had managed to let sleeping lust lie; one thoughtless, misjudged step and the beast might awaken with a vengeance and all would be unravelled. But now at last, with Amanda's departure from Morley Comprehensive, she would be out of sight and, eventually, out of mind. Hyde had been restrained and Jekyll had emerged victor; though it was a victory that was more than a little ironic.

In the first place, he knew he had nothing to offer Amanda but one or two lustful encounters; lust was temporary and fleeting when the object of desire was one person alone; the feeling simply could not last and the passion would burn out leaving nothing but an empty shell, and after that they would move on. Suppose they moved on together? But the idea of leaving Sally for Amanda was absurd; a life with Amanda would settle into the same boring routine he had known so long, and longed to escape from; and the collateral damage entailed was unthinkable: Sally and Pete would be thrown into an emotional turmoil from which they could never be expected to recover, because no one recovers from divorce, while at the same time he himself would secure only a temporary release from his frustrations, and Amanda might be stuck with a much older man who had nothing more to give. Giving in to his lust would be too destructive to contemplate, and it would leave him a lonelier man than he was already. No, he was doing himself and everybody a favour in leaving well alone. His relationship with Amanda was so far quite innocent, and should end that way. But the cold, iron gates of irony creaked on their hinges once more.

Amanda got into her car. They promised to keep in touch, a promise neither intended to keep, and Jack bent down to kiss her goodbye, on her cheek. The kiss was anything but passionate; a mere formality of friendship, a simple parting gesture. 'Perhaps in another life,' Jack muttered. Amanda just smiled that irresistible smile, the smile that had first caught his eye and which he now saw for the last time; but in such matters, Jack felt, the more irresistible a thing was, the more it had to be resisted.

But that innocent peck on her cheek might just as well have been a steamy embrace. Sally had been parked on the opposite side of the road for the last hour, half hidden in the shadows of the night, and she saw what was for her the most damning evidence of her spouse's infidelity. The light from the streetlamp and the pub windows revealed what she had long suspected. Jack had told her he'd be meeting Patel in The King's Head, and she had decided to drive over, park in the shadows and await developments. She could, of course, have entered the pub, bold as brass; but then, had she been wrong about him, she would have looked ridiculous; and, if right, too upset for words – to have made a scene in the pub could never have been lived down, and she had her career to think of. No, it was important not to be seen; in any case, the last thing she wanted was for Jack to think she was taking an interest in him and his movements. Her patience and detective work had been most revealing. The young and alluring creature Jack had kissed looked nothing like Patel; Jack was caught red-handed and was dangling on the hook.

Sally drove off discreetly. She had seen enough to last her a lifetime. There would be no fuss, no domestic explosions. On the contrary, she would act as though she'd seen nothing at all. But her mind was finally made up. The way ahead was clear. She owed that much to Pete, and of course to herself.

So it was that Jack became the victim of his own keen observations. For he had often mused on the ironies of life. His adultery had been no more than cerebral, and a man or woman cannot be held culpable for mere thoughts – thoughts dictated to them by their very natures, for the fundamentals of human nature are unalterable, dictated to us by that very nature. He had never really intended betrayal, and that simple parting kiss was no more than it seemed. Yet what a thing seems is not necessarily the same for everyone; and for Sally it seemed other than it was, perhaps because it was in perfect accord with her expectations – perhaps even in perfect accord with her wishes.

12
The Triggers of Fate

There was no outward sign that Sally was reacting to what she took to be Jack's amorous liaison with Amanda, which is just how she wanted it. The less Jack knew or suspected about what Sally thought she knew, the stronger the rope might become that would hang him; not that the rope wasn't thick enough already, for Sally had definitely made up her mind to break the matrimonial knot; but the stronger the rope, the more certain the outcome. She was in no great hurry; besides, there were things to sort out, plans to be made, moves to consider on the chessboard of her life. The decision to make the break was the inevitable result of an accumulation of factors, and the more Sally thought of them, the more determined she became to take the action they seemed to dictate. Yes, his liaison with that slip of a thing, whoever she was, and his bare-faced deception concerning it, were merely the trigger of the inevitable. The explosive charge had already been set and now the hand of Fate was at work to bring matters to their inevitable conclusion. The build-up to the inevitable was clear, and Sally was at pains to enumerate to herself the factors involved in the emergence of the inevitable: their continuing to lead separate lives; his disregard for his son's future, indeed the contempt he repeatedly showed for success and achievement, and the fact that he refused to take a parental hand in such matters and left everything to her, who, not herself being a teacher and not having had the advantages of a higher education, was not so well-placed to offer guidance to Peter, vulnerable and impressionable as he was; Jack's inability to sort things out with his mother and, if necessary, to put her well and truly in her place, instead of playing the role of dutiful son to someone who didn't deserve to be treated with even a modicum of respect; her own growing financial independence; and the growing physical coldness between them. This last was by no means least: at no stage of her life would Sally have described herself as even moderately oversexed, but she had certain needs, which Jack seemed to be entirely oblivious to, making no attempt even to address the subject, let alone satisfy her. It was as though she and Peter were no longer items of consideration in his life; it seemed a very long time since they were, and a longer time still since she and Jack spoke together in anything other than clichés. He had never shown more than a passing interest in her career moves, preferring to complain of his own tiredness and dissatisfaction at work while at the same time doing nothing whatsoever about it. In one way or another, he had lived for himself. And now Sally was determined to follow suit and, as she put it to herself with ever-increasing emphasis, 'Not before time, either.' The ease with which Sally now planned her own future was therefore highly suggestive; it was as though she'd been relieved by the 'discovery' of Jack's infidelity, for it seemed to signal a new and better life, perhaps incidentally for him, but without question for her. Someday soon, on a day of her own choosing, she would simply disappear from the scene, taking Peter with her, and Jack would get the shock of his life – and good riddance! Such thoughts half-filled her waking hours and did more than a little to deprive her of much-needed sleep.

* *

Meanwhile, Monday mornings for Jack were becoming increasingly heavy, taking their toll mentally and physically. By the time he'd cycled to school, he'd feel like turning round and cycling home again, exhausted and quite out of sorts. Gone were the days when sleep refreshed him; for now he awoke in the mornings feeling much as he had when the heavy blanket of sleep had descended the night before. 'It can't go on like this much longer,' he'd murmur to himself; but then, he'd been saying that for years, and here he was still! Was there to be no respite?

'I'll be off this week, then,' said Jacob, as Jack clicked shut his cycle-lock for the millionth time on the millionth Monday morning. It was Jacob's last week, and he was determined to let Jack know about it. 'Before spring, too. Pity!' Jacob added, with the look and intonation of one who was commenting derisively on the idiocy of another.

'Typical of the loony-bin,' said Jack.

'Eh?'

'I said, you'll be sadly missed, Jacob. Very sadly missed.' Jacob just shrugged his small, round shoulders and trundled off with his wheelbarrow.

Things were certainly in a state of flux at Morley Comprehensive; but change was one thing, improvement quite another, as Jack felt he had to tell Gladys a few minutes later. 'Not every change is a change for the better, Gladys.'

'I suppose not,' said Gladys, 'but there's not a lot we can do about it, is there?'

People were quiet and stiff in the staffroom these days, and even Gladys had lost the little lustre she once had. True, avuncular relationships had always been few and far between. But it was all staleness and manners now. What jokes there were now sounded as though they'd been carefully rehearsed, like tired questions and answers from Christmas crackers, which people laugh at merely because it's inappropriate not to. The heart had gone out of things. When Davenport was present, the staffroom resembled a morgue, political correctness being the order of the day, which meant that jokes and quips at the expense of what people generally call left-wing politics were not only permissible but well-received, while no one dared poke fun at the other end of the political spectrum; with Davenport out of the room, the pendulum might swing the other way; either way was of little interest to Jack, who tended to lump all politics together into one amorphous and irrelevant heap. Left-wing quips and barbs directed by a handful of staff members against the powers-that-be inside and outside Morley Comprehensive failed to impress Jack, who believed, rightly or wrongly, that anyone who truly claimed to be left-wing needed to fulfil at least three criteria: they had to be highly intelligent, they needed to possess a profound moral insight, and they were obliged to practise what they preached; since these criteria were markedly absent in his colleagues, he refused to believe that any of them could lay claim to being of that political persuasion – on the contrary, they were as far removed from the Spiral of Consciousness as it was possible to be.

Be that as it may, instances of political incorrectness would be carried forthwith by Davenport to Watkins, Davenport functioning robotically in the interests of quality control. But, these days, people were so much out of humour that the effort to crack a joke at anyone's expense seemed hardly worth the trouble.

But the atmosphere in the staffroom wasn't merely on account of Patel, who was by now considered to be well and truly out of the way, defunct as far as Morley Comprehensive was concerned. The 'incident' concerning him was merely a signpost on a long, straight road of fatigue and disillusionment, a road which seemed to offer little in the way of respite; the policing of the teaching staff, under the label quality control, and the amount of red tape that teachers were now engulfed by, were by now causing many to question their choice of career. Jack, unsurprisingly, decided to avoid the staffroom as much as possible from now on. But where could one possibly hide in a loony-bin?

With Amanda gone, he had no one to confide in apart from Gladys, whose moods were unpredictable; she would make a good listener only if she considered her horoscope for the day sufficiently favourable. Even so, Jack decided to tell her about Alf and the Big Truth from which, Alf had allegedly said, all smaller truths must flow, like tributaries from a vast ocean:

'Yes, I know, Gladys, but it's really quite amazing what he came out with, considering he was uneducated in the conventional sense. For instance, he'd say, "People worry about their mortgages, and because of this they worry about their jobs; and because of that, about how others see them – all that worry, as though they were going to live forever. If only they knew," he said. "If only they really *knew*!"'

'Knew what?' asked Gladys, softly and with knitted eyebrows. She looked and sounded like someone humouring a mental patient.

'That's all he'd say, Gladys – "If only they knew!"' Jack was playing with her, and enjoying it.

'Well, he must've meant something!' she said, after a pause. The fact that she wanted to invite further comment suggested that her horoscope might easily have been worse that day.

'Gladys! He meant: if only they knew how important it is to acknowledge the Truth that's inside them!'

'Oh!'

There was a long pause. There was a very real danger that she wouldn't go on to ask the question that begged to be asked, the question Jack wanted her to ask. So Jack decided to answer it anyway. 'The truth about the reality of death – that they are really going to die!'

'Oh, is *that* it? Well, I should think they know that very well and need no reminders,' said Gladys, with a nod or two.

What was Jack doing? Was he playing the hyperactive schoolboy who thinks he has something to say when he does not? Perhaps he was testing Gladys's receptivity, as though he wanted her to understand that Alf was no ordinary guy. If so, it was doubtful whether it was working. The phrase 'Spiral of Consciousness' flashed through his mind, but this was no time to come out with it; Gladys was already unimpressed, and any reference to a spiral of consciousness would have put her off completely. He continued nevertheless.

'Of course they *know*, Gladys! But they hide what they know and pretend it isn't there, as if it isn't really going to happen to them at all but is something that only happens to someone else, or as though it's so far off it isn't worth thinking about. But if they acknowledged it, looked at it squarely, they'd see things differently, and they'd understand the futility of anxiety and worry, and of the wickedness of man's inhumanity to man. Above all, they'd see the futility of fear itself. Life would be richer than it ever could have been before. Nothing can prevent death coming, but as long as you're afraid, you can't even *begin* to live. You see, people think Jesus Christ was promising them life after death, which is like promising to square the circle – when all the time he was trying to get them to acknowledge the reality of death; because if they can acknowledge that, they can start to live – to live without fear, worry and anxiety. You can't understand the meaning of life until you understand the meaning of death, you see?'

The expression on Gladys's face suggested that she was having difficulty seeing any of it. But Jack persisted:

'Look, the ability to live, *really* live and not just go through the motions, requires a certain acceptance, knowledge, understanding, perception, acknowledgement – call it what you will – of death. Well, people don't want to acknowledge the reality of death because they're afraid, and it hurts, at least at first; it's like looking into a box of bright, white light – it hurts your eyes, so you close the lid quickly, put it back on the shelf and try to forget it – see? Well, there are consequences. I mean, if people did acknowledge the reality of their own demise, it'd be the worst possible news for money lenders and insurance brokers, because it's fear, worry and anxiety that sustains all that stuff and keeps the system going. But acknowledging the reality of our own demise would mean a new beginning, a new life, the beginning of life, because when you're afraid you can't live properly. People will see that they can't afford the time to worry, to be afraid. We'll all see how ridiculous our fears are, fears about how we should see ourselves, about how others see us, about our jobs, about the future – well, all sorts of fears. Even the fear of death – because we're only afraid of it so long as we think it might just be avoidable, something we might just be able to put off for good, something that might not really concern *us* at all – only *others*. We'll be able to live in the present moment, and that'll be right, because the present moment is all we've really got. Or as Alf put it: the past is frozen, the present is fluid, and the future borders on eternity. See what I mean?'

Poor Gladys, whose lunchbreak had been ruined by what she thought was a rivulet of confused ramblings. She had been a good listener, but secretly hoped that Jack had no more to say on that subject – whatever that subject was. What's more, it was hard to believe that Alf had come out with all this, especially the last bit about the past being frozen; she was right, Jack had picked up the line from something he had read long ago, which had obviously stuck though the source was long forgotten.

Wishing to be polite, all Gladys could say was, 'Oh, I don't know. All sounds a bit depressing to me. Anyway, must dash!' And Gladys was off and away. So was Jack, for the bell signalled the end of the lunch-hour.

In all fairness to Jack, it did indeed occur to him that any more of this kind of talk and he might easily lose credibility; Gladys might think he was going off his chump, and she might even say as much to someone else, and who knows where it would end? The thought of leaving Morley Comprehensive for good was most palatable, but he wanted to choose his own time, and not be forced out on grounds of early-onset dementia. No, all that stuff he'd spouted to Gladys sounded confused, and he was far from sure how to put things. It was all very fluent, right enough, but there were too many ambiguities, too many obscurities, too many opportunities for getting it all wrong – and that was the trouble with putting things into words. Words were a problem. All he was sure about was that there was something somewhere in all that stuff; some germ of something vital, and that, in one way or another, Alf lay at the bottom of it; and that, whatever it was, it had something to do with the spiral of consciousness; the very thing he'd come out with as a schoolboy was somehow waiting all this time to be discovered, to be defined, and he, Jack, had been chosen by the Hand of Fate to be articulator *par excellence*. He did not put it to himself in quite these terms. But that is how he felt, and it was hard to get away from the feeling, for it refused to be stifled.

If, he thought, what he told Gladys had been said to Alf, Alf would have nodded in agreement without further ado. So perhaps what he told her was not as obscure as all that, after all. There was even a moment when he felt he wanted to reproach Gladys for pretending not to understand him, for wilfully missing the point. What was that about seed falling on stony ground? But the seed, some kind of seed, had certainly taken root in Jack's restless and overworked brain; it was like taking a glimpse of Heaven and being unable to forget it, the memory following you about and not letting you go, or you not letting go of it – like a catchy tune. Well, that was Alf all over. Alf was the catalyst to end all catalysts. Alf would start you off asking questions, and then there was no end to it. That was the power Alf exerted, bless him – or curse him.

Jack gave up trying to communicate such thoughts to anyone, and the fact that he now took to staying in his classroom before, after and between classes didn't seem to worry Gladys unduly; perhaps she felt relieved. Jack noticed that she didn't try to seek him out. No matter, he was alone with his thermos, and was intrigued, not to say strangely comforted, by a feeling of inevitability about events. His self-imposed exile from the staffroom, however, was a habit of which Davenport decided to take a dim view.

'Oh, you're in here, then!' said Davenport, feigning surprise and poking his head round the door near the end of the mid-morning break. 'I've been looking high and low for you. Harris's mother called to say he's off-colour and won't be coming in today.'

'Right.' (If it had been anyone other than Harris, Davenport wouldn't have bothered to convey the message, thought Jack – possibly unfairly, though Davenport was looking for an excuse to convey a message of his own.)

'Well, I expected to find you in the staffroom, of course. Hope everything's alright. It's better if staff take their breaks there. Makes liaison easier, don't you think?' Jack didn't reply, but continued marking a bunch of essays. Davenport walked out with the utmost dignity, determined not to show how ruffled he was.

Jack's new habit of solitary confinement gave Davenport an opportunity to fulfil his robotic function of reporting all possible signs of dissension to Watkins and, at the same time, to assert his own authority. Jack had noticed Davenport's shoes out of the corner of his eye – suede, a bit dusty and, in Jack's view, uncared for – so different from Patel's which, like his own, were a highly polished leather. Jack used to look at Patel's shoes and feel in good company, as though a man who looked after his shoes was to be trusted in a world full of uncertainties. Patel, like Jack, used to polish them every night, ready for the next day, as though he were after some kind of reassurance, and as though a bit of polished leather could make all the difference. Patel's shoes were part of his armoury, but they clearly hadn't done him much good. Jack decided that he would no longer polish his shoes.

His decision to neglect his shoes was perhaps connected with his intention of reading a poem to 5C that afternoon, during a lesson which was supposed to be about the growth of Nazism in pre-war Germany. It was a little poem by W. H. Davies, which began: *All from the cradle to his grave, Poor Devil, man's a frightened thing.*

'No, the poem isn't negative at all,' Jack insisted – though nobody had said it was; in fact, nobody had said anything at all, nor did anyone have the slightest intention of saying anything. The class was full, but Jack was on his own and talking to himself. 'It's a diagnosis,' Jack went on, 'Davies is diagnosing a kind of disease. The name of this disease is Fear, and it's entirely up to us to do something about it. In fact, his poem is entirely positive – no, Davies is saying that we should fight against fear and intimidation. He's writing about what he knows best. Fear's like a prison, and I'm sure he managed to break out of it, and he's telling us that we should do the same.' Jack was addressing a sea of blank faces and would have fared marginally better with Gladys. Perhaps Watkins and Davenport would have said it was not really a fitting subject for kids, especially for kids whose minds were full of yesterday's routine doings and the mediocre dreams of tomorrow. And it was not that no connection at all could be made out between the poem and the rise of Nazism – far from it. It was only that Jack had not succeeded in making a connection, so that the poem hung in a state of limbo. But Jack was really addressing himself, or had, to an observer, simply and unaccountably gone off at a tangent. In any case, before anyone might begin to suspect that premature senility was beginning to make itself felt, Jack actually started to address the growth of Nazism, and all went smoothly for the rest of the lesson. But he ended on what 5C would have regarded, had they been paying attention, a most obscure note:

'Now, we may well ask ourselves how we can put up resistance to something like the horror of Nazism. Well, despite the best efforts of the lunatics, of the Shadow People and their two-for-the-price-of-one appreciation of the gift of life, I can tell you that it's a single memory that can stand up to it, a single idea that can shape your whole life and make it unshakeable. Yes, one good memory can save us. I can picture my own father, for example: his gentleness, his light blue eyes. He never raised his voice against me, or anyone else for that matter; my mother would catch him reading his Bible and scold him for not finding something more useful to do – she was much younger than he was and never really understood him. Yes, I remember him: quiet, slow, tall, with sharp features, and with all the gentleness of a lamb and the integrity of a saint.'

Jack paused, and when he spoke again, his voice had softened and he was unlike himself, as though someone else was speaking from deep inside him, just using his body for the purpose, just the way he had told Amanda that spirits and ideas seem to use bodies as vehicles.

'In fact, a whole life can be built around a single memory, a single picture. A whole life can be built on a lie, too, but the Truth inside you will come out in the end – if you let it, if you don't stifle it, or suffer it to be stifled. But if you try to stifle it, it's fear that makes you do it. But the Truth inside you will never let you go – not willingly, anyway. And it's the same Truth, that's the point – it's the same Truth for us all, and the tragedy is that we spend our lives trying to hide from it. But I hope you will never stifle the Truth inside you. And that's not the same as your father telling you that you must always tell the truth, when you've lied. It's not the same. It's not the same at all. We all know there are times when we might just as well lie – to help a friend, for example. But acknowledging the Truth inside you is different – there's never a justifiable alternative, never such a thing as a white lie; you can never help yourself or anyone else by stifling the Truth. There's no acceptable alternative. Only Shadow People recognise alternatives. And we're all in danger of becoming Shadow People; the greater danger is that once we have become one of them we shall always remain so – the temptation being so great – the fear of fear itself. But we must all try to break out. I hope you will all manage to break out. Because it's not *knowing* the Truth that's so hard, but living *by* it. Living by it is the hard part – living by the ultimate Truth, that Truth which always has a capital letter – the Truth that's inside you.'

Then he paused, as if musing, and then wound up in a noticeably hesitant and apologetic tone: 'Yes, well, a memory like that, a single memory, can help you stand up when everything around you is falling down. That's the way to… er… defeat something like Nazism or… or stand up to any… er.'

5C certainly did stand up, for Jack's last few words were uttered on the bell, and there was the customary scramble for the door, leaving Jack somewhat stunned, in a kind of semi-hypnotic state.

Needless to say, the lesson would hardly have been considered a model for any inspectorate worth its salt. Was the man demented? Was he ill? The best that could be said of his lesson was that it resembled the Curate's Egg – it was good in parts. But all that stuff about Shadow People and the Truth inside you and his father – no, it was just as well that 5C were as inattentive as usual. He was certainly eccentric, and there may well be a place for a certain degree of eccentricity – perhaps as a motivating factor, for dramatic effect; but there was precious little evidence of any effect at all on 5C, dramatic or otherwise. It was also just as well, therefore, that neither Watkins nor Davenport had been sitting in on the lesson. Jack was making a noose for his own neck. And because Jack once again had the feeling that he was standing outside himself, listening to himself and watching himself, he was well aware of the noose he was making.

Yes, the lesson could easily have gone very badly wrong. If someone had raised his hand and asked, 'What Truth is that, then, sir? The Truth that's inside you?' it would at least been evidence that someone was listening fairly intently. Young Potter, for example, was always good for a question. However, Potter's mind, like everyone else's, was very much outside the classroom and could not be induced to enter it. But had such a question been asked, Jack might have felt inclined to talk again, as he had to Gladys, about the 'reality of death', and goodness knows what further mess he would've got himself into. Had the mess been reported to parents, Watkins and Davenport would have intervened with a vengeance. After all, teachers, and history teachers in particular, should stick to hard facts and allow themselves only the most orthodox of interpretations. They should certainly not personalise matters or philosophise on things that sixteen-year-olds could hardly be expected to make head or tail of; for they were only on the threshold of life and could only be expected to cope with facts.

Yes, all things considered, Jack was fortunate, though it was becoming increasingly unlikely that he would bestow on poor Fortune the gratitude she so richly deserved. Jack was bending under the weight of something extremely heavy, and resistance was becoming increasingly futile.

At the end of the week, he said goodbye to Jacob, who was in his shed, cleaning his gardening tools with a damp old rag, ready for the next incumbent; for he believed that he was to be replaced, that his job was not to be left vacant, and in this he was not altogether mistaken. He smiled as Jack approached, and it looked like the first smile he'd managed for a long while. Only platitude and cliché passed between them, though there seemed to be a mutual understanding behind and between such mundane exchanges, like a good filling in a sandwich of stale bread. Jack found it hard to actually say anything very meaningful; it was like trying to talk of future plans to a dying man. As he walked away from Jacob, however, he called out, 'The Truth inside you, Jacob!' Jacob who was, at the best of times, hard of hearing, just smiled and said 'Yes!' scratched his forehead and went on cleaning the gardening tools with the damp old rag.

As Jack made his way to the bike shed, Watkins passed him, seeming studiously to ignore him. Then Jack made his way home with Jacob very much on his mind; thoughts of the old gardener coloured his weekend an even deeper shade of grey.

* *

Jacob's departure was nothing compared with the earthquake and the emotional tsunami that awaited him the following Monday morning. The first tremors began with Harper's casual remark to Gladys.

'Well, then I realised it *was* him,' said Harper, 'I mean, from the general description – and it occurred to me, we haven't seen him around here for while.'

'Poor old boy,' said Gladys.

Jack, en route to his classroom, had just walked into the staffroom to pick up his class register, and picked up this piece of the conversation as well. He casually looked towards Gladys.

'Bit of bad news, it seems, Jack,' she said.

'Oh, really?' He sounded a bit absent-minded.

'Read about it in last night's *Evening News*,' said Harper. 'It's the old boy who used to lounge about at the gates.'

'Alf,' said Gladys.

Jack said nothing, and waited. There was a pause.

'Anyway, it seems some yobs beat him up – no half measures,' said Harper.

'He's hurt, then?' Jack asked, with obvious concern.

'Worse than that, I'm afraid,' said Gladys, looking at Jack sympathetically.

'Kicked and battered, apparently. Anyway, the police are treating it as foul play.' Harper sounded too casual.

Jack said nothing. He just stared at Harper, and then at Gladys, and at Harper again.

'Bring it in for you to see, if you like,' said Harper.

'I'm so sorry, Jack,' said Gladys, sincerely.

'Well, er... I mean, it's not as though we were related, is it?' Jack said with a dismissive laugh. There was a pause.

'The silly old bugger!' Jack suddenly shouted, as if to himself. Davenport had just opened the door, and stood stock still, as though the remark were meant for him, like an arrow which struck home in a vital place, deep and sharp.

'I told him! I told the silly old bugger to be more careful. Wouldn't listen, would he? And he gets himself...' Jack stopped suddenly, looking Davenport straight in the eye. He marched out of the staffroom, leaving Davenport to be filled in by Gladys and Harper.

Just how Jack managed to last out the day apparently intact must remain a testimony to the mysteries of the human psyche. His brain froze that day, and he had what people call 'a glazed look', and he felt strangely ill. He might have gone home on the pretext of an unmanageable attack of migraine; he was not in the habit of doing this, though it wouldn't have been the first time. But he was too dazed to consider pretexts of any kind, and of course a pretext was not put to him. The fact that he stayed in his classroom all day was not, by now, considered particularly abnormal.

When 3C started acting up later that day, he couldn't have cared less; or it was as though he was watching it all on film and it didn't concern him directly at all; had his lesson been observed, he would have failed miserably on Classroom Management – a box that had to be ticked if a teacher was not to be hauled over the coals. He simply told the class to read and summarise chapter three of Wheeler's *History of Roman Britain* – an order which most of them refused to obey, preferring instead to chat noisily or lose themselves in their smartphones. He didn't raise his voice, let alone lose his temper; the veins in his hands, which normally bulged under pressure, were barely visible as thin blue lines – not that it noticed. Nothing was clear; no two things were clearly distinguished one from another. For all the difference it made to him, he could have wantonly slaughtered the innocent, or delivered the Sermon on the Mount as though it were fresh from the press of his own intellect. 'Silly old bugger. Oh, silly old bugger!' Jack murmured to himself off and on throughout the day. The phrase seemed to be intoned differently as the day passed, sounding at first like a reproach, and gradually becoming a sad and reflective incantation for the souls of the dead.

In short, then, Jack managed to survive the day by switching to automatic pilot. He managed his lessons by refusing to teach; he gave every class work to be getting on with, and it didn't matter in the least whether the work set was done or not, or how quiet or boisterous his classes were. He had a lot of thinking to do – or 'thinking' of sorts and he felt bound to do it. Or perhaps he had a lot of *feeling* to do – for thinking and feeling are not necessarily strange bedfellows. But one thought did strike him, in a vague kind of way. What had happened to Alf inclined him to believe that the only kind of beauty that mankind would suffer to exist is natural or physical, like trees, flowers, landscapes and seascapes; and it only remained for the more thoughtless of the species to complete the job of destroying the planet before even that kind of beauty ceased to exist as well. As for a kind of moral beauty, perhaps that was something you made yourself, inside yourself, and once made it could not be unmade; you were stuck with it; stuck with the pain of the intolerable contrast between the beauty inside you and the ugliness you saw everywhere around you. Was the beauty you perceived, the beauty you made inside yourself – was this the offspring of the Spiral of Consciousness? Jack had to blink to restore his sanity and his awareness of his surroundings. But his thoughts rambled on with some purpose of their own.

For instance, if anyone was a silly old bugger, Jack felt it was he himself. It wasn't Alf who hadn't heeded advice, but Jack. It wasn't so much what Alf had *said* that was pushing him in a certain direction, but rather what Alf *was*, what he *represented*; and it was a direction in which Jack was himself unwilling to go, in which he was afraid to go. Sally, Peter, his other, his job, Watkins, Davenport – all were mixed up in Jack's mind like a toxic cocktail, a compound which prevented him from being what he wanted to be; for it was not so much *doing* as *being* that was important. If he could manage to be what he wanted to be, then what he wanted to do and what he wanted to say would follow naturally. The name of this cocktail was Responsibility; but it was poisonous because its chief ingredient was fear and intimidation, and it left no room at all for the Truth that Alf was getting at, or the Truth that Jack *thought* Alf was getting at, whatever that was, exactly – because he was still trying to work things out to his own satisfaction. But, somehow, it was the Truth that everyone really knows and hides away from until it's too late.

Jack had always acted responsibly, as though by acting responsibly that toxic cocktail might somehow be endured.

'I understand you, Alf, but I can't go that way, I really can't!' Jack was thinking out loud, in the classroom and with a full class.

'Sir?'

It was Harris, who'd already finished an essay Jack had set. He brought it to Jack and wanted it looked at.

'Huh? Yes, well, take it back and check the spelling thoroughly.'

'I have!'

'Again, then!' Jack looked at him scornfully and sounded reproachful.

This was just about the last straw for young Harris. Harris was an extremely conscientious pupil, and he had important connections, his father being one of the school governors. Harris walked smartly back to his seat, wondering what to make of Mr Jack Barker, whose head was now bent over a pile of undisturbed and unmarked essays from a previous class, and who seemed to have no intention of marking any of them. Harris had hardly recovered from the first bout of smarting, and now old wounds were reopened with unwelcome vigour.

When Alf had looked at him and smiled behind that grey-white beard, Jack couldn't have said whether it was a smile of sympathy or of mild contempt. He might have enquired, but was too scared to. What worried Jack most was that he might be betraying the old fellow, and Alf's death seemed to give the notion some added poignancy. Jack felt that he owed him something and should pay up. In Jack's weird imagination, Alf resembled Jesus Christ, and if Christ had stayed with you, spoken to you, offered you a way out of your perceived malaise, offered you pearls of wisdom in shafts of bright light, and then suddenly you said, 'Well, that's very nice of you, but there's Sally, and Peter, and my job and…' – if you said something like this, it would seem like some kind of snub, a kind of ingratitude. But Alf would just smile, and he didn't even move his head when he smiled; there was no movement to accompany the smile – just the smile, pure and simple, and most disturbingly ambiguous. Now the man to whom that smile belonged had up and left for good; he had sailed into eternity, leaving Jack to feel hollow and some kind of cheat. But who had he cheated? 'Always be true to the Truth,' Alf had, allegedly, said. But how could you be true to the Truth unless you knew what that Truth was? The Truth must be known before it can be told, and it must be known before you can pay allegiance to it. Or, it was like being told that you must be true to yourself. How can you be true to yourself unless you know who you really are? Did the toxic cocktail of Responsibility bar the way? Did it charm you into lying to yourself?

* *

'Silly old bugger,' Jack muttered tearfully, as he cycled home.

He hadn't seen Gladys or Harper since first thing that morning. He had spent the day inside himself; as usual, his thoughts were confused and confusing. He needed to talk to someone. Not to Sally; she was the last person on earth he could talk to about things like this. 'What? Alf dead? Good riddance!' No, she wouldn't say that, but she would think it, and you would sense it and it would spoil everything.

The house was empty when Jack got home; it was Pete's sleepover night and he'd made an early start, and it would be another hour before Sally was due home from work. Jack thought of Amanda. She had moved and was staying with friends. He was about to call the number she'd given him, but he thought better of it; he walked round the living room once or twice and finally decided to give her a call; he began to splutter a message into voicemail, which he interrupted when the front door opened and Sally walked into the hallway. Sally greeted him coldly, sensing his nervousness with the phone still in his hand; she gave the situation her own, silent, interpretation.

'You're early,' Jack said.

'That's right.' No more words passed between them that evening.

* *

Between classes next day, Tallis's 'Solfaing Song', Jack's favourite Elizabethan piece for viols and lute, was heard loud and distinct through the corridors on the approach to his classroom. Yes, it was loud – to hell with complaints, to hell with Davenport. Jack felt that there was in such sounds a kind of truth; not perhaps the Truth at which Alf had hinted and Jack was attempting miserably to elaborate, but something serene and divinely eternal nevertheless – and therefore deeply reassuring.

13
The Mechanism

In the mornings that followed, Jack found himself cycling more slowly than ever en route to Morley Comprehensive, and particularly slowly over the grey stone bridge that spanned the river; and he would peer into the bus shelters as he cycled past them, or glance at the clearings between the trees where Alf used to pass the night or take his ease during the day, as if he might still catch a glimpse of his great mentor there and prove that it wasn't he who had been kicked to death and left to die in some cold backstreet on a dark and windy night, but some other unfortunate, nameless and unknown. But he sensed it was all in vain: everywhere felt empty, some endless vacuum. Something had been torn out of the mornings, leaving them bereft of a presence bordering upon the sacred.

For some days now he had played his Elizabethan music loud, or it would be better to say, as loud as he dared. For how long can a man grieve? How long can he be shocked and shaken? Yes, it was loud; but it was not too loud for too long. Jack, in common with the vast majority of mankind, had developed an in-built guidance mechanism that would dictate the limits of dissidence and protest, of open rebellion and overt disquietude, and it was fear that had programmed the mechanism. He knew all about the mechanism, or at least sensed its effects, and he felt uncomfortable with it, not to say at times tortured by it. But the mechanism was alive and well, its heart still beating with his own. This cybernetic mechanism had itself developed a system of signals to warn of overheating and approaching danger. Jack might protest, he might demonstrate, he might raise his voice. But when he felt his lips begin to tremble, or when his tongue began to stick inside his dry mouth, he knew it was time to back off, and he acted accordingly; for the mechanism would be overburdened, and what was likely to happen next would almost certainly not be to his advantage. For if he exploded, the game would be all up, and this could not be allowed to happen. After all, did he not have responsibilities to shoulder, a family to look after, and a future, his and theirs, to consider?

It was not long, therefore, before the music began to drop to a more acceptable level of decibels. As a counterbalance to this gesture of moderation, however, he still took to remaining in his classroom during the breaks, and would continue to do so until such time as the mechanism would begin to advise a tactical retreat even here. Davenport soon found it unnecessary to approach him over his music. But there remained the question of the breaks.

So far he had been left alone, and not even Gladys – probably his last, though admittedly flimsy, contact with normality, not to say sanity – had troubled to seek him out… until now.

'Mind if I come in?' she asked, sheepishly poking her head round the classroom door. Jack smiled and shrugged his shoulders. She walked in. Jack was sitting at his desk.

'Just wondered if you've seen this,' she said, approaching him. She handed him a piece of paper she'd taken down from one of the staffroom noticeboards. It announced in bold letters that Davenport had formally been made Deputy Head of Morley Comprehensive. Jack took the paper, gave it a cursory glance and handed it back quickly – as though it were contaminated.

'Careful, Gladys! This is subversive activity, you know. You'd better pin it back up ASAP.'

'Well, what do you think?'

'Think? Nothing! A foregone conclusion, wasn't it? He's been toadying long enough. He deserves it.'

'You're happy about it, then?'

'Hm? No, you don't get my meaning, Gladys. You see, not long after Davenport first arrived here, when he was still just about human, he and I had a longish chat. Watkins had given him extra responsibilities, and I could see where it was all going – his face obviously fitted. Anyway, Davenport actually asked me for advice – well, I was an old hand compared to him at that time, and still am – anyway, he asked me whether he thought he was up to the task, and I told him he had all the necessary qualities in abundance, and that pleased him, because he thought I was complimenting him.'

'You were being sarcastic.'

'I meant, he had all the qualities of a first-class crawler (toadying to Watkins, not to mention the governors), the sort who'd throw his weight about all over the place given half a chance, and have people like you and me for breakfast. He's subtle, of course, and eloquent –

he probably gets that from the classics. Power always brings out the worst, Gladys, never the best. I'm just sorry I turned out to be right.' And then he added under his breath, as if to himself, 'The Truth can be so damned pedestrian.'

'You don't think he'll settle down, then? You know, become a kind of counterbalance to Watkins?'

'That's wishful thinking if ever I heard it. No, come on! He'll go from bad to worse, if anything. Haven't you heard the way he speaks these days – that tone of authority, with some of the stock phrases Watkins himself uses? No, he's unshakeable. The cries of a dying infant wouldn't produce in him an ounce of self-doubt, even if he was himself responsible for the poor kid's plight. There's not the slightest quiver in his voice, and his eyes burn through you like hot coals. He has about him a permanent aura of superiority – the brazen bugger oozes self-assertion.'

'That's a bit strong, Jack!' Gladys frowned. Perhaps he had indeed gone too far. But Jack was as yet receiving no danger signals from his in-built mechanism, so presumably it was safe to continue.

'Is it? I don't think so. I told him, on one of those early days, I was interested in Greek philosophy, and he asked whether I knew ancient Greek, and when I said I didn't, he seemed to smirk, as though I'd come out with a silly non-starter. But crawling and toadying, hypocrisy and duplicity – these aren't Socratic virtues, I can tell you that much, Gladys. No, Davenport acts out virtue as though it were a part in a stage play – and only one part amongst others, at that! You know, when you think of Alf...'

Gladys smiled sympathetically. She sensed how deeply Alf's demise had cut, and she thought she now knew where all that strong stuff about Davenport had come from, or where Jack was coming from. Davenport, fairly or unfairly, was 'taking the rap'.

'You know, when you think of Alf – well, it's just... You know what Alf told me? As a kid, he went out shooting rabbits, but he never managed to come across one. Then one fine day he saw a rabbit and aimed his gun. He looked into the rabbit's eyes, pulled the trigger and sent the creature into eternity. He said that when he looked at the rabbit lying there lifeless, it was like looking into the eyes of some benevolent priest. But he'd killed it, and he couldn't reconcile the life he'd seen there a split second before with the nothingness he'd created – created in ignorance. He actually lost sleep over it, sold his gun, gave up hunting. Now I ask you, Gladys – how can one man feel so deeply, suffer such guilt, and all about such an insignificant thing, while most men would have seen nothing other than the eyes of a rabbit and remembered nothing about it afterwards? Alf said he'd killed a rabbit but gained his own soul. Such sensitivity, Gladys! Such sensitivity. Do you think Watkins or Davenport would lose any sleep over a thing like that? Christ, they can't even treat human beings with dignity, let alone small woodland creatures. Yet Alf gets kicked to death while Davenport gets promoted and Watkins goes on lording over us all!'

'There's no justice, Jack – we all know that. Not in this world, anyway.'

'Well, there's no other.'

'Anyway, you wouldn't want Davenport or Watkins to be beaten up in some dark alley, would you? Right – I'd best be going.'

Jack smiled. 'Sorry, Gladys, it's just…'

'I know.' And with that, Gladys smiled and left.

Jack had been rambling on again, as he was well aware. Moreover, he had lied. The story about the rabbit had been an episode in his own life, not in Alf's. But it was a lie that didn't seem to matter. Gladys wouldn't suspect anything, and, as for his rambling, she hadn't, as he might have feared, even dreamt of reporting it to a higher authority. Not that she wasn't concerned. On the contrary, she had mentioned to Harper that she was worried about Jack, that perhaps he had been overdoing things, though what things exactly she was unable to say. That's all she said to Harper; the rest she kept to herself. She suspected that something deeper might be wrong with Jack. After all, if Alf's demise had knocked him for six, there was no very obvious reason it should have done so. To have felt sorry for the old fellow was one thing, but the effect on Jack was quite another and suggested something else. All that venom against Davenport, for example, was – well, it just wasn't on.

She popped in again the following morning, with a piece of friendly advice.

'No, he didn't make a special point of it. He just came into the staffroom – I was packing up to go home – and asked if I'd seen you,' she said.

'Ah! He knows you'll pass it on to me. It's his way of telling me to toe the line, or else. He wants me in the staffroom where he can keep his beady eyes on me.'

'Well, anyway, Watkins has put him in charge of monitoring classroom management. There's a list up in the staffroom with names of teachers to be observed, and times. Your name's on it, Jack – I'm not sure but I think it's right at the top. But really, Jack, you ought to put in an appearance, you know.'

'So, if Davenport's gunning for dissidents, he'll have all the authority of his position to back it up.'

'We all have to toe the line, Jack.' She sounded like an older version of Amanda. 'But of course, whatever Davenport says or does, Watkins will back him up – I know that. He gives Davenport a free hand in everything these days. Watkins has the utmost faith in him.'

'Ah, you're learning, Gladys. Would you expect anything else? They're two of a kind.'

'Oh, I don't know,' she said in a tone of frustration. 'It's all getting to be too much, isn't it? Appraisals, observations, assessments. An overload!'

'It means there's no hiding place anymore – nowhere where you can be yourself. They don't trust you to be yourself. It's not enough to be a good teacher and just get on with your job. You have to be seen to be good – constantly on trial, constantly having to prove yourself. Everything has to be structured and formalised – and that rips the heart out of it all; externalises everything. The best discipline comes from the inside – self-imposed, self-judged. From the inside where it can't be monitored; impose it and you've lost it – I mean, it's like ripping the personality out of teaching and replacing it with something regulated and standardised – so no differences, no variations from the "norm" can be tolerated; differences are rejects, like objects which turn out wrong on the assembly line. But these people won't understand that in a thousand years. No hiding place, Gladys. We can't even hide away in our classrooms anymore – yes, we have to be viewed, observed, assessed, because all trust is gone. I mean, what happens in a marriage if all trust has gone?' Jack paused. 'Well, anyway, Patel wanted to do just that – hide away, I mean – and who in their right minds could possibly blame him? Just wanted to be a good teacher, the kind of teacher he'd always been. Well, what's the use?'

'I wonder how he's getting on.'

'Don't know. He won't let me call him. I can't even text him, either. His phone's off most of the time. He just doesn't respond. It upsets him to be contacted.'

'Really? Excellent teacher. Been here for years. Then suddenly he's gone, and nobody cares. It's amazing,' Gladys mused.

'Amazing, Gladys? The problem is, it's much more amazing than most people would or could acknowledge it to be.'

'Right!' said Gladys, not hearing or not quite understanding what Jack had said. Then she scuttled off, just as the bell for morning classes sounded gratingly in the corridors.

Gladys was alright, Jack thought. He'd had some misgivings about her from time to time, and there were limits to the philosophising, or the confused rambling that passed for philosophising, she could take. But she was alright – she was alright just in the way Amanda was alright. Gladys didn't have Amanda's youth and beauty; in this respect they differed markedly. But they were on the same kind of level: uninspired and uninspiring, but safe. They were unremarkable; but they were 'good sorts'. Had Jack been a climber, he would have aimed for the very highest peak, and the conquest of formidable but lesser summits would have failed to gratify him. He was forever on the lookout for models he might emulate, and neither Amanda nor Gladys could inspire him to emulation. But by the same token, neither could they inspire fear. He could therefore feel quite free in what he said to them; it was necessary to have someone to smile at from time to time, and someone to smile back; they fitted the bill nicely. And above all, his in-built mechanism was content.

Gladys was clearly discontent with the way things were going at Morley Comprehensive, though it was just as well that she didn't complement Jack's own ramblings with ramblings of her own, otherwise they might drive each other into some kind of cerebral abyss from which there could be no return. Jack was thankful that she wasn't into that kind of thing. It was enough that she felt restless, insecure and intimidated, like everybody else; but she clearly felt comfortable confiding in Jack. In that respect, she reminded him of Patel. Patel! Ah, yes, Patel! Yes, he'd better pay Patel a visit quite soon – if Patel didn't contact him first, and there seemed little likelihood that he would. On the other hand, a visit could easily wait a few days more.

*   *

Meanwhile, Jack's built-in mechanism was being subjected to further testing. He set one of his classes an essay on the purpose of education despite the fact that the subject had little to do with the Glorious Revolution of 1688. The title read: *It is often said that education is 'a preparation for life'. What does this mean, and how far do you agree?* For his class, it was a bolt out of the blue. Young Harris, still smarting from his most recent rebuff, might even have raised questions about its relevance, but for the fact that Jack had shown a particularly firm countenance and spoken in stentorian tones, a combination which seemed to defy all questioning and preclude all criticism.

It was a rash move, as indeed was a lecture given later that day to 4B on the evils of unemployment. It started as it was meant to go on – as a lesson on the Elizabethan vagrancy laws – but after only ten minutes he was well into an all-out polemic on the government currently in office. He had consciously gone off at a tangent and was thoroughly enjoying it. But children, arguably more than their adult counterparts, have a strong aversion to party political broadcasts. He asked the class what the primary causes of unemployment might be, and the general consensus was 'laziness'; Jack saw red, and it was his cue to attempt to show that unemployment was still the social stigma it was when the Protestant Ethic had first raised its ugly head. His pupils, at first poised to write history notes in their history notebooks, found themselves unable to write a thing, and, at the end of the lesson, were no wiser about Elizabeth's vagrancy laws than they were at the outset; nor had they understood Jack's tightly knit ramblings. Had Jack been inspected, and judged, concerning how far he had succeeded in meeting the aims of the history curriculum, he would have failed miserably. He had not only failed to throw light on the topic he should have taught, but also on the topic he had seen fit to teach instead. But, if education should concern itself with the reasoned removal of prejudice and myth, Jack felt he'd given it one of his very best shots.

The mechanism was tested once more when the essays on education were handed back to pupils later that week, having been marked and graded. Young Harris, the apple of his father's eye, one of the brightest sparks in the school, with a future predicated to be brilliant, was given a D-minus instead of his customary straight-A. Naturally, he was thoroughly deflated, despite having gorged himself during lunch-hour. Yet, still the mechanism exhibited no real signs of strain, and consequently none of the usual warning signals were issued.

Not, of course, that the mechanism was defunct. Mid-morning Thursday, Gladys popped her head round the classroom door again to say that Davenport had been asking his whereabouts for a second time.

'Ridiculous. He knows where to find me, Gladys. It's not as though I've left the planet. Unless Davenport has finally lost his bearings due to overwork.' It was a poor joke and had no effect.

'But it's no good hiding yourself away, Jack.'

It was this last remark of Gladys's that seemed to give the mechanism a bit of a jolt, like a loose tooth you've temporarily forgotten about getting a bump from a peanut. The fact is, it reminded Jack of his own words to Patel concerning the boiler room escapade. And look what happened to Patel! Was he going down the same track? Was his classroom for him what the boiler room had been for Patel? Yes, but he *wasn't* Patel, and he had better prove it now. Jack was made of different stuff, and he would prove it by the words he spoke.

'He knows where to find me. After all, Gladys, people like that have people like us looking forward to retirement at least twenty years before it's due. Yes! You actually start wishing away twenty years of your life, just so you can get away from people like that. Not to mention the very real possibility that you won't even reach retirement age. Come to think of it, I've got a tingling sensation in my left arm, a tightness in my chest, and my blood pressure's rising by the second, and… Oh, come on, Gladys, people, like him – they're just not worth it!' Jack's joking continued to fall on stony ground.

But despite the jolt it had received, there were still no clear warning signals from his in-built mechanism. Perhaps he was so beside himself that the normal settings on the programme were being overridden. Nevertheless, he said no more, and Gladys left him with his thoughts, amongst which was the notion that ten thousand Davenports could never equal a Patel or a Jacob – and as for an Alf, well… Davenport and Alf were just worlds apart. Yet it was Davenport who had helped to get Patel crucified, Davenport who lived in the peace and tranquillity of green suburbia, while Patel dragged out the poor remains of his life on the rim of a motorway, with nothing but pictures of his late wife in silver-plated picture frames as a means of consolation. It had really been Davenport's budgeting proposals which had yanked old Jacob out of his shrubberies and thrown him smack into the arms of cold solitude – and the duplicity here was that it had been done on the pretext that Jacob was to be made redundant, while the intention was to replace him with a cheaper and younger version of himself. No, it was always the wrong guys who got crucified.

Jack continued to console himself with the thought that *he* wasn't Patel. The trouble with Patel was that he had had faith in those that had brought him down and sent him packing. But Jack clearly had no illusions about Watkins and Davenport. He could cite his own words to Gladys as proof positive that he was clear about the nature and extent of the opposition. To quake and shake before the likes of Watkins and Davenport would be nothing short of an act of betrayal, a betrayal of what he knew to be right. Alive or dead, Alf was his guiding star, and he could plot his course by him. If Jack's own father had simply left home to wander the streets for good, instead of dying in his armchair with his Bible open at the thirty-fourth reading of Ezekiel, he might have turned out pretty much like Alf, and got himself killed in the same way, too. It was hard to get away from the feeling that every day, every hour, every minute that passed in submission to the likes of Watkins and Davenport, was a further day, hour and minute of betrayal, a betrayal of what his father and Alf had stood for – yes, betrayal, at the very root of which lay Fear masquerading as Responsibility.

*   *

'It has been brought to my attention,' Watkins began, in his slow, meditative manner. Jack was sitting in Watkins's office in the mid-morning break, not voluntarily this time, but having been called there by Watkins himself, and the experience was already unpleasant even before Watkins got round to stating his business. Jack's built-in mechanism was very much on the alert.

'It has been brought to my attention that you have been – how shall I put it? – er… *politicising* your history lessons, and to a rather considerable degree, and er… well, causing some offence in the process.'

The question, 'How do you plead?' flashed across Jack's mind, but there was no time to be amused by it. Jack simply raised his eyebrows but said nothing. Watkins then spoke quickly.

'Well, naturally, it would be a breach of confidence to reveal my sources, not to say invidious and irrelevant. I have tended to assume their reliability, though I would of course be interested to hear your version of events.' So this really was a version of the question, 'How do you plead?' Watkins was shuffling some papers about on his large metallic desk as he said all this, an action which was perhaps calculated to produce some unsettling effect upon the listener, as though Watkins was a very busy man who had no time to spare for this kind of nonsense and was therefore most annoyed that he should have to deal with it at all. In any case, Jack found it unsettling.

'History…' Jack began, pausing fatally.

'Yes?' Watkins put in sharply. Jack found this unsettling, too.

'History…' Jack began again, this time speaking the word slowly and reflectively, as though he were about to deliver a highly reasoned, not to say weighty, proposition.

'I am not a historian,' Watkins cut in again, 'but I believe I can confidently assert that history is history, which is to say there are many things history is *not*. With respect, I did not ask you to come here to talk about history. No, we are not talking about history now. History excludes party political comment, and the charge brought against you – if I may put it like that – is that you have been indulging in party political comment, and in no small measure, either. But perhaps you wish to deny the er… charge?'

'I might have drawn certain parallels with the present in some of my lessons, or… or drawn out certain inferences, yes.'

'Yes, and pursued them at considerable length, some accounts would have it.'

'I might've gone a little overboard on occasion, yes.'

'Quite, quite. But, really, insofar as they are current parallels and er… inferences, as you call them, they are not strictly speaking *history* at all, are they, Mr Barker? And apart from that, we must remember that we are dealing with children who are barely into their teens, who have very little experience of the world in which they live. No, no, it's quite inappropriate, even if it were ethical, which I earnestly believe it is not.'

Jack later wondered what Watkins had meant by 'ethical' and thought he should have asked for clarification. But the conversation, or what passed for conversation, was moving apace, and the word was allowed to pass muster.

'They are young, certainly—'

'I beg your pardon?' Watkins cut in again. And again Jack was unsettled, and his mechanism was twitching with disquietude.

'I said, I know they are young, but they should at least start to become *aware*.'

'But the question is, aware of *what*?'

'History cannot exclude personal opinion, and it cannot exclude its relevance to the present,' Jack said, speaking quickly and clearly, anxious to avoid unsettling requests for repeats. Jack began to feel his lips tremble. His in-built mechanism was telling him something, loud and clear; it was flashing a red light.

'But it must exclude mere propaganda, should it not?' Watkins was a paradigm of coolness and firmness; he was entirely in control, while Jack was beginning to feel anything but cool, calm and collected. If Watkins had a built-in mechanism of his own, it was very much in the background, smiling complacently.

Jack thought quickly, attempting to cope with the messages delivered by his mechanism, but his brain seemed to spin round like a bicycle wheel making no contact with the ground. He was silent, but not through choice. He just couldn't get things together.

'History cannot exclude politics – or excludes it at its peril.' Jack spoke quickly, as though it were a reflex action and entirely involuntary.

'I beg your pardon?' Watkins had only caught the last word – 'peril'.

'History cannot exclude politics.'

'Well, history cannot exclude the history of politics. If that is what you mean, I agree entirely. But that is not at all the same thing as party political electioneering.'

'It wasn't electioneering.'

'Since I was not present, I'm hardly in a position to contradict you. But that is evidently how it came across.'

Jack was the historian, but Watkins seemed to be giving him a lesson about what it means to teach history. Jack was smarting, and here at least he had something in common with young Harris. Jack's mouth was dry and his heart seemed to be pounding, sure signs that his mechanism was beside itself. This session with Watkins was anything but a shouting match; no, words were exchanged in friendly tones; friendly, but firm; firm, but friendly. Even so, it was one of the most stressful experiences that had fallen to Jack's lot in recent times.

'Well,' Watkins went on, after a painful pause, 'let's stop pussy-footing around, shall we, Mr Barker? Alright, you have a political opinion. You are perfectly entitled to it, whatever it is. But however tempting it might be to parade one's own views, one must consider the time and the place – and one's audience! School desks are not hustings, classrooms are not party headquarters, classes are not political rallies. That much, at any rate, is clear. But you know this. This much is common ground between us, is it not?' If Watkins expected a nod of assent, he didn't get it. 'Alright, you probably went off at a tangent, lost your sense of direction, and committed a grave error of judgement. But the question is, where do we go from here?'

There had been no tone of compromise in his words; yet, from this point on, his tone seemed to change and he began to sound almost avuncular. Even so, Jack found the transition unsettling, as though someone had answered the simplest of questions with a 'Yes, and no'.

'Bear in mind our duty of care, Mr Barker. Our duty of care. I remember making the point to you not long ago that the parents of the children under our charge have every right to expect the highest standards of educational care, and educational care includes academic objectivity. Put bluntly and simply, they expect their children to be taught English in English lessons, biology in biology lessons – and *history* in history lessons – party politics is nowhere on the school's curriculum. Think it over, Mr Barker. Think it over.'

According to custom, Watkins got up to signal that the discussion was at an end, and they both walked to the door. 'Oh, one other thing. I am given to understand that you have begun to take your breaks in your classroom of late. No doubt you find it easier to work there. Commendable. Highly commendable. However, it would be much appreciated if you would observe the custom of spending them in the staffroom; easier to find you in an emergency, easier to disseminate information – that sort of thing. Yes?' Again, a nod of assent from Jack was not forthcoming. Watkins had a smile on his face, but it was rather thin and limp; the kind of smile one might wear when the only alternative is a scowl of contempt, which is why the lame little thing melted away even before the office door was shut on Jack, who was, as before, left standing in the corridor.

*   *

This was not just another betrayal. It was an abject betrayal. If Jack had been religious, he might have counted it a sin against the Holy Spirit, and therefore unforgiveable. Suddenly, he thought he knew what he should have said: that there is all the difference in the world between mere propaganda and reasoned argument; that history is not and cannot be the mere parading of names and dates; that unless history is shown to have parallels in the present, it counts for nothing; that history is related to the present as upbringing is to adulthood; that an understanding of the present is ample justification for a study of the past; that some attempt, however tentative, should be made to get children to see the whole point of history; that the point of history lies in the present; that history repeats itself and does so because mankind and ideas are slow to change if they change at all.

He reproached himself for thinking of the right things to say only after the event, because to say them now was no more than preaching to the converted, namely himself. Why hadn't he said them? He didn't say them, because he hadn't thought of them, and he hadn't thought of them, because fear had reared its ugly head yet again. Fear of Watkins and his big metallic desk, of his hollow smile, of the consequences had he said them, of all these things. Was fear at the bottom of abject betrayal?

With bitter self-reproach came a modicum of consolation. After all, had he said any or all of these things, it was very unlikely that much of an impression would have been made on Watkins. Was not Watkins, like his acolyte Davenport, worlds apart? Jack couldn't have done better than Socrates during his trial, and look what happened to him? It was like knocking your head up against a stone wall; when people with power have it in for you, you've had it.

In fact, in some frustrating sense, Watkins couldn't really be faulted. He was playing a game, and he had played it rather well. It might be a silly game and one deficient in logical rigour, and even lacking in moral responsibility towards the young in particular and humanity in general. But it was a game he was paid to play, and just the game parents expected him to play. He had played it straight down the line, producing all the form and cliché expected of him; parents would have applauded him for it, and undoubtedly some parents more than others. No, questions about the logical and moral validity of the game apart, Watkins was doing a superb job, with not a word, much less a sentiment, out of place. Yes, Watkins had handled it beautifully.

Yes, but supposing someone didn't like the game? Jack, for example, loathed it. Well, then it wouldn't matter how well it's played. Jack compared the game with football, a game of which he was no great fan. If you don't like football, it doesn't matter to you how well, or how badly, it's played, for it's just as well to you if it isn't played at all. That's how Jack thought of Watkins's performance. Watkins wanted to play, and Jack didn't. By the same token, Watkins didn't want to play Jack's game, either, so that even if Jack had said all he was capable of saying about the point of history, it wouldn't have made a bit of difference to Watkins. On the contrary, it would only have been confirmation for Watkins of the rightness of his own stance, which, luckily for him, was the stance that parents and people in general would expect him to adopt. Which boils down to saying that Jack was very much in the minority and felt he hadn't a leg to stand on. Jack had to admit it, at least to himself. He knew he had gone too far in what purported to be a history lesson; he had gone too far, and that is why he had enjoyed it. But that is just what he wanted to do – to go too far, to kick over the traces; he had subsequently been squealed on, and he felt as though he should be saying, 'It's a fair cop, guv!'

But none of these cerebral meanderings helped to mitigate his sense of self-betrayal. Jack felt scolded, like a small boy found with stolen apples. He had engaged in political sniping from behind bushes, and he had been found wanting when discovered by the opposition. He had broken down under light interrogation, and he felt he had given away far more than his name, rank and serial number. If he didn't like the game Watkins was playing, he could at least have said so, and walked out. He hadn't done so, and this made it appear that the game was perfectly acceptable after all, and that he had really deserved the scolding he'd received. And then there were the signals that his built-in mechanism had given out – his quivering lips, his dry mouth; they were, no more, no less, signs of abject fear.

They were signs of deep, volcanic anger, too.

Jack felt low. He was prevented from tumbling even further into an abyss of despair and self-reproach by the casual and momentary appearance of someone who was perhaps as near a precipice as he.

Jack marched into the staffroom in a huff at the beginning of the lunch-hour, and interrupted Llewellyn Jones, a tall, lanky fellow in his mid-fifties, who taught French, in the act of screwing the cap back onto his hipflask. Jones had managed to dismiss his class a few minutes before the bell, to be first in the staffroom with a minute or two to spare, just enough time to take a swig or two, and then quickly mask the odour with a strong coffee. He was standing by the window on the far side of the room, and Jack's entry had taken him completely by surprise. In a nerve-racked flash, Jones shoved the flask back into his pocket, though the cap had been screwed back askew and might cause the flask to leak – luckily for him, it didn't. Jones had never been a paragon of composure and stability, but he had been particularly jittery of late, and his sentences were delivered in an ever-increasing staccato. But he not only spoke in staccato; he moved in staccato, also – a walking framework of frayed nerves. How he could teach French, or indeed anything necessitating the use of words, was a continuing and deepening mystery. But he was still there, and, if not going strong, was at least going. Jones had a crippled wife who had to be taken everywhere in a wheelchair; the washing, cleaning, shopping were all down to him, not to mention the routine care of his wife. And all this on top of an increasingly stressful workload in a context of observation, assessment and appraisal. No wonder he fancied a wee dram to help see him through the day, though he did his level best to control the quantities he drank at night, for he had soon learned that the more you drink at night the less capable you are on the morrow; such dependency burned an unwelcome hole in his salary, but he felt it helped keep him going. Little wonder he was forever crunching extra strong mints and looking flushed and apologetic. But it was surprising he hadn't yet been caught out and 'approached' by the powers-that-be. One whiff of Jones's breath and Davenport would be off to Watkins like a shot, and the consequences would be unthinkable despite all that talk about 'teacher support', which was yet another instance of pure cant and hypocrisy. Even to be seen with a bottle of alcohol would occasion a remonstrance; to be caught imbibing would result in instant dismissal. Jones, it might be said, was playing with fire-water. Scalpels are used to heal, knives to hurt, maim and kill. Had Jones been caught, the knives, not scalpels, would have been out. When it came down to hard facts, and, for Watkins, it seemed, hard facts was what history and every other school subject was about, *teacher support* was a dream come false.

Later that same lunch-hour in the staffroom, Jones crept up to Jack and tried to start up a conversation, and before long asked him whether he had a local and what his favourite tipple was. He tried so hard to make it sound like idle chatter; but Jones was at great pains to point out that he hardly ever indulged much himself. Jack's powers of observation were clearly being tested. How much did he know? How much had he seen? Jack, for his part, tried equally hard to give him the impression that he hadn't seen anything at all, and he did this by appearing to swallow the lie that Jones was peddling to the effect that he was practically teetotal. Jack said that he was practically teetotal himself, but added that there was nothing wrong whatsoever in an occasional and moderate indulgence. Jones even went so far as to say that he had the strongest possible views on overindulgence. Jack changed the subject, and Jones looked decidedly more relaxed at the end of this apparently casual small-talk than he had at the outset. But poor devil! Had Jack stared at him disbelievingly and reproachfully, the fellow might have fallen on his knees in front of him in a posture of solemn contrition, delivered a full confession, undertaken to wear sackcloth and pleaded with him to say nothing. Jack afterwards entertained the thought of taking him aside, telling him frankly that he was in the know and offering him the hand of genuine friendship. But he judged it was not the better course. Poor Jones was too far gone, far too fragile for mending, his tissue too delicate for the surgeon's skill; Jones probably wouldn't have trusted him, and a heart-to-heart might have sent him irrecoverably over the top.

But every cloud has a silver lining, Jack reasoned. Jones had been caught in the act of taking his daily nip – or thought he *might* have been. He would be more careful in future. The wolves might catch up with him and bring him down in the end and tear him limb from limb, but he, and therefore his crippled wife, had been given a further period of grace.

On the one hand, there were people like Watkins and Davenport: cool, firm, self-assured; on the other, people like Llewellyn Jones. Yes, the strong and the weak co-existed nicely at Morley Comprehensive. Was not the school a microcosm of the world? Jack regarded his experiences that day as poignant reminders of life's rich and tragic tapestry. But Watkins and Davenport were not alone in their strength. For there was Lloyd, who taught mathematics. Lloyd was Patel's replacement. Lloyd was tall, straight and solid as a telegraph pole, and in his mid-thirties. The man exuded confidence. He was mathematical certainty incarnate. Why, even Watkins and Davenport gave him deference to a degree not enjoyed by the rest of the staff. Unlike Jones, he was able to dress up, go to the pub, limit himself to one pint only, drink it slowly, and firmly, and sincerely refuse the offer of another one, in the conviction that he was unique in his moral rectitude, and then leave with an unshakeable belief in the dignity of his own being.

But for all that, no, *because* of all that, he wasn't a patch on Patel, or on old Jacob, or for that matter on Jones. Above all, he wasn't a patch on Alf – no, no chance, no chance at all!

Yes, Patel. What about Patel? Jack decided that he really must pay him a visit. But first he would try to contact him, despite Patel's insistence that he'd rather he didn't.

14
A Force Unleashed

Jack managed to compound his self-reproach still further: he should have expressed righteous indignation at having his integrity challenged; nor had he questioned Watkins's sources. Watkins had told him that his sources were reliable and that to reveal them was irrelevant. But that was not good enough. Jack now thought he should have insisted on knowing them. It was too late now. But it was not too late to wonder. It was unlikely to have been a pupil who'd reported him directly to Davenport, much less to Watkins. It was far more likely that a pupil had spoken to his parents or had been grilled by them. Harris had an axe to grind and was a chief suspect; he might well have had a long story to tell his father. Watkins had seemed to imply that there was more than one source. Well, there was Ferguson, a sneak if ever there was one – one of those pupils that appear to go about with a permanent chip on their shoulder and an inexplicable scowl on their face. Jack thought he would look about him for signs and leads. On the other hand, what did it really matter? The damage had been done. Having to inch one's way into the place every morning and teach irrelevancies to a sea of blank faces was off-putting enough, without serving oneself a cocktail of malice and suspicion. But if little brats like Harris and Ferguson thought for one moment that he would be frightened into servitude by this whole affair, they would be seriously mistaken.

More important than the question of sources was the matter of his personal shortcomings. He had lacked spirit – not, of course, for the first time – but it worried him more than ever. What he saw as a major deficiency became an obsession, and he felt contemptuous of himself. On a positive interpretation, he had carried himself well with Watkins, showing remarkable restraint and self-control, perhaps even humouring the opposition; but he could be positive only by being superficial and dishonest, for inwardly he knew he had acted like a rabbit caught in the glare of a headlight, unable to move until the vehicle had passed and lucky not to have been flattened by the wheels.

As a new week began, his self-disgust was further augmented by the short-lived relief he felt at finding Gladys wrong. He wasn't at the top of Davenport's list of observations which was pinned to the staffroom noticeboard. The indescribable honour of that position fell to Llewellyn Jones, who, upon seeing it, had turned pale; but Jones then immediately recovered his composure when Davenport informed him that the observation was to be postponed; Jones, who had pretended indifference, could be seen, after a discreet allowance of time, walking about with an expression of curious benignity. The fact is, Jones was now to give first place to Jack. Jack was to be first in line after all. He did not wonder why. This was clearly a follow-up to his meeting with Watkins – a policing job, and no mistake.

Jack determined to take it with a pinch of salt this time. He thought of Jones's reaction and how repulsive it had seemed. It was fear – that's what it all boiled down to. Bloody silly fear. And fear of what? What had Socrates said? A good man cannot be harmed. Yes, that was it. A good man cannot be harmed because he has nothing to fear, and he's got nothing to fear because he's dead already – dead to the *Self*. A good man puts himself so far into the background, he negates himself, and a man can't die twice. If you are nothing already, no one can make you less than nothing. Yes, you conquered fear by rubbing yourself out, so to speak. Whether Socrates or his expositor Plato would have agreed with this interpretation is perhaps debateable, but the only philosophical training Jack had was that which he gave to himself, and self-negation is how he understood the idea that a good man cannot be harmed, and it was good enough for him. Jack thought it was an ingenious notion, but he had always wondered who on God's earth could ever really manage self-negation. Alf, perhaps, had come close; he had died to the Self; he had negated himself. Well, many would have said he was dead already, what with sleeping in bus shelters and under trees on frosty nights and having to beg the price of a cup of tea. That was no life at all. But precisely because Alf had nothing, he had nothing to lose. And he had *chosen* to have nothing. All he had was what was left of him when possessions and greed were stripped away. He had nothing to lose, except his life – and we all have to lose that in the end, anyway. He could have had more than nothing if only he had conformed. Alf wanted none of the trappings of conformity. But Alf was gone now, and that was hard to accept. He had no doubt been cremated, because it was the cheapest way to be shipped off. Truly a case of dust to dust, ashes to ashes. Now he was in the air, flying about in particles. He was still trying to get up people's noses, in death as in life. Jack determined to do the same – to get up people's noses, a least while he still lived.

* *

'Well, I'm not quite sure,' said Gladys, looking around furtively. 'But I definitely heard him say "Patel" – yes, I think Watkins mentioned his name. They were definitely talking about him, but I couldn't catch what they said – and I could hardly stand next to them and listen, could I?'

Gladys had caught a few words of the conversation between Watkins and Davenport as she passed them in the corridor, and she was keen for Jack to know that the subject of that conversation was in all probability Patel. Perhaps, she thought, Patel was coming back. 'Oh, I don't know about that,' Jack said. 'I don't think it's at all likely – but you never know…'

But this reported reference to Patel was enough to push Jack to action. He resolved to call Patel that very afternoon, using Patel's landline number. But when he did, all he got was a pre-recorded message in a nondescript voice telling him that the number he had used had either been disconnected or was otherwise no longer in use. It would have been less puzzling to have received no answer at all. Had Patel gone so far as to change his number? Or had he got himself disconnected? That would have been consistent with his retreat to the boiler room and his nervousness about being contacted by phone. If so, was this a step further along a downward path? Or had he up and left altogether? But where would he go? As far as Jack knew, he had no relations to go to, and no offspring who might take him under their wing. In any case, moving away takes time; it didn't seem feasible, let alone likely. There was only one way to find out.

That evening, Cherrytree Road was as busy as ever. Jack chained his bicycle to the post that only just managed to hold up Patel's garden gate, walked up the weedy garden path, blanketed in a light covering of frost, and stood at the front door for a moment before knocking. The place looked deserted, and the garden as unkempt as ever, though few improvements could in any case be expected before the spring. Bubbles of paint had started to crack open here and there on the red door, a condition to which the freezing temperatures were bound to contribute. There were no lights from inside; Patel might be out, or he might be reading somewhere in the darkened bowels of the place. Jack knocked hard. No Patel. Access to Patel was never easy. He knocked again, and waited. Still no Patel. Perhaps he was out, after all. Jack walked round to the side door and banged on that. He put his ear to the door to see if he could hear anything, though the persistent roar of the traffic not too far behind tended to drown out or obscure every other sound. Yes, Patel was probably out. Jack decided to return to the front door, give it another good bang and return again next day. He was stopped in his tracks by a high-pitched voice behind and to the right of him, though the intrusive noise of the traffic prevented him from making much sense of it.

He turned and saw a frail, elderly woman, wrapped in cardigan and shawl; it was Patel's neighbour, Doris, looking over the hedge that separated them. He approached her, almost slipping on a frosted flagstone.

'Sorry – it's the traffic,' he said.

'I said, you won't get an answer.'

'Out, then, is he?'

'Relative, friend or caller?'

'What? Oh, yes, I see. Er, friend. I'm a friend of Mr Patel's, yes.'

'You don't know, then.'

'I'm sorry?'

'Mr Patel's… Look, you'd better come in for a minute.'

Jack stepped through a gap in the hedge and followed the old woman into her house, which, contrary to his immediate expectations, was light, warm, cheery and clean as a new pin. She closed the door on the traffic and the cold, and they stood in the living room. She and her husband, Ted, were a simple and kindly old couple, and they might have had a thing or two to say about the traffic and the freezing temperatures had there not been something infinitely more pressing to say.

'I'm afraid poor Mr Patel's passed away,' she said. Jack gaped in disbelief. 'Oh, yes, a week or more now.'

'A week exactly,' said a voice from the kitchen.

'My husband, Ted,' she said, introducing him as he joined them; he was stout, clean-shaven and round-faced, and looked as neat as the house itself. 'Yes, and it was Ted who found him, wasn't it Ted?' Ted nodded. 'Wouldn't you like to sit down?' Doris said. Jack remained standing and didn't flinch.

'Well, it was Doris who first saw him,' said Ted.

'Hadn't been well for a long time,' she explained. 'Expect you know that – what with him losing his wife. They were very close, you know. Yes, he had a weak heart, apparently. We used to chat over the hedge from time to time. Quite enjoyed those little chats, and—'

'We hadn't seen much of him recently,' Ted put in. 'And then Doris went out to the garden and she sees him sitting on the bench under the tree. In the freezing cold, mind you.'

'Under the willow tree,' said Doris.

'That's right, and she calls to him—'

'Very quiet, he was.'

'She calls to him, and he didn't move, did he Doris?'

'Well, I thought he was asleep, at first. Well, you would, wouldn't you? I never dreamt—'

'Then you got a bit worried, didn't you? And she calls me.'

'Ted went to see.'

'For all the world as though he was sleeping, you know. But cold he was, cold as ice, poor chap,' said Ted.

'We didn't know what to do – so we called the police, and they came and—'

'A heart attack, they said.'

'Yes, heart,' said Doris.

'But what he was doing in the garden, I don't know,' said Ted. 'Mystery to me.' Ted scratched his head. 'In the middle of winter. But there he was, like taking a nap on a summer's afternoon. Not even a warm coat on. But peaceful. Very peaceful. Strange.'

'You'd like a cup of tea, I'm sure,' said Doris, who hadn't had a visitor in ages.

'Oh, no. Not at all,' said Jack, giving an inappropriate response, having heard very little since the mention of the bench under the willow tree.

'What they'll do with the house, I don't know,' said Ted.

'It's not as though he had anyone to leave it to, is there?'

'Anyway, the police went in and turned things off and then locked it all up.'

The kindly old couple might just as well been talking to themselves or commenting on the state of Doris's rose garden. Jack was under a spell; he felt lost, and presumably looked it.

'You look a bit under the weather. You'll take a cup of tea, won't you?' Jack looked puzzled. 'I said a cup of strong hot tea would do you good.'

'No, I must be going. But thanks all the same. You've been very kind, explaining everything.'

'Came as a bit of a shock, I suppose,' said Ted. 'You must have been a very good friend of Mr Patel's.'

'Yes, that's right. A very good friend.'

'Didn't have many friends, as far as we could tell. Bit of a loner, you know,' Ted added. Jack nodded in response.

Jack managed to drag himself away; it was not because the old couple were insistent upon his lingering, but he could simply have stood there forever, thinking of one thing, staring fixedly at one mental picture in particular. He unlocked his bicycle from the gate and began to ride away. But then he stopped, and returned. He returned and found himself looking down, down at the empty bench under the willow tree in the garden that used to belong to Patel, everything now draped in the darkening shadows of a winter's evening. Had the old couple seen him, they might have thought such behaviour suspicious, or thought him crazed. He rode away again, this time for good. He cycled home, though it was a journey he would never remember having made.

Home, but still shocked and dazed, he began to make his way upstairs, there to stay, and there to open, at last, a bottle of expensive single malt he'd been keeping for a rainy day, for this was, without doubt, a thunderously rainy day.

Before he reached the top of the stairs, he heard a voice behind him. 'Home late, then?' said Sally, cold as ice. She stood looking up at him from the hallway below.

'Patel,' he said, weakly.

'What?' she said, sharply.

'Patel. It's Patel!'

'Of course it is. It's always Patel, isn't it? Or *is* it? Is it really Patel you're talking about?'

'What?'

Without replying, she walked out of the hallway into the living room. Jack descended the stairs and followed her. 'He's dead. Patel's dead.' Sally looked at him as if he were making it up.

'So you can't use him as an excuse any more, then – can you?' she said, with her back to him, pouring herself a drink. Her tone was subdued, almost as though she were addressing herself. But she wouldn't have cared had Jack heard.

But he didn't. He had already turned away to climb the stairs again. It wasn't at all like Sally to disrespect the dead or to pour scorn on someone she hardly knew except by name. But, alive or dead, the very mention of Patel's name was anathema, being a reminder of Jack's assumed infidelity and duplicity. If the poor fellow was no longer in the land of the living, Jack would need to find some other excuse for his clandestine flirtations; though the time was fast approaching, Sally would have said, when no further excuses would be necessary.

Jack lay awake all night on his side of the bed. They still slept together, but this was no euphemism, just a cold, physical fact.

The same picture dominated his thoughts and was the hinge on which all other thoughts swung to and fro relentlessly – Patel sitting alone on the bench under the willow tree, staring at a rundown garden which used to be tended with such loving care by hands that were no more, by someone he used to know and love so deeply, by someone who was far more than his better half. Didn't Patel wonder, as he sat there, how it could possibly have happened – this disintegration of his world, or that part of his world that sustained all the rest? He must have looked around him, unable to find form or substance or sense; a life had disappeared, taking with it everything that had surrounded it. His world was now as cold and bare as that frosty winter day. His heart had been yanked out of him, the heart that was not to be confused with the weak thing that beat grudgingly inside his chest and would itself give up as if in protest and despair.

So now Patel, too, was no more. He who had best remembered his wife was soon to be forgotten. For years, 'Patel and Misbah' might have been a phrase which seemed as inviolate and fixed as a mountain range; and now it meant nothing; just a mere sound. No one now would remember Misbah; and after Jack, Ted and Doris and a handful of others, who would remember Patel? And so it would be with all of all. That was the gigantic flaw in what people called history – because it was what history left out that was important: all those names and all those faces to which the names belonged, and all the hearts that once beat and gave those faces life and enabled eyes to see. There was much more on earth than books could tell, because there was much more on earth than books could ever hold. But it seemed unforgiveable that history should leave out so much, as though it were maintaining a treacherous and ungrateful silence.

Such was the colour and texture of Jack's thoughts that sleepless night. Nor was he neglectful of Alf. Alf and Patel were too good to die in the way they did. Jack took a modicum of comfort in the thought that all men are mortal, if only because it meant that even the likes of Watkins and Davenport could never escape the Grim Reaper. Yes, their turn would come, too, albeit in kinder circumstances, perhaps pampered and cosseted in private beds in private wards in private hospitals, with their spouses and offspring seated around them, shedding tears and holding hands; that seemed unfair. It was unfair, too, that Alf and Patel should have to die before Watkins and Davenport – as though they were gate-crashers in the party of life and were inferior or had less to commend them, and were therefore kicked out before the party had even got underway. That the good die young was not a sentiment that Jack found in any way consoling as he tossed and turned and stared into the darkness. No, Alf in particular should have gone out in style, like a Viking chieftain in a burning longboat, with battle-flags flying, and everyone singing his praises to Wodan and Baldar. Yes, like that – not with a lonely whimper, as though his life had meant nothing. The unfairness was intolerable.

Jack's tossing and turning was also intolerable, which is why Sally was obliged to remove herself downstairs, taking the top quilt with her. He said nothing, pretending not to know, or not to care.

* *

He was about to open the door of the staffroom the following morning when he checked himself, did an about-turn, and made for his classroom instead. Which is where Gladys found him during the mid-morning break; he was sitting at his desk, his head buried in his hands. A sleepless night was now added to his shock over Patel, and he looked decidedly the worse for wear.

'It's about Patel – it's terrible,' said Gladys, tapping him on the shoulder. Jack looked up. 'Davenport's just been in the staffroom,' she said, 'and told us Patel's passed away. I can't believe it!' Her eyes welled up and she fiddled with a paper handkerchief. Jack looked at her. Yes, Gladys was a good sort, and the good sort were in very short supply.

'I know. I went round to his place last night. The neighbours told me. Yes, it's terrible. Look Gladys, I'm very sorry, but I've got a mountain of marking to do.'

'You're not coming to the staffroom today, then?'

'No, I'm staying right here, Gladys.'

'It's just that Davenport said something about a memorial service – for Patel.' Jack just nodded. She left, closing the door gently behind her.

Jack buried his head in his hands again, as though it were weighed down by the picture inside it. What had Patel been doing? Why had he gone out there into the cold and sat there all alone, without even a coat and Nature's indifference? What had he been thinking? And how had it started – the pain? – the pain in his chest that had killed him? Had it been dull or sharp? And had he cried for help? Or had he dozed off and died peacefully in his sleep? Yes, but in that cold? Or was such a sweet death in any case and everywhere quite mythical? He should not have delayed his visit. Had he been determined to die? Might a visit have made a difference? Or was this mythical, too? *And David said to Solomon, his son, Be strong and of good courage: fear not, nor be dismayed: for the Lord God, even my God, will be with thee, nor forsake thee.* 'I find great comfort in words like that,' Patel had said. But obviously, not *that* much comfort. Words had not saved him; and there was an even slimmer chance that Jack would have done so. Had God forsaken him? But Jack would not have done so – if only he had known. Had he not befriended him, advised him, met him in the boiler room? Had he not visited him, not once, but twice? And how was he to know it would be too late that second time?

Jack was tired, alright. And on top of all these diseased thoughts, he was to be observed by Davenport that very afternoon.

* *

'Well, it was a real fiasco,' said Davenport, following the observation. Watkins was listening intently behind his large metallic desk. 'Yes, a complete departure from his lesson schedule.'

'We're all entitled to depart from our schedules, and frequently do,' Watkins remarked.

'Yes, but this was ridiculous. It had nothing to do with history at all – absolutely nothing,' Davenport said, with a dismissive wave of his hand. 'It was supposed to be about Cromwell's Protectorate. But he told them he'd changed his mind and was going to tell them instead about the Shadow People.'

'What's that?' Watkins looked bemused.

'The Shadow People – at least that's what I think he said. Crazy!'

'Extraordinary. And what are they supposed to be these, er… Shadow People, visitors from the next world?' Davenport began to laugh, but he cut himself short, because Watkins was frowning.

'Heaven knows!' said Davenport. 'It was just – well, politics, religion, and I don't know what – just a jumble. But whatever it was, it was as far removed from a history lesson as a history lesson can get.' Davenport was now ready to deliver the *coup de grace*. 'The point is, it couldn't be described as a history lesson at all.'

'It's not as though he hasn't been warned.' Watkins was expressionless, and spoke quietly and slowly in a tone of grim determination. 'It simply won't do. It won't do at all.'

Davenport had a point. Measured against the canons of acceptable practice, Jack had begun his lesson most obscurely and provocatively, losing his audience almost immediately. But it must be said that Davenport had exaggerated things for dramatic effect. Jack had only mentioned the Shadow People in a quick preamble, because he intended to speak, not about them, whoever they were, but about the Digger Movement:

'...yes, Shadow People lack all substance; they're as much committed to the fight against man's inhumanity to man as to the shadows on the wall. No, I'm going to tell you about the Diggers, who believed in the brotherhood of man, because they were in complete contrast to the Shadow People. This is really all about British communism. And I'm not supposed to talk about it. You see, communism is not the evil foreign import they'd like you to believe it is. No, it isn't evil, and it isn't foreign. No, it's the voice, the deep voice of good old British common-sense socialism.' At this, Davenport had twitched in his seat. 'Yes, we need the likes of Diggers nowadays to put some life back into the body politic.' Another twitch. 'The Diggers wanted everyone to be treated with equal respect, equal dignity, and nothing, least of all money, should put one man above or below another. The true basis of this equality is Christian love. And suppose someone says that the Diggers had sentiments that were morally obvious? Well, I say that we should never give up saying the obvious merely because it's obvious. Because if you give up saying the obvious, the danger is that it'll soon stop being obvious. No, we must go on saying things like, "Love they neighbour as thyself." It's rather like praying – because if you give up praying, you'll soon forget how to, and if you forget how to pray, well then the things in which prayer is rooted begin to wither and die, like plants derived of water. If you think the Sermon on the Mount is too obvious to bother quoting, too simple to talk about, too obvious for our oh-so-cultivated minds, then we'll find ourselves on a slippery slope, and there'll be no return from the oblivion that results. Well, so I'm going to talk to you about the Diggers, and then you can go home and tell your mothers and fathers about them, too.' Davenport, seated at the back of the classroom, was by now twitching so much that he was in imminent danger of contracting a permanent condition. He managed to hold on for most of the lesson, and then he decided he had heard more than enough and, without waiting until the very end, made a swift exit, heading for Watkins's office; there was not a moment to lose.

No, judged by the canons of acceptable practice, this was not the sort of stuff to mere sixteen-year-olds, who had never heard about the Sermon on the Mount, let alone knew what it was about. Jack sounded more like a preacher than a history teacher, and a confused one at that; all that stuff about the Shadow People sounded like something from a sci-fi comic. True, he did go on to talk about the Diggers, even mentioning some dates and names, but such scraps of history were obscured because they were mingled with what Davenport could only describe as political claptrap. It was natural, therefore, that Davenport should wonder whether Jack's political tirade was meant as much for himself as for the class. He received the clear impression that Jack was being deliberately provocative and willingly charging over a precipice like a lemming. Well, whatever his intentions, he had bungled his so-called history lesson, and Davenport would waste no time saying so. Having gathered what he considered to be overwhelming evidence for the prosecution, he was more than ready to state his case.

Jack seemed to have reached the conclusion that it was no longer possible to acknowledge something vital in one half of himself and deny it in the other; no longer possible to lay claim to something deep within himself while at the same time behaving as though it didn't really matter. Something had clicked, some trigger had been pulled, some catch released, some force unleashed. The canons of acceptable practice were no longer acceptable, and he would not pretend otherwise. He might be right, he might be wrong; but it was at last enough that he *felt* he was right. As Alf had so graphically put it: nobody should give up the ghost before giving the Shadow People a kick in their shadowy balls. And these were not words that Jack had made up and attributed to him, but Alf's very own. Not that Alf had actually managed to kick anybody anywhere; on the contrary, they had kicked him, and had done a lasting job of it, too. Alf would no doubt have smiled to hear Jack speak as he did about the Diggers, and he would have relished Davenport's twitches – presumably because it was pleasing to witness the discomfort of the ungodly.

Jack's muddled lesson had been preceded by a couple of pints in The King's Head at lunchtime. He had been tempted to ask Gladys to join him, but he had thought better of it. But a spot of lunchtime drinking perhaps explains why it had been quite congenial to ever-so-slightly wobble through the insane asylum that afternoon; why even the inmates seemed rather pleasant at times, their abnormalities almost benign; and why Davenport, sitting right at the back of the classroom, seemed so very remote and just about as important as the flaking paint on Patel's red front door. But the beer, though pleasant and enhancing, had not been the driving force that day. 'You've got to fight them, Jack,' Alf had said. He never actually got round to saying who exactly should be fought, or how they should be fought; and Jack had never asked, for such questions hadn't seemed at all necessary. They didn't seem necessary now, either. It was hard to grow up, Jack reflected as he cycled home, and harder still to stay grown up – but the process seemed to be getting easier.

Anyhow, Jack was certainly feeling a freer man, refreshed and invigorated. He might even say as much to Sally. For perhaps it was high time they talked: there was some explaining to do; and there were fences to be mended, and axes to be buried, some bridges to be built. Llewellyn Jones had once quoted from the *Mabinogion*, ' A vo ben bid bont' – *He who leads must be a bridge.* Jack wanted to do some leading, having been led long enough. Yes, he would try talking to Sally, and maybe they could both look forward to better times. The way things were going, which was the way he felt they had to go, his job might soon be on the line. But it didn't matter – they'd be able to work something out, together. He would tell her about Patel – in particular about the bench under the willow tree. They would talk about the future, a better future, and plan it all out. Yes, that's right, he would talk to her. Well, *perhaps* he would talk to her – he would see.

15

Disintegration and New Birth

Cycling home that Friday evening was unusually heavy going although the short respite of the weekend was in view; but then, the atmosphere at home was relentlessly grim, divesting the weekend of all claim to restful retreat; the old illusions that had persistently enveloped weekends were finally relegated to the nursery of naive suppositions. And then, as he pushed the reluctant pedals forward, he remembered that he had neglected to make his weekly pilgrimage to 92 Cutters Way. It had been a long time since he'd missed a visit, and then only because, on one occasion, he'd been laid up with influenza, and, on another, because he'd been kept in hospital overnight. His mother would never contact him to enquire why he hadn't called in; she would simply wait until the next visit, and complain then; and her complaints were made indirectly, by grumbling about real or imagined expressions of disloyalty, and about the trials of loneliness.

The left fork in the road ahead would take him to Cutters Way; all he had to do was follow it. He took the right fork instead, and cycled homeward, in anticipation of the soothing sounds of Elizabethan lutes and viols.

He arrived to find the house empty, and, since this was not unusual, thought little of it. As the hours passed with no sign of either Sally or Pete, he began to look here and there for an explanation. He eventually found it in the kitchen. The note was nothing if not succinct:

I have gone away. I need to think things through. Peter is with me. DO NOT try to follow us – Sally.

The capitals said it all. She didn't say where she's gone; Jack presumed it was to her mother's, though that would entail an improbable daily commute for them both; it was more likely that they'd gone to stay with one of her former schoolfriends who was herself a happy divorcee. The note made it all sound a temporary departure; but temporary or not,

Jack felt strong enough to leave well alone. Things would eventually work out – or not.

Sally had thought the note rather clumsy and amateur, as though it lacked sufficient bite or dramatic effect. She had wondered what to write. At first it hadn't occurred to her to write anything at all, perhaps because she thought him undeserving of any communication whatsoever. But then, he might think she'd been kidnapped and feel obliged to report her missing, and then the police would be involved and her whereabouts traced – and that would spoil everything by making it farcical; Sally was an intelligent and determined no-nonsense woman; so there could be nothing farcical about the life-changing decisions she made. In fact, it was Liz, Sally's old schoolfriend, who had suggested the note in the first place; 'If I were you, I'd make it simple and straight, nothing fancy,' she'd said. Sally had confided in her from the start, a confidence that Liz had much appreciated; Liz was more than happy to offer advice; after all, it came from one well-versed in such matters, for Liz had liberated herself from the shackles of an unhappy alliance – though not, it must be said, without considerable struggle, not to say pain; but there is no gain without pain, and Liz was delighted to tell all and sundry, in fact anyone at all with sufficient stamina to listen, that her gains far outweighed her losses. She considered herself, then, free from the yoke, and, in an evangelical spirit, felt bound to help others who had fallen into marital ruts from which they could with a little extra help to extricate themselves. Sally considered herself fortunate to have kept in touch with her, and gave her Best Friend status. Their friendship was further cemented by the fact that Jack and Liz had taken an instant dislike to each other from their first meeting, Jack thinking her irresponsible and woolly-minded; Liz thinking him too introvert and distant, the kind who enjoy their own company – the sort who had no right tying the knot in the first place. Liz had plenty of room to spare for Sally and Peter, and over the last couple of weeks they had moved some of the more essential clothing, study materials and other bits and pieces to Liz's place, so that only the exact time of departure and the question of the note remained to be sorted. Sally's stay was not meant to be permanent; anything more than a temporary separation from Jack would necessitate Sally finding a place of her own.

For all her posturing as a no-nonsense woman who knows her own mind, Sally relied very heavily on Liz, almost holding her up as a model of liberated woman. Such reliance suggested uncertainty. In fact, the physical act of leaving Jack seemed very different from what it had been in the planning, and this was mirrored in an inconsistency of attitude and design: was she content merely with giving him some shock treatment, to be followed by reconciliation – or did she intend a separation ending in divorce? Such ambivalence, though not at all uncommon, is almost always confusing and unwelcome. Even in the planning stage, she had thought now this, now that. She had thought of having it out with Jack and giving herself an unforgettable send-off. Liz had advised against it, for Peter's sake – suggesting that it was better to make the break without prior warning and then just await developments, and further advising that she should take Peter with her to dramatise the event to the fullest possible extent. It had not occurred to Sally to question whether Liz was the best source of advice on this or any other related matter. She simply agreed with Liz that something dramatic should be done, that things could not possibly be left as they were. Peter had always been closer to Sally than to Jack, a fact Jack had mildly resented but could, despite his best efforts, do little about; and in more recent years father and son had grown steadily further apart, which perhaps explains why, after the matter had been repeatedly explained, Peter fell into line and went along with his mother's strategy. For all that, Sally felt deep down that the wisdom of the entire venture was not so easily or so completely demonstrable. But leave she did, and the die was cast. To be in two minds was one thing. To be in no mind at all – well, that was just not on.

In the event, the intended shock fizzled out and was much milder than either Sally or Liz might have hoped. Jack didn't even resort to choice expletives on reading the note, much less to tears. Neither did he immediately rush about the house desperately looking for evidence that would confirm the authenticity of the note; confirmation was conducted calmly; true, his heart did pound inside his chest as he quietly checked the wardrobes, though whether this was anger or anxiety or a mixture of the two is impossible to say. The wardrobes were lighter, but far from empty, and some books and a school backpack were missing from Pete's room; but this was all the confirmation he sought or needed. He returned to the living room, grabbed a bottle of single malt, poured himself a drink, sat down, got up and sat down again, his heart still pounding. One quick neat drink later, he made a grab for his phone; he could just phone round Sally's friends and… but he put his phone back into his pocket and left it there. He paced about a bit, sat down again, and poured himself another drink. No, this was something he could and would manage, without getting into any fluster. Because it was no use – these attempts to try and convince himself that he was devastated just wouldn't work. Alf's question, 'Are you afraid of losing your wife?' had lost the poignancy it once had; it was now more on a par with, 'Are you afraid of losing your passport?' Losing your passport was certainly an inconvenience, and in some circumstances it might be a serious one; but it was an experience you should and could survive. No, there was no fire in Alf's question now, no sharp ends that ripped the flesh of his emotions – and to think that he'd once hated Alf for asking that very question! Yes, now it felt different – and it wasn't simply the effect of the single malt, either. Not so long ago, he might have collapsed in an emotional turmoil to receive a note like that. But if Sally, and Pete for that matter, felt it was time to go, if it was what they really wanted, if they were better off for it, then so be it, and who was *he* to complain? The complaints he'd made for years on end had gone unheeded. Why should he be listened to now? As for living alone – well, many people had to live alone and just get on with it; poor Patel had had to manage alone, and with the knowledge that his wife had suffered miserably; the poor woman had passed on without having brought children into the world to lighten her passing, or to console Patel in the long hours of his loneliness, which then loomed ahead like a dark, unforgiving cloud. By contrast, Sally and Pete were alive and well, and they wanted to dump him; not to mention the fact that Sally had a good job with prospects and was hardly wanting materially; and she was happy in her job while Jack had never been in his. Jack surprised himself with this line of thinking, which was much more positive than he would have anticipated. And because thinking and feeling are ideal bedfellows, he began to feel stronger than he would ever have expected to feel. Yes, all in all, he was taking things very well. Very well indeed.

Not all *that* well. He spent the entire weekend on a diet of single malt. Yet, despite this, the clarity of his thinking was unimpaired; on the contrary, his ability to think, to sense, to feel, was if anything heightened. There were bouts of anger alternating with periods of quiet acceptance and a strong desire to let things ride. The split should have happened years ago. Precious lives had been tied down to nothing, through sheer force of habit, respect for social expectation, and false personal expectation, as though they had had a thousand lives to live, and nine hundred and ninety-nine of them to go. As he moved from room to room he sensed the sameness of every day they'd spent in them, a sameness that had been confused with comfort and security and fulfilment; false security, and false comfort, like the familiarity of an old fairy tale that comforts a child in the dark and affords an unjustifiable degree of complacency in the face of the unknown. If sameness and familiarity were in any sense good, it was also possible to have too much of a good thing. When sameness begins to cloy, one might as well be insensate. What was the point in living many days if one day were indistinguishable from the next, or distinguishable only by misadventure and catastrophe? Life, the fact that they had been living at all, had been noticeable only when a leak occurred in the plumbing, or when the washing machine refused to work, or when they were waiting for the all-clear following an X-ray. If life was a machine, it could only be appreciated when it began to fold up. And when Pete came along, yet another sameness had set in, birth, like, death, being little more than a nine-day wonder. Alf had been right: treadmillers just trod the mill to maintain the sameness; and the sameness was punishing. Sameness could not allow discovery. Predictability was the antithesis of discovery. When life disallowed discovery, it was as good as over.

One of Jack's persistent mutterings was the phrase 'Too late', which he repeated now with vigour, now with quiet resignation. He and Sally had never been much good at talking, and attempts to talk through important issues seemed to leave each of them feeling that the real nuts and bolts hadn't been addressed and never could be. No, it was in any case too late for talking. And there were too many disappointed hopes and dreams, too many thwarted expectations, the dictum 'Better late than never' had no application. It was just too late for mending – like mending a garment that was threadbare and which should have been discarded at the outset. Such thoughts only served to confirm Jack's conviction, already formed, that any beauty in the world belonged to only to Nature and the creative arts, not to personal relationships.

If, at bottom, Sally's state of mind was muddled by uncertainties, Jack's mind fared no better. It was a tortuous weekend, Jack's mood shuttling restlessly from anger to benevolence and back again, and there was really no telling where, if at all, it would come to rest. Exhausted and nerve-racked and addled with an uncustomary overdose of whisky, he absented himself from school on Monday and Tuesday.

Gladys was the first to notice his changed appearance on Wednesday morning, his beard untrimmed, his hair surprisingly long and unkempt, his shirt collar and cuffs a little worse for wear and his tie a little askew; but whatever she saw, she kept to herself. Watkins intended to speak to Jack after school that Friday afternoon. He had been given the green light by an Extraordinary Meeting of the school governors, during which Harris Senior had been most outspoken in his advocacy and defence of educational standards, and his denunciation of Loony-Left teachers – of whom he considered Jack Barker an outstanding example.

But Jack's execution was to be preceded, on Thursday morning, by a short memorial service for Zanjik Patel. Patel's demise was now generally known by staff and pupils alike, and he was to be afforded in death an honour generally reserved for all those who are no longer in a position to inflict injury upon the living. Gladys reminded Jack of the service, to which reminder Jack responded by quoting a line of an obscure poet: *The living, some wise man has said, delight in speaking of the dead.* Morning assemblies, in particular those that sought to thank the Christian God for all things bright and beautiful and to invoke His assistance in what was further needful, were now things of the past, though not yet a past dim and distant. But it was still customary for assemblies of the whole school, like parliamentary sittings of The Whole House, to be organised for something eventful, like the acquisition of a new playing field, or a high rating from the inspectorate, or a death. It was only a minor organisational hassle, and a small price to pay for what both Watkins and Davenport agreed was an appropriate expression of regard, an indication of competent and compassionate leadership, and therefore excellent PR.

* *

All the staff, both teaching and ancillary, were gathered in the hall. Watkins climbed the steps onto the podium and stood there alone, waiting for complete silence. Pupils were seated in rows below him, while teachers stood against the walls. Davenport stood below and slightly to the right of the podium. Watkins nodded down to Davenport, Davenport nodded left and right to teachers, who in turn gave threatening looks to any lingering whisperers and shufflers in the ranks. Jack, still looking the worse for wear, stood next to Gladys, looking fixedly at Watkins; Jack looked pale and his face more deeply lined, and his eyes were rather menacing – a countenance that might easily have been mistaken for an expression of normal early-morning offishness. Davenport finally nodded back up to Watkins, who cleared his throat in his customary manner and began. He had mentally rehearsed his speech several times, but he spoke slowly, as though he were putting it together on the spot and weighing the import of every word. After the expected eulogy to the dearly departed, his tone would become more stentorian, for he planned to extol the high academic standards to which he and, he sincerely hoped, everyone else was committed. But first, the eulogy.

'Once again,' and here he cleared his throat a second time, 'once again, we gather together on a solemn occasion. It falls to me to announce that Mr Zanjik Patel, who taught mathematics at this school for a considerable number of years, who started teaching here long before the school reached its present size and complexity, has passed away. I remember very well the day I myself started at Morley Comprehensive, as a teacher myself, when Mr Patel was kind enough to take me under his wing. He was indeed in many ways my mentor. I admired above all his industry and dedication, his kindness and selflessness. Yes, it is hard to accept the departure of a valued member of staff, and one who still had years of valuable service to give, and someone who has consistently given so much of himself in the interests of others, who has dedicated his portion to the education of the young…'

Gladys noticed that Jack was arching his back; at any rate, he seemed a bit restless. She knew only too well how boring and long-winded Watkins could be, and right now he was particularly slow in his delivery; but, after all, he was doing his best to sing Patel's praises; she wished Jack would keep still, and she felt slightly annoyed.

'…someone who has always been at pains to give of his best in the challenging but essential business of educating young people who will one day replace us and carry the flag of civilisation onward and upward to even greater heights of accomplishment. Yes, we…' he cleared his throat again, for now he was in his stride and was preparing for a memorable crescendo of self-congratulation, '…we mourn his loss, and—'

'Do we indeed?!' Jack shouted. The question, entirely ironic, broke the air like a streak of lightning and stopped Watkins dead in his tracks. But so unexpected was it, and so shocking, that Watkins repeated himself, thinking perhaps that what he heard was not in fact what it sounded – perhaps a loud cough or splutter from the ranks. Everyone else, of course, knew different.

'…we mourn his loss—'

'I think not!'

This time Watkins could not allow himself the luxury of doubt. Gladys almost swooned. Jack stepped out of the line of pedagogues, approached the podium and stood in front of Davenport, who was sufficiently beside himself to take a step or two backwards out of the way. So traumatic was the event that not so much as a giggle could be heard from the serried ranks of pupils, not so much as a shuffle of feet, not even the faintest whisper from the most boisterous and unmanageable of boys or the most capricious of girls. The teaching staff were likewise stunned into silence. So, Fate, Destiny, Providence or his God, had at last given Jack his stage, his audience and his cue.

'Yes, that's right. I challenge you, Watkins. Oh, you, too, Davenport,' he added, looking quickly over his shoulder. 'You are up there, Watkins. Patel is down, and will stay down. He can't speak for himself, but, then, I believe he never could. Not like you. No, you can speak for yourself, alright. Patel was gentle. He just didn't have it in him to make speeches – about anything, and least of all himself. He depended on the goodwill and support of others – "others" means you, too, Watkins, and lesser evils like him,' he gestured derisively with his hand towards Davenport. 'He trusted you, and look where it got him, poor little bastard. Did you ever show the kindness to him that you said he showed to you? No, fat chance! No, you can't say you mourn his loss – I won't let you get away with that, though I daresay you'll get away with everything else. No, to mourn you must love and respect. You had neither love nor respect for Zanjik Patel. And do you know how he died?' Jack turned round to the pupils and staff. 'I'll tell you how he died. He died as he lived, and he lived as he taught in this place – alone, unwanted, neglected! Oh, Patel's not alone in that. In fact, there are many uglier lives and deaths than his. But a school is no place for hypocrisy, not if you really care about education.' He turned to Watkins again. 'All that stuff about supportiveness! What does it mean? What on earth can you possibly mean when you talk about taking civilisation to even greater heights? I won't have it, Watkins. I won't have cant and hypocrisy. Not here – not here, of all places!'

Jack stormed towards the exit, turning round at the door. 'You're a Shadow Man, Watkins – and all *you* who are taken in by him.' He paused for just a moment, eyeing the assembly accusingly, before walking out briskly.

It was just then, as if the audience had been given its cue, that the giggling, the whispering, the shuffling, began. Davenport rushed up to Watkins, who whispered something in his ear, and then rushed down again to restore order. It was the longest minute in Watkins's life, but order was indeed restored, at least sufficiently for Watkins to say that Mr Barker's outburst was quite understandable given that he had been such a close friend of poor Mr Patel. He hastened to add that it was, however, unfortunate that the graceful solemnity of the memorial service should have in any way been marred by unwarranted expressions of regret or bitterness; but Watkins reminded everyone that the expression of grief was a house of many mansions in that it took many forms, and that appropriate allowances must therefore be made. He attempted to finish on the kind of crescendo he had intended:

'For all that, I should like to take this opportunity to applaud the school, the staff, and the pupils, for their dedication and combined commitment to a better future in a challenging but better world. Permit me to say that the ship is on course, and that the captain and first mate are at the helm, forever conscious of the need to steer our vessel through the storms that can be expected to assail it from time to time...'

After which, the school song, entitled 'Towards the Light', was sung with as much gusto as could be managed.

Shaken but not stirred, Watkins had gone on for as long as he felt strictly necessary; for the so-called memorial service had now become an exercise in damage limitation. He excelled himself, demonstrating his qualities of leadership and his vision as educationalist. He had, in his own estimation and to the admiration of others, not least Davenport, managed to turn things round. He could not, of course, prevent the subsequent talk, the giggles and the whispers in corridors; but he could set all that in a more favourable light. The man was a rock and a shining example to all. He even began to feel that he owed Jack Barker a favour, though it was a debt he never intended to repay. Jack had also done him the favour of irreversibly ejecting himself from Morley Comprehensive. If Watkins had managed to set the whole incident in a more favourable light, it was also possible to set it in a much less favourable one. The incident was therefore like an object that could appear differently depending on the way one turned it – now this way, now that. In its worse light, it was a flagrant challenge to the integrity and authority both of Watkins himself and of Davenport, and, as such, was a rejection of the very ethos of Morley Comprehensive and of every other educational establishment worthy of the name – a stark denial of its educational standards, aims and direction. In these terms, Jack was simply refusing to be a teacher! What was more, his refusal had been made in front of the whole school, so what better corroborating evidence could there be?

Even Gladys had more or less regained her composure by the time Watkins finally descended the podium and walk with strident dignity out of the hall. Jack might be upset, but an outburst like that was... well, it was... Gladys struggled to find the right word inside her head, and settled for 'wrong' instead. Jack was obviously not himself. She liked him; she had *always* liked him; but he had gone way too far, and it was really hard to see how he could be forgiven. In front of the whole school, too! Harper and Llewellyn Jones agreed with Gladys. Harper felt a sneaky admiration for him, but didn't let on, for one never knew who might tell who what, and it would never do to risk implication by association; besides, for Harper, rebelliousness was entirely out of character, and it was in any case too late and much too dangerous to change. As for Llewellyn Jones, he continued to thank his lucky stars that his skeleton still remained securely inside the cupboard; any sympathy he might show for his colleague would at best be muted.

*   *

Jack grabbed his bike and cycled straight home after his outburst, and there was no going back. Whatever qualms he might still have had, the die was well and truly cast now, and there was no undoing what had been done. It was a bitterly cold day, but the sun was shining, the air was clear, and it was curiously satisfying to be going home again when the day had hardly begun.

He found himself in the living room again, sitting in his armchair, with a glass of whisky – everything so contrary to all the mornings of a lifetime. It was pleasant to sit there quietly, listening to the calming blend of lute and viol. But in this very pleasant state there came to him an intriguing, not to say disturbing, thought.

When he had told Gladys about Alf and the rabbit, he had lied, but not just because the episode had been an event in his own life and not in Alf's. He'd lied about the gun, too. He told her the gun had been sold. The shotgun was made so that the stock could be easily unclipped from the barrels. After the incident with the rabbit, he returned home and disassembled the gun, putting the two parts, together with the remaining cartridges, in a canvas bag, and he tied the bag round tightly with thick string. He'd hidden the bag in his room, in the house he then occupied with his mother. It lay hidden and undiscovered, for his mother hadn't taken the slightest interest in his belongings and was unlikely to find it; the pride she had taken in her home seemed to stop short of her son and his small domain. But

P. R. BROWN

when he'd left home, he'd hidden the bag in the attic of his mother's house, finally re-housing it in the loft of his own, dusty but otherwise intact, as were, he presumed, its contents.

Watkins and Davenport would meet next morning in Watkins's office, as they invariably did first thing on Friday mornings, to review the week that had passed and preview the week ahead. They would be comfortably settled, no doubt looking forward to a comfortable weekend – Watkins behind his large metallic desk, Davenport seated obsequiously before him, like a novice before a Father Abbot. Without doubt, they would have far more to discuss this week than ever before, Jack's outrageous behaviour and thoroughly blighted career being the principal topic of conversation.

I could do it, Jack thought to himself. He could reassemble the gun, walk indifferently into the school building, with the gun hidden beneath his coat, casually enter Watkins's office and blow them both to Kingdom Come, and so deprive them of the last laugh. The world would be rid of them. So quick. So simple. And Jack? Jack had long decided that he himself had nothing to lose.

No. No, that was not at all possible. But he could at least fire into the metallic desk, or into the ceiling. No, that was not possible. Or it might be enough just to point the gun at them. But that was not an option, either. The gun need not even be loaded. No matter, it was still not an option. Perhaps that would be enough to shock them into a new and better understanding. Yes, and pigs might fly.

When darkness fell that evening, Jack stood on the stone bridge that spanned the river that ran through an outlying village. He held the dusty canvas bag under his arm; looking carefully left and right, he opened the bag and emptied half its contents over the bridge into the river where he believed it was deepest; then he walked to the other side of the bridge and emptied the second half. He was glad; it was long overdue.

*   *

Next morning, presumably just as Watkins and Davenport were having their weekly meeting, Jack walked into his garden. It was sunny again.

Spring was too far off, but then he noticed some buds on the garden hedge, some of which were already beginning to open, as though spring had decided to do an early reconnaissance before taking the plunge. Winter follows autumn, but spring follows winter, the faithful ebb and flow of darkness and light, of light and darkness. There would always be a Watkins, and always a Davenport. But always a Patel, too; and, above all, always an Alf. Besides, Watkins and Davenport and people like them, were not the worst of the worst, not the lowest of the low. Their foolishness ranked far about their capacity to do wrong; their ignorance dwarfed their malice. In any case, what could not be cured amongst men like that had to be endured. Jack contented himself with the conviction that he didn't have it in him to kill a rabbit with impunity, let alone a man, not even the semblance of a man, not even a Shadow Man. And as for shock-treatment, no shock could cure the Shadow People – at least, the shock had to come from the inside, not imposed externally. Yes, but was it right that Alf should be ignored, that the gentle Patel should be neglected, while Watkins and Davenport enjoyed respect and admiration for their cant and hypocrisy? But then, was it so bad to be ignored and neglected by the society of the unwise? After all, the world was not, and never had been, ready for wisdom, and even those who were judges amongst us were not yet so wise. If Alf was a model of beauty, it was beauty of a kind that had perforce to be appreciated at a distance.

Jack refused to chide himself for entertaining such thoughts about the gun, because he had known at once that the options he had considered were unreal. They could never be real, because they were forbidden by the Spiral of Consciousness, which, if it meant anything at all, implied sensitivity at the highest level, a degree of humanity which outlawed any action that compromised the dignity, not to say sanctity, of human life.

Jack took a deep breath and found the air invigorating. An early spring was unquestionably on the horizon, and it was good. The beauty of Nature was something to look forward to. Jacob would be looking forward to it. Alf and Patel could not.

But as he enjoyed the prospect of Nature's wonders, it struck him that the beauty of Nature was not the only beauty, nor was it the most significant. He had been wrong to deny the beauty of man; for the beauty in man was precisely his capacity to recognise it, and to recognise it not simply in Nature but in humankind. Was not love the recognition of beauty in another? Had he not loved Alf and Patel for what he found in them? Was not the love of one person for another the recognition of beauty? But the love which flowed from the recognition of beauty was unconditional; it did not depend for its existence and continuance on its being reciprocated. *The beauty in man is his capacity to recognise it*, at once became his mantra. And was not this capacity what the Spiral of Consciousness was all about? The greater the capacity, the further the upward spiral would soar; yes, that was it: the Spiral of Consciousness is an infinite capacity to recognise beauty in another; when you recognised the beauty of man you also acknowledged his dignity, and then you could not tolerate any violation of that dignity. Slavery, for example, was anathema to the Spiral of Consciousness; it was an absence of the capacity to recognise the beauty of man, and therefore it was a violation of his dignity, of his essential worth. It was the difference between treating people as you wished to be treated yourself, and treating them as though they were saleable or marketable commodities, something lesser than yourself.

Jack felt he understood Alf better now, and understood better why he had to take Patel's side and not that of Watkins or Davenport. He understood better the differences between these people. Alf, one might say, had softened Jack's 'Weltbild'. For the lines of the ancient Buddhist poem now required more generous reading. True, *'Friends who seek naught are scarce today'*. But, though scarce, they did exist; the trick was to recognise them if and when they ever crossed your path – to recognise the beauty within them. The poem enjoined us to *'Fare lonely as rhinoceros'*; but Jack was destined to fare lonely; there was really no choice in the matter, for that is what the Spiral of Consciousness entailed – a narrow and lonely path, one which was not given to all to walk, and one which required courage; but it was on this path that one was likely to encounter like-minded people.

He breathed deeply once again, relishing even more the promise of spring.

16
Full Circle

In the fullness of time, further changes were brought about in the staffing of Morley Comprehensive, with the skill that one might expect from leadership at its very best. The proverbial gun was not applied to proverbial heads, but nothing was done to discourage the departure of both proven and perceived stick-in-the-muds, and every facility was afforded to those who believed they had reached the end of their tethers; and to this extent, the concept Teacher Support was given a further and unflattering twist. Watkins informed the governors that 'new blood' was required, at which point Davenport nodded in unambiguous approval; the 'transfusion' he had in mind required that 'dead wood should be cut away', for then and only then could he pursue his flight 'onwards and upwards' to even higher standards of academic accomplishment, and this astonishing cocktail of metaphors seemed not to trouble him in the least. The attempt to achieve such standards might well entail hitherto undreamt of thresholds of stress for teachers and pupils alike, but such standards were designed to secure a better future in a better world. Such talk was so habitual and conducted with such forceful determination that it occurred to no one to question the ideas that underpinned it; no one, for example, saw fit to ask for a clarification of 'better'; but it was stressed that should some pupils, or for that matter teachers, fall by the wayside, it must be considered by all and sundry to be a perfectly acceptable hazard, even by those who fell headlong into the Slough of Despond. (The time was not far off when even Watkins himself would be showing unhealthy signs of stress, and when those who pointed this out comforted themselves with the thought that Davenport was waiting reliably in the wings.)

Within weeks of Jack's outburst in the memorial service for Patel, Gladys was offered early retirement, and took it. Davenport joked to Watkins that she could spend her time more profitably tending to her vegetable garden; Watkins kept a straight face, as proof of his authority, but enjoyed the jibe behind Davenport's back. It was not that Gladys was an ardent opponent of change and upward flight, but neither was she a keen advocate; besides, as an old bird, her flight could hardly be expected to be steep and sustainable. The truth is, Gladys had for a long time reserved her enthusiasm for her vegetable patch, but her limitations hadn't been so noticeable, or hadn't seemed so important, until Jack's departure, when she found herself next in the line of fire. Gladys's early retirement might well have had something to do with her little visits to Jack's classroom; these and the rapport that seemed to exist between them had not gone unnoticed; and Davenport's observations and impressions had, of course, been duly conveyed to the man behind the large metallic desk. Gladys, however, saw nothing of Jack since his outburst and was in complete ignorance as to his whereabouts or his state of health.

She spent part of her retirement tending her vegetable garden at appropriate times of the year, and, when indoors, watched old movies on her television; or played Patience at the kitchen table. Playing Patience gave her time to think of the past; she had a sneaking admiration for Jack, entertaining fond memories of him which grew fonder as time passed. Jack had had, she thought, a kind of courage; perhaps the kind of courage that is gradually acquired over time, a kind of 'creeping courage', she called it; not the kind that is a quick flash of bravado, or the kind of false courage that alcohol can produce and which is regretted as soon as sobriety kicks in. Yes, it was hard to make much sense of it all, but there was something admirable in it, though it was difficult to articulate precisely what.

Though younger than Gladys, Llewellyn Jones was also considered to be a dead weight on the nimble feet of progress. Yet he was lively enough and his teaching was unimpeachable, and, miraculously, he was never caught on the act of imbibing the devil's brew. Just as it seemed that Morley Comprehensive would be stuck with him for another decade, he announced that he would give up teaching to look after his wife full-time. A marked deterioration in his wife's condition was therefore good news for Watkins and the governors, who were now relieved of the obligation to find something that would either blacken his name for all posterity, or to pave the way for approaches on the subject of early retirement. Llewellyn Jones therefore departed Morley Comprehensive, his reputation untarnished, his hair prematurely white, and his nerves quite beyond repair.

Next for consideration was Harper, who had surprised everyone, not merely by dramatically changing his daily lunch from egg to pilchard sandwiches, but by actually announcing, in one of Watkins's so-called Progress Seminars, that he had been in education all his life but was only now beginning to question its purpose. Now, there were doubts, and there were doubts; but this was definitely one doubt that Watkins, as supreme advocate of unlimited and unstoppable flight, could not allow, for it smacked too much of possible negativity; and that would not be at all consistent with the 'positive thrust onward and upward' that Watkins now emphasised in this and similar swashbuckling phrases. Davenport even suggested, in camera with Watkins, that Harper's negativity was quite possibly linked to an incipient senility which might soon impair Harper's ability to teach at all. Watkins pretended to take this seriously, and he agreed that meanwhile Harper had developed 'an attitude problem' that might easily affect the morale of the increasingly youthful staff. Harper began to be frozen out by Watkins and Davenport whenever they addressed the staff collectively at meetings. To pierce his flesh even more effectively, Watkins suddenly called him into his office and had a few dry words with him, after which Harper was happy to confine his attentions to his recent preference for pilchard sandwiches, making no further statements about the purpose of education that could possibly be construed as an incitement to rebellion. But Harper very quickly became something of a curiosity; and because he was actively treated as one, he began to feel like one, until, when early retirement was at last mooted, it seemed to him an inevitable, not to say desirable, conclusion to a long and spectacularly uneventful career. He retired, but had little to retire to, and died almost a year to the day.

As for Jacob, like many of the plants he had tended, he would gradually go to seed. To keep active and useful, he would take the dogs of the local elderly out for walks; but, despite the fact that he had hardly two pennies to rub together, he would flatly refuse to take payment for this service. 'Not everything has a price,' he would mutter, as he led the dogs out of the garden gates; but, given his frailty, he would not lead them far, and it would become questionable as to who was leading who.

Apart from the dogs, there was nothing and no one in his life. Such was his loneliness that every evening he would talk to the dead, not merely because he found them a more receptive audience than the living, but because he owed them his solicitude, feeling that he had not bestowed sufficient attention on them while they lived; and because, quite simply, he missed them so deeply. He continued to speak to the dead until he himself joined them, when his communication could at last be reciprocated.

Jack, of course, had not darkened the doors of Morley Comprehensive since his outburst. Sally returned to the house a week later, only to pick up some odds and ends; she found the house empty, and a note in the living room even more succinct than her own. Eventually, she and Peter would return for good, encouraged by the near-certain conviction of finding the house permanently empty. Sally would focus a large proportion of her energy on Peter's future. She would not find it too hard to wean him away from his fascination with philosophy and what she considered to be other juvenile indulgences. She would convince him that advertising and marketing were the way to go, and that is the way he went, and in a short space of time Peter would be infinitely more concerned about market downturns and spiralling prices than his father was in the so-called Spiral of Consciousness.

If Jack was no more than a ghost in the corridors of Morley Comprehensive, his subject was hardly much more in evidence. History had been 'absorbed', Davenport's term, under the all-encompassing title General Social Studies, and this category was regarded by staff and students alike as a soft-option catch-all for anything and everything that did not address the infinitely more relevant domains of the business of science and the science of business.

To Alan Sedley, Jack's replacement, fell the task of teaching General Social Studies. Sedley was tall, slim and wore a neat moustache under an aquiline nose; his thin, long, sharp facial features gave him an aura of intelligence, which was not belied by his conversation, which proved incisive and inquiring. He had just moved into Morley with his young wife, and they were expecting their first child. For the Sedleys, the future seemed very promising. They had discussed things fully together, or as fully as was needful, and it had been decided that Anna Sedley would try to pick up the threads of a career in commercial law once the baby was old enough to be child-minded; she was fluent in Spanish, for her mother was Spanish, and she fully intended to make use of her education and talents in an ever-expanding business environment. All they had to do was to steer a steady course.

*   *

It was early Monday morning, and Harper had only one week left to go. He had managed to befriend Sedley, and Sedley had taken to him despite, or perhaps in view of, the quiet but unmistakeable derision in which he was held by the younger elements in the staffroom. Sedley was a champion of the underdog, and this trait in his character was not always one that Anna readily understood or approved of.

Harper and Sedley stood together in the staffroom, helping themselves to coffee from a pot placed on the table next to the window. As Sedley waited his turn, he glanced out of the window. He saw a figure standing alone down at the gate. It was hard to make out, and the early morning haze did nothing to improve visibility. It wasn't a pupil – that was fairly certain; in any case, it would be another thirty minutes at least before the first lot started to file reluctantly through the gate. The mist cleared a little, and, as far as Sedley could tell, the fellow was some kind of down-and-out. As he strained to see, the figure turned a little in his direction. Sedley thought that the fellow was bearded, with a scruffy haversack or bag on the ground at his side. Sedley turned to Harper.

'Who's that?'

'Hm?' said Harper, unconcerned and half asleep.

'There. Down there by the gate.'

'Dunno.' Harper was leaving at the end of the week, and was interested in nothing save the freedom that dangled in vague prospect before him.

Sedley poured himself a coffee, and when he looked out of the window again, the figure had disappeared, like a spectre in the mist.

~ ~ ~ ~ ~

ND - #0277 - 270225 - C0 - 234/156/14 - PB - 9781780915920 - Gloss Lamination